AMARANTH

BOOKS BY TIM FRANKOVICH

Heart of Fire
Until All Curses Are Lifted
Until All Bonds Are Broken
Until All the Gods Return
Until All the Stars Fall

Dragontek Lore
Viridia
Incarnadine
Auric
Onyx
Amaranth

AMARANTH

DRAGONTEK LORE, BOOK 5

by Tim Frankovich

To all the guys
(You know who you are)

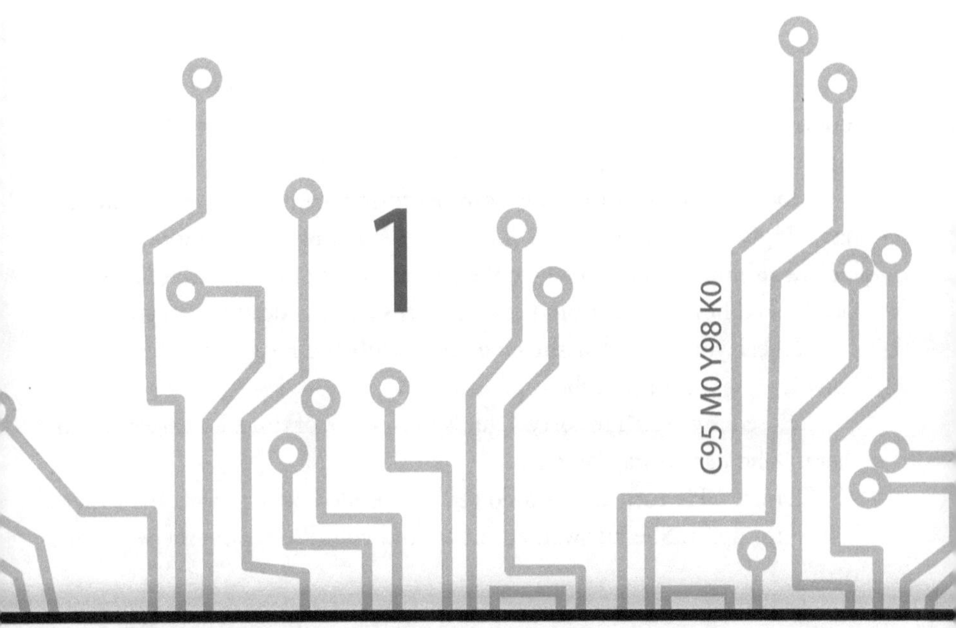

I swung the sledge hammer at the broken edge of the platform. A few rocks crumbled off with the impact. I grunted, added a boost to my arm, and swung again. This time, the hammer smashed through, and a chunk the size of my head came loose. I watched it fall to the mountainside below.

I swung again but did even less damage this time. My aim wasn't the best. Having only one working eye and hand will do that to you. I let the hammer rest while I looked over the mountainside. Only a few patches of snow remained here and there, including piled up around the tower's door behind me. Any day now, we should be able to leave this tower and head toward our "real" home. Good thing. Every day we spent here was one more day that a dragon might come swooping down on us. I'd feel more comfortable in a place not built by one of them. "Onyx Tower" had a lot of nice amenities, but its previous owner would come home someday.

We'd been here almost two months. Two. Months. A whole new year had begun in the time we'd spent in this tower. I knew Kelly needed time to recover from her surgery, and the weather trapped us after that. But even so, I chafed at the delay. We had work to do.

Caedan approached me, pulling his coat tight around him, hands stuffed inside. "It's still too cold out here!" he complained.

"You always think it's too cold." I waved my useless left hand at the landscape around us. "It's nowhere near as cold as it was a few weeks ago."

"Back then it was insanity to be outside. Now it's just stupid." He looked at my progress. "So… after all this time, you've succeeded in knocking down… maybe six square feet? Think that'll make a difference?"

I looked around at the enormous platform meant as a dragon's landing pad. "It gives me something to do," I said. "A way to get frustrations out." I looked at him, and he casually looked away. I didn't blame him. I knew my face looked horrendous from the acid burns and the dead cybernetic eye.

"I hear you." Caedan shivered, even with the heavy coat. "But, you know… it's your turn at the top."

I closed my eye. "I'm sorry. I guess I lost track of time. I'd better get up there. Who had to stay late?"

"Lainey." He turned and followed as I headed back toward the tower. "She's not upset. She just wanted me to find you. Pretty sure she was worried."

At the top of Onyx Tower, we'd discovered a room where we could watch all of the cities within The Circle from above. All of them except Viridia, though, and that bothered me. Out of all the cities, it was the one I most wanted to know about. I still didn't understand how the viewing screens were even possible, but we'd decided someone should keep an eye on them as much of the day as possible. It would be good to know in advance when a dragon took to the air.

I made it inside and stomped snow off my boots. I peeled off my coat and left the sledge hammer by the door. Without waiting for any more words from Caedan, I hurried up at the stairs to find Lainey sitting in the easy chair, watching the screens.

"Smashing rocks again?" she asked without turning around.

"Yeah. Getting my exercise." I came around the chair. "Anything interesting happening out there?"

She yawned and brought the chair upright, retracting the foot rest. "Not a single, solitary thing," she said. "Maybe all the dragons are dead."

"We've seen Auric and Incarnadine." Both had emerged from their cities and flown off somewhere before returning. But neither of them had done it at the same time, and their movements had been spread out over weeks. At first, I thought this watching the cities would be exciting. After two or three days of nothing, I realized how boring it could be. No one relished the job, except Lovat, who had great fun pushing the buttons on the chair that operated the screens.

Lainey got up and offered me the chair. "Your turn."

"I'm sorry I was late. I'll stay longer."

"I didn't mind. This time." She hesitated. "In fact, do you want me to stay?"

I sat in the chair. "I never want you to go." No, I didn't say that. It's what I should have said. What I knew I should say, at that exact moment. Not five minutes later. I knew it right then. But I didn't say it. Instead, I said, "If you want to. I could use the company."

I looked over the screens at each city, trying to ignore the screaming voice inside my head demanding to know why I hadn't said it. Over the past two months, I'd gained a lot of clarity on my own feelings. I knew what I wanted. I knew who I wanted. But… I was a fool. I was stupid. And I knew it. But I didn't know why.

With Rick gone, I'd been sort of expecting Kelly to want to re-new our previous relationship. But in the past two months, she'd shown little to no interest in doing so. Granted, she did have a lot of other things on her mind. But… I think I'd resolved my lingering feelings, at least. Kelly and I were solidly good friends now, as it should be. That left me completely free to pursue Lainey, and I knew it's what she wanted. But I didn't do it. Because I was an idiot. And a coward.

"Oh. Well. If I want to," Lainey said. "Maybe I should just go find Glacier."

I reached out with my good hand. "Stay."

She smiled. "That's a little more like it."

She sat on the arm of the chair. I should have pulled her into my lap.

"Are you still finding enough food for Glacier?" I asked.

"That's another reason we need to leave soon. We've about used up every bit of frozen meat we found in the storage."

"That cat's growing bigger every day." I pushed the button to bring the city of Amaranth in closer to my view. "Her teeth too. If we don't keep her fed, she might eat one of us."

"She'd go for the smallest and weakest first, you know."

"Well, that's dark." I raised my eyebrows at her. "Why are we even talking about this?"

"You started it."

I guess I had. I studied Amaranth. "Why hasn't she moved at all?" I wondered. Out of all the remaining dragons, she'd never left her base since we'd been watching.

"Maybe she's still nursing Onyx back to health."

"And keeping him a secret from the other dragons. I mean, if Incarnadine knew… maybe we can make use of that when we get out of here. I could have Stacy spread the story. We could get Cerise and Marcus in on it too."

"Beryl…"

"What?"

"We've been stuck here for weeks. My father is missing. I want… I need…" She looked at me with those green eyes. "Why won't you talk with me about… about us."

"I don't know. I guess…" I lifted my useless left hand. Some bandages remained, but most were gone now, revealing the metal skeleton within. I'd lost my mental connection to that hand and couldn't use it. And the combination of injuries and burns had taken off much of the exterior skin and muscles. "I don't think I deserve it. I'm in pieces, Lainey. And half of my pieces don't work."

She slid off the arm of the chair into my lap. "I don't care what you look like," she declared, looking straight into my ravaged face. "I care about what's inside." She poked my chest.

I swallowed. I didn't know how to respond. I knew I didn't deserve her care, her love, if that's what it was.

She pulled back, a mischievous grin on her face. "Besides, what parts of you aren't working besides the hand and the eye?"

"I guess that's all," I admitted. "Maybe it's not half."

She leaned in, her face almost touching mine. "Are your lips working?"

I let her discover for herself. We sat there a little while, the kiss going on longer and longer. A lot of pent-up emotion came through that kiss. And even as it continued, part of me still resisted, worried about what might happen next. The very fact that she was even willing to kiss me when half of my face looked horrendous blew my mind.

When we finally broke apart, Lainey giggled and ran a finger along my lips. "Have you ever tried boosting these?"

"Pretty sure that wouldn't work."

"Why not? They're muscles, aren't they?"

"Hunter and Loden didn't cut open my lips so I could boost them. What good would that do?"

"Good? I don't know. Fun? Maybe."

"You're ridiculous."

"What? You don't wonder about things like this? It's your body."

I rolled my eye. "No, I can't send boosts to my lips. Or any other part of my face, except my eyes."

She leaned in and kissed the good side of my face. "Well, then, what about—" She broke off.

"What about what?"

"Oh, look here. We're not alone." She got out of my lap.

What? Who would come all the way up here? I turned around.

"Come here, little one," Lainey called, moving toward the stairs.

An eighteen-inch tall baby draconic pulled itself up the last step and stood there, staring at us with its enormous eyes.

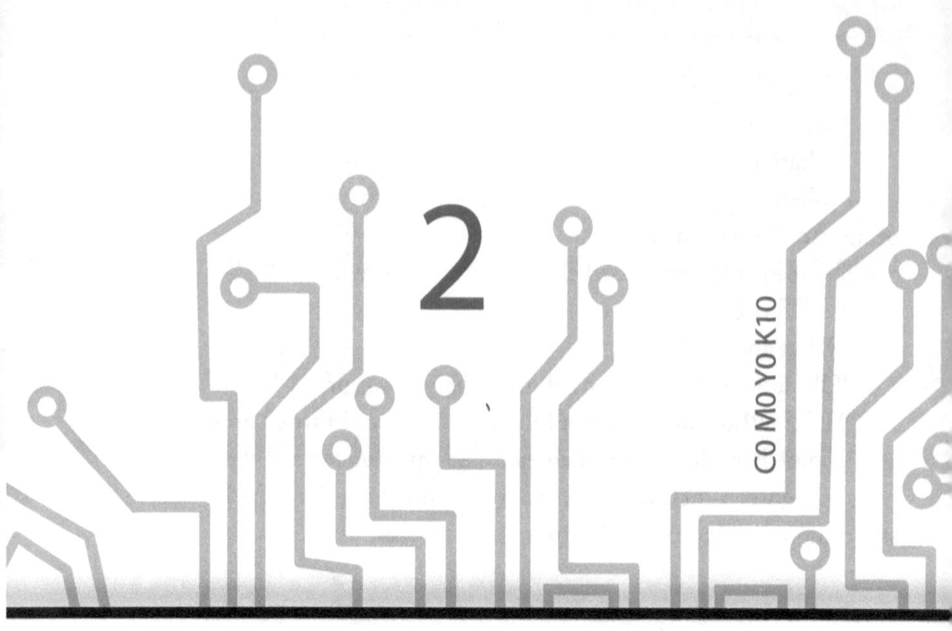

Not a day went by when I didn't question my decision to let the infant draconic live. I bore full responsibility for the decision. Kelly, if she'd been conscious, would probably have made the same decision… but we'd never know what she would have done, because she hadn't been there. In fact, she hadn't come out of her coma for over a week. By then, it was far too late to suggest killing the infant. And once she saw him, she didn't want him to die either.

When I held that newborn in my arms, I didn't know what to do. I asked myself what Bice would say, if he were there. And I knew. He'd say that the dragons have been killing our children for generations. Would we be any better if we killed theirs? And with an image of blood dripping from golden curls in my mind, I decided the baby would live.

Kelly named him Chance. I guess it made sense. We had a chance with him: would he become an evil tyrant like the other draconics, or a great ally to humans, maybe the greatest ally ever?

Chance toddled toward Lainey, and she swooped him up in her arms. But no sooner did she have him than he turned to look at me. He'd been fixated on me from birth. Maybe because I held him first? Or did he somehow sense that I was the one responsible for his life?

"Aw, do you want your daddy?" Lainey cooed.

"I'm not his daddy."

"You're the closest thing he has to one. That's important."

"His real daddy wouldn't think so."

Lainey continued to play with the infant, making silly noises and bouncing him. She and Kelly both treated him almost entirely like a human child. Fern, Kelly's mother, remained adamantly opposed to his very existence. Once Kelly recovered and declared her intention to raise Chance, Fern didn't talk to her for over a week. Even now, their relationship remained cool.

Hunter saw the child as a fascinating medical study. To his knowledge, no human doctor or scientist had ever been given the opportunity to watch and study the draconic growth process. Caedan and Lovat didn't know what to think. Lovat played with the child on occasion, but told me Chance was creepy. Caedan just avoided him.

"Draconic children grow so much faster than humans," Lainey observed.

"Do they?" I focused my attention on the screens.

"Sure. No human baby would be walking and climbing stairs at two months!"

I knew this, though my experience was limited. My baby sister hadn't lived long enough for me to learn of childhood development, and I'd never been around any babies since then. Nor did I have any great desire to change that.

"Does your mother know you're up here?" Lainey talked to Chance in a ridiculous voice. "Does she? I don't think she does!" Why did babies make girls so… silly?

"Kelly's probably asleep," I pointed out.

"And everyone else was busy?" Lainey asked Chance, as if he would answer.

Yes, all right? I was annoyed that Chance interrupted the romantic moment. I finally push past some of my reservations to truly enjoy Lainey and then this. My life was cursed.

"I'll take him back downstairs." Lainey carried Chance back to the stairs.

"Will you come back?" I asked, hoping I didn't sound whiny.

She stopped, two steps down, and smiled at me. "As soon as I can," she promised. "But if Kelly's asleep and no one else is around, I may have to stay until she wakes up."

I nodded. Of course. Lainey and Chance disappeared down the stairs. The room suddenly felt a lot colder without Lainey in it. I sighed and looked back at the screens.

For the first time in days, my thoughts wandered to my still-missing friends, Bice and Don. If they were still alive, which of these cities held them? I glanced at the one dead screen. My attempts to find them in Viridia had proven fruitless, but they still might be there, held by Troilus Green in some secret prison. It seemed unlikely, though. If Troilus Green had captured "the heretic" Bice, it would have made sure I knew it.

I turned my head to the opposite end of the screens. Auric. It seemed the most likely possibility now. I'd met the gold dragon and talked with him. He seemed different from the others somehow, but very confusing. His agents knew the general vicinity of our headquarters, the Achromatic Asylum. It's possible they'd seen when Onyx attacked, kept an eye out for survivors, and found Bice and Don when they emerged alive. If so, I thought it very likely that Auric would have kept them alive, waiting for me to come for them. I knew I needed to get there, sometime soon, or send a message, at the very least.

My eyes wandered from city to city. I knew the least about Atramentous, the black dragon. I wondered what he thought about the return of Onyx, if he even knew about it yet. Atramentous had also been allied with Viridia in the war we sparked. By now, I strongly suspected the dragons had put aside their differences, though I hoped not. The longer they focused on fighting each other, the more likely we could make progress against them. In that, Onyx and I were alike. He'd used me to promote that infighting. But it really was the best outcome for all of us.

I skimmed over the blue city of Caesious. We'd killed the blue dragon to start all of this. With no dragon, the city was a hotbed of revolution, according to Caedan and his recruits. His absence for this long might hurt that cause, though. And technically, the red dragons had taken the blue city as part of their domain.

The red dragons: Incarnadine and Amaranth. I'd met Incarnadine and almost gotten eaten. And I'd looked Amaranth in the face when she rescued Onyx from me. I had no doubts that the two of them had returned to her city. How long would it take Onyx to recover from his wounds? Would both of them come back to destroy us?

Onyx wanted his child most of all. As long as we held it, we had bargaining power. I'll admit that aspect had not occurred to me in the moment I chose to keep the child alive, but it certainly affected how I felt about him now. Onyx couldn't just destroy the tower with us in it, not as long as Chance was here. Did he know we'd kept the baby alive? Was there a connection between the child and his father even now? Maybe his fixation with me had more to do with his father's thoughts than his own.

No. Protogonus Blue, the one good draconic I'd known, had never mentioned a sustained mental connection between draconics and their dragon father. But they did make such connections at times, particularly when a draconic reached the age where his previous lives' memories came flooding back. I'd assumed we'd have many years before that eventuality, but at the rate Chance was growing, it might be much sooner.

Lainey had been gone for a while now. She must have stayed with Chance to let Kelly sleep. Even though I felt sorry for myself, I knew Kelly probably needed the rest. Hunter said she'd made good progress in recovering from Chance's birth, but she was still pretty weak. Any extra sleep would do her good.

I shook my head and turned my thoughts back to the dragons. Incarnadine and Amaranth had always been said to be close; their cities were side-by-side, even. But as I'd just told Lainey, Incarnadine certainly didn't know about Onyx. Could we get that information to him somehow? Would it spark a war between the two red dragons? That would be something to see.

I heard footsteps coming up the stairs behind me. "Lainey?"

"No such luck," Caedan answered. "Just me. Sorry."

"Fewmets."

Caedan laughed as he came around beside the chair. "You two getting closer?"

"Maybe. I don't know."

"That's the problem with you and girls. You never seem to know what's going on."

"Because I don't!" I really didn't. Kelly. Olive. Lainey. None of them made sense to me.

"Look, girls seem complicated, but they really aren't."

"Is that why they flock to you all the time?"

"Hey, you've never seen me in action with them. How would you know?"

"So… you and Sapphire?"

He gave me a stern look. "That's not streak, man. She's too young for me."

"Too young? By how much? Three years?"

"It's enough. Look, girls just want one thing. It's—whoa."

"Whoa what?" He stared past me at the screens, so I turned to look. "Oh."

Amaranth, the red dragon, rose out of her nest—I still didn't know what it was called—and took to the skies above her city. She circled it once, and then shot away toward the east.

Straight toward us.

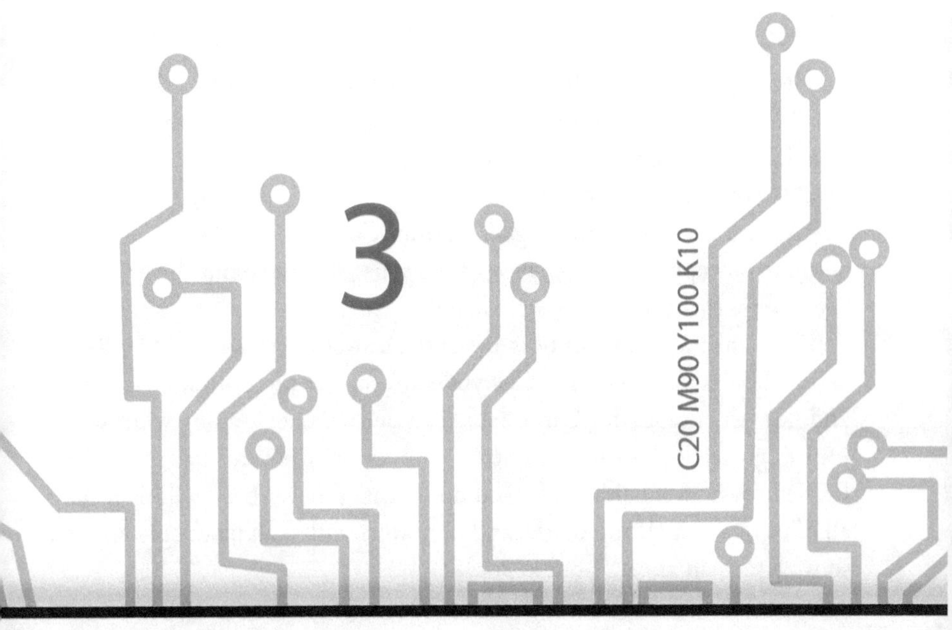

"Go, go!" I yelled at Caedan, scrambling out of the chair. "Get every-one down to the lower levels!"

I didn't trust any of the tower to protect us completely, but the lower levels were built into the actual side of the mountain. I figured that might give us a little more time, at least. Time for what? I hadn't figured that much out yet.

We tumbled past each other down the stairs. I stopped at the next floor for a moment, not expecting to find anyone. The only room of note here was my bedroom. No one else should be there, but sometimes Glacier liked to use my bed. Not seeing her, I chased Caedan down to the next level.

He was already heading further down, but I met Lainey hurrying to the stairs, carrying Chance. "Kelly's in the shower," she reported.

"I'll get her," I said, starting to push past.

"Beryl!"

I stopped, and Lainey shoved Chance into my arms. "Take him. I'll get her."

I took a look at the draconic. He smiled at me with a surprising num-ber of tiny sharp teeth. I hadn't even noticed he'd grown any yet. I tossed him on my shoulder and ran down the stairs.

Caedan shooed Hunter and Fern out from the next level, and all of us hurried down two more flights. "Is this far enough?" Hunter asked.

"We're in the more secure area now," Caedan said. "Only one more level left, where Mazarine and friends are hanging out."

"Is Lovat down there?" I asked.

At his nod, I descended again. "Lovat! Come on up!"

The boy appeared at the base of the stairs. "What about them?"

"Leave them for now. Come here!"

Not until we were out of range of the unwelcome guests did I tell him about the dragon. Mazarine Chalybdeous, former high priest to Caesious and now chief toady for Onyx, had been our prisoner—along with two of Onyx's guards—since we'd arrived in the tower. The three of them stayed in the lowest level behind a locked door. They'd never been willing to face all of us in a straight-up battle, and they apparently had plenty of supplies, so we left them alone… but kept a watch.

The level on which we gathered held storage rooms. We'd searched them, but hadn't found much of interest: some tools, including the sledge hammer I'd been using, blankets and other necessities, and lots of dry food products. Between that, the freezer of meat, and running water, we'd wanted for nothing in our time here.

Lainey and Kelly, her hair still dripping, tumbled into our group. I handed Chance to Kelly as soon as I could.

"Anyone seen Glacier?" Lainey asked.

"She's not with you? She wasn't in my bedroom."

"Did you check the far side of your bed? She sometimes pulls the blankets off and lies there instead."

I had forgotten that.

Lainey turned. "I'll go get her."

I grabbed her arm. "The dragon could be here any second. I'll go." I boosted my legs and shot up the stairs, feeling like an idiot. Why was I risking my life for a cat? Because the cat belonged to Lainey, of course.

I yanked open the bedroom door again. "Glacier! You stupid cat! Get out of here!" I took a few steps around the bed. Sure enough, the white saber-toothed cat lay curled up on top of a pile of my bedclothes. She looked up at me, but didn't move.

"Come on! Lainey's worried about you! Let's move!" I yanked the blanket.

Glacier snarled at me as I forced her off. She sauntered toward the door as if it had been her idea all along. I followed, flicking at her with a corner of the blanket to keep her moving. She didn't appreciate my efforts.

As we reached the stairway, the tower shook around us. An enormous impact sounded just outside the door. Glacier shot down the stairs. I started to follow.

"Beryl Godslayer!" The voice boomed through the walls. "Beryl Godslayer! I would have words with thee!"

Thee? None of the other dragons talked like that. Of course, none of the others had such a distinctive feminine sound to their voice either. Amaranth still sounded enormous, but her intonations weren't as deep as the others. I couldn't explain it very well.

"I'm not interested in conversation," I muttered as I bounded down the stairs.

"If you do not come speak with me, I shall be forced to rip this tower apart, stone by stone, until you do."

I stopped.

Lainey's voice came up the stairway below me: "Don't do it, Beryl!"

What choice did I have? If I could protect her and everyone else by potentially sacrificing myself, I'd do it. Every time. Of course, I had no reason to trust this—or any—dragon.

"I will not wait for long!" Amaranth declared.

I retraced my steps. I glanced at the sledge hammer leaning beside the door, but left it alone. It wouldn't have been much of a weapon. Even my sword, safely back in the bedroom, would be useless against one of the immortal dragons. Unless, of course, she transformed into a human. I didn't see much likelihood of that.

I pushed open the door and stepped out.

Amaranth, the red—reddish, really… maybe almost orange… maybe copper?—dragon, perched on the landing pad in front of me. She looked terrifying, like all the other dragons. Enormous, fierce… and were those feathers? Or just scales that looked like feathers? I raised my head to look all the way up at the dragon's face. I'd forgotten my coat, but I didn't need it. Warm air and a smell of decay filled the atmosphere.

"What do you want?" I asked.

Steam erupted from her nostrils in a snort, adding to the warmth. "You are either very courageous, or very foolish to address me in such a manner. Perhaps thou art in need of a lesson in manners."

I blinked. "Thou art?" I had a vague recollection from my Learning Years of being forced to read a story where people used that kind of language. Wasn't it a thousand years ago or more? Oh, right. She'd probably been there. "When you allow all the humans under your rule to make their own choices in life, then you can talk to me about manners," I countered.

"Onyx informed me that you possessed revolutionary ideas. I see he was truthful in this." The dragon spread her wings momentarily. "I am here for the child. Thou wilt bring him to me at once."

"Child? What child?"

More steam emerged from her nostrils. "Do not test my patience. Onyx is aware of his child's existence. The older the child grows, the stronger the connection between them will grow."

Hm. That might complicate things. Also, she confirmed that Onyx was definitely alive.

"Regardless, bring the child to me," she went on.

"That's not going to happen."

Amaranth's head went back on her neck, and the scales around her neck bristled like feathers. "Do you actively desire death this day?"

"You already threatened to tear the tower apart," I pointed out. "So you've already threatened me with death. But to do that, you would also kill the child. If he's that important to you, I don't believe you'll do that."

"I could slay thou in an instant."

"You could. But then what? You're back to tearing down the tower. You accomplish nothing."

The dragon blinked. She really wasn't used to anyone defying her. She came here believing that all she had to do was make demands, and we'd comply. Surprise, surprise.

"My will cannot be opposed."

"And yet here I stand, opposing it."

A few tongues of fire erupted from her mouth with the nostril steam this time. If I pushed her too far, I'd end up incinerated. But what else could I do? If I kept her talking, maybe we had a chance.

"This is outrageous!"

"Look…" I took a deep breath. "We're not getting anywhere here. What if we discuss this in a more civilized manner? I'm getting an ache in my neck from looking up at you, and that makes me cranky. How about if you transform into a human so we can talk face-to-face? You could even come inside the tower then."

She stared at me, unmoving save the tip of her tail, which twitched back and forth. At last she spoke: "I am trying to determine whether you believe that thou art clever, or whether you are making an attempt at humor."

"Maybe I'm being sincere."

"I find that unlikely."

I couldn't think of what else to say. Too bad my boosts couldn't make me smarter.

"I will return to Onyx and discuss this," she announced. "Do not think this means we will allow you to keep the child. He belongs with his sire, and it will happen eventually."

"If you say so."

"Regarding your other suggestion… shouldst thou ever come to my city and seek me out,"—she lowered her head down to look at me up close—"something you should consider most earnestly… Should you come there, then I will allow you to gaze upon my alternate form and perform your worship there."

I felt a strange feeling wash over me. The idea of visiting the city of Amaranth and seeing her human form suddenly seemed like the most logical and desirable thing I could do. I wanted to say that I had no interest in worshipping, but no words came out when I opened my mouth.

"We shall meet again," she said. She spread her wings and launched from the platform. The wind from her motions threw me back against the door. I watched her depart, wondering what had just happened.

4

Back inside the tower, I descended the stairs and found the others waiting. Lainey rushed to meet me. Everyone clamored to know what had happened. I summarized the conversation.

"We need to get out of here now," Caedan said when I was done. "She'll go back and talk with Onyx, and he'll send her right back."

"Can we even get out fast enough?" I asked. "If she caught us out in the open, it would be far worse."

"We make a run for it," he argued. "Find a place to hide if we spot her coming."

"Sounds risky," Hunter put in. "Is not the tower the safest place to be?"

"In some ways," I admitted. "I don't know that it could stand up against the force of an angry dragon, but it is stronger than any other place we've lived in."

"The downside is they know we're here," Lainey said.

"And Onyx knows where his child is." I glanced at Kelly, who held Chance close. "I didn't want to believe it, but she claimed they had a link."

"So no matter where we go, it'll lead the dragons to us?" Fern exclaimed. She scowled at the draconic.

Kelly's expression hardened. "I will not abandon my child!"

"We're not asking you to!" I said quickly.

"Then where does that leave us?" Hunter asked.

"Shouldn't we be watching the city?" Lainey chimed in.

"Yes, someone should—"

"I'll go!" Lovat volunteered, and took off up the stairs.

"We shouldn't be wasting time talking," Caedan insisted. "We should just go!"

"To where? It'll take days to get to the Asylum, even if Kelly can move as fast as the rest of us." I knew she'd been doing much better, but she'd nearly died when Hunter had cut Chance out of her.

"We can't just hide here!"

"I know, I know! We don't have any good options."

"Could we somehow—I do not know—convince them that we are gone, while we stay hidden?" Hunter suggested.

I considered it. "If no one appears when she returns, she'll probably start tearing it down to be sure."

"Will she?" Kelly asked. "Would she go that far?"

"I don't see why not. These are the dragons. They've been committing atrocities for a thousand years."

"What if we sent Mazarine out there to tell her we're gone?" Caedan grinned at the thought.

"Why would he do that?"

"Oh, I think we can talk him into it."

"What good will that do?" Fern shook her head. "As long as we're with that creature, they'll know where we are."

"To be completely fair, she didn't say Onyx could sense Chance's location," I said. "Only his existence."

"But you don't know that he can't."

"No, we don't know anything for sure."

"If Mazarine won't do it, maybe one of the guards will," Caedan added. "They've got to be tired of being cooped up in there."

"You're just postponing things," Kelly said. "Even if that works, they'll still come back eventually."

"It buys us time," I said. "That's what we need right now. Once we've got some time to work things out, we can figure out our next moves. We need to get back to the Asylum, and maybe visit Auric, and then go to Amaranth."

"Why would we go to Amaranth?" Caedan gave me an odd look. "What good would that do?"

I blinked. "I don't know why I said that."

"Did you mean Incarnadine?"

"Maybe?" I shook my head. "We're wasting time. Let's visit our prisoners."

Caedan and I tramped down the stairs to the lowest level. "Let me try," he said to me, and approached the door.

"Hello in there! I have a one-time opportunity for only one person. Who's tired of that room and company? Anyone want to get out?"

"We have no interest in—" Mazarine's voice began.

"What are you offering?" another voice interrupted.

Caedan grinned at me. "All I need is for you to tell a lie to someone. One lie, and you're absolutely free to go, anywhere you want."

"Do not listen to him!" Mazarine insisted. "He will lead you away from the true faith!"

"Shut up," the guard said. "What has that true faith gotten us?"

"This is not a good idea," said a third voice, the other guard.

"I think it's a great idea," Caedan said. "I can't imagine what it's been like for you guys cooped up with Mazarine, of all people."

"That's, that's—" Mazarine sputtered.

"He's got a good point," the first guard said.

All three voice erupted in a sustained argument, talking over each other, increasing their volume, and growing more and more angry. Caedan let it go on for a few more minutes before interrupting: "I did say this was a one-time opportunity. And it's a very limited one. I'll give you another thirty seconds to step out here if you want it."

From behind the door came the sounds of a scuffle: rustling, grunts, and a solid impact. Then we heard something being moved away from the door.

"You're a fool!" Mazarine screamed. "You're betraying your god! Your very soul is at stake here! Don't do this!"

The door opened, pushing something else aside as it did. Mazarine continued to rant, but I tuned him out. Out stepped a tall man with long reddish-blond hair, two months' growth of facial hair, and a red chromark. The door slammed shut behind him.

He looked from Caedan to me, then quickly back to Caedan. "What's the lie, and who do I tell it to?"

"That's the hard part," Caedan said.

"Amaranth," I said. "You have to lie to the red dragon."

His face paled a little, but he nodded. "And if I do that, you let me walk out of here?"

"Absolutely. Anywhere you want to go."

"What's the lie then?"

I looked at the door behind him. It had gotten quiet in there. Mazarine was no doubt listening to us. I'd probably let him hear too much already. "Come this way," I said. "And we'll explain."

He stepped forward, then hesitated. "What if I change my mind?"

Caedan patted the door behind him. "Then you go back in here with your best pals. I'm sure they'll be very happy to see you again."

He winced, then followed me up the stairs. Caedan trailed behind until we reached the next level.

"What's your name?" I asked, turning to face him.

"Carmine." He wouldn't look me in the eye, but who could blame him for that?

"Which of the red cities are you from?"

"Incarnadine." That was a bit of a relief. If he'd been from Amaranth, I don't think I could have trusted him for this.

"All right, Carmine. Here's the deal." I outlined what we wanted from him.

"You're going to let me walk out there alone and talk to the dragon?" He shook his head. "What's to stop me from telling her the truth?"

"Me," Caedan said. He held up a crossbow. "I'll be watching and listening the entire time. You say something wrong, give one hint that you're lying… and I'll put a bolt through you."

Carmine wrinkled his brow. He started to say something, then thought better of it.

"Yeah." Caedan grinned. "You're getting it. We've got absolutely nothing to lose. If you don't convince her, we're all going to die anyway. So I'll just make sure you die first."

"Right. Um… can I have something to eat first? All we had down there were crackers and some kind of protein paste. It got old after the first couple of days."

I laughed. "We can do that."

Caedan led him to the pantry, and I reported to the others.

"Can we trust him at all?" Fern asked.

"No idea. But it's better than doing nothing. We'll just have to wait and see what happens. In the meantime, start packing up the essentials. I don't know how soon we'll be leaving, but I want everyone ready."

While the ladies and Hunter all set about gathering their things, I made my way up to my own bedroom. Once there, I took a brief look around at everything. I had to admit: it had been nice to have this bedroom for the past two months. I would miss it. Despite the cold and the circumstances, this had been the most luxurious living I'd enjoyed since this whole thing began. At first it bothered me that everything in this room had been built for Rick, but I got over it after a few nights sleeping in the bed.

It took me less than five minutes to pack up my belongings. Everything I owned right now consisted of some clothes, camping supplies, and my sword. I made one last stop in the bathroom, and stopped at my reflection in the mirror. Being here among friends the past few weeks, I hadn't cared much about how I looked. But now, as we were about to re-enter the rest of the world… Ugh. I looked horrible.

Starting just below the hairline on the right side of my face, the scarred area formed a rough triangle, ending in a point in the middle of my cheek. Throughout that area, clumps of scar tissue formed ragged patches, interrupted here and there by spots of dull metal. My cybernetic eye appeared white and unmoving, regardless of what I did with the other eye. It provided an odd contrast to the multi-colored chromark on the left side of my face.

People would just have to get used to it, I supposed. I shoved a towel into my bag and headed to the top of the tower.

I met Lovat halfway up as he rushed down to meet me.

"She coming!"

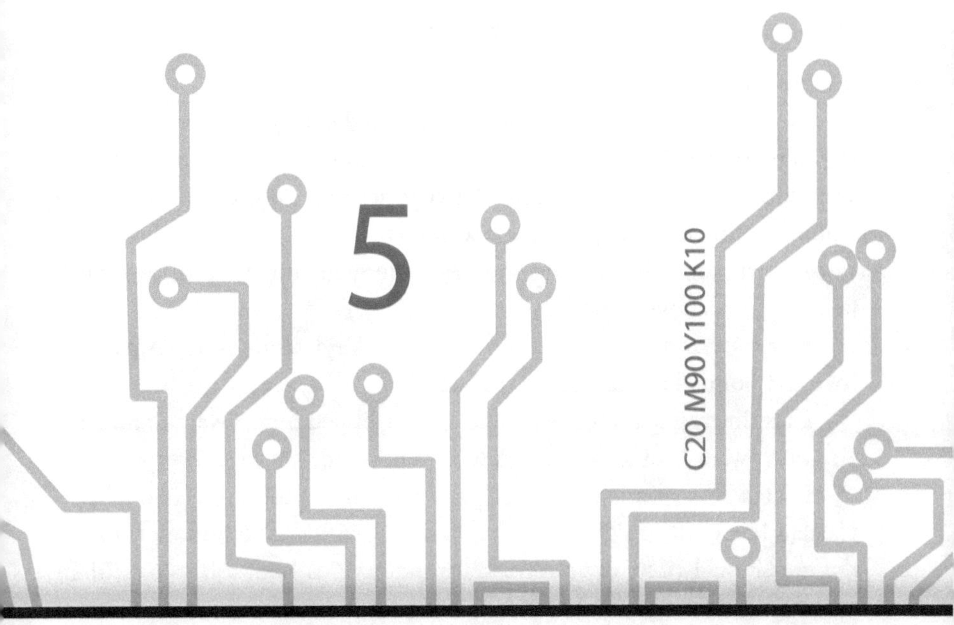

5

I sent Lovat down to join the others. Caedan brought our former enemy to the door leading to the landing pad.

"She'll be here in a few minutes," I told them. "Carmine, do you understand what to do?"

"Yeah, yeah, I think so." He squinted at the door, noticing the sledge hammer beside it, maybe. "I tell her all of you are gone, and I'm the only one left behind."

"You can tell her we've kept you a prisoner all this time," Caedan added. "That part shouldn't be hard."

"Since it's true?"

"Mixing a lie with the truth is the easiest way to tell one."

"Sure. Anything else I should know?"

"She'll ask about the draconic child," I said. "Tell her we took it with us."

His eyes widened. "You kept it alive? I thought killing it would be the first thing you people did."

"We're about life," I told him. "If we can get freedom for all of us without any killing, we'll do it."

"Except the dragons," Caedan said.

"Obviously, the dragons have to die."

Carmine looked from me to Caedan again. "I don't know what to think of you people."

We waited in silence after that. I considered telling Carmine more, trying to persuade him of the rightness of our cause, but doing so might also sway him in the other direction. Better to let him do his one task. There would be time for talk later… if it worked.

At last came the rushing sound of the giant impact outside. "She's here…" Caedan whispered.

I put a hand to my ear and waited. "Beryl Godslayer!" Amaranth roared. I pointed at the door and nodded.

Carmine reached for the handle, but I stopped him. "Wait a moment. You don't want it to look like you were waiting for her to show up."

I let a few moments trickle past, and then pulled my hand back. Caedan knelt out of sight from the door, but with the perfect angle to fire the crossbow. I drew my sword. Carmine gave us both a last look, then opened the door and went out.

"Who art thou?" the dragon demanded.

From my angle, I couldn't see him, but I imagined Carmine bowing. "I am Carmine of Incarnadine, your greatness." His voice wavered just a little. That was okay. Anyone would be nervous facing a dragon.

"Has Beryl Godslayer sent thee in his stead?"

"Uh, no. He is gone, majesty. He and all his people."

"Gone? Where?"

"I don't know, sire. I was in service to Onyx. My fellow guard and I have been prisoners in the basement for the past two months. I only just got out and discovered them gone."

"Where is this fellow of yours, then?"

"He's still in the basement. He's too weak to climb the stairs right now. I was searching for more food for him when you showed up."

"He's good at this," Caedan whispered.

I nodded, but the longer this lasted, the more nervous I grew.

"Did the rebels take the draconic child with them?" Amaranth demanded.

"I haven't seen a draconic child," Carmine answered. "I haven't searched the whole tower yet, but I think I would have noticed that."

The dragon didn't respond for a while. I resisted the urge to peek around the doorway. "What's happening?" I hissed to Caedan.

"She's just staring at him," he whispered back.

"They cannot have gone far," the dragon burst out. "I will seek for them. Thou shouldst stay and take care of thy friend. Onyx will reward thee for thy perseverance."

"Thank you, your majesty."

With an enormous rush of wind from her wings, Amaranth took to the sky again and swept away. Carmine was knocked prone. He struggled to his feet and returned to the tower door.

"You did great," I told him. "Thank you."

"So I can go?"

"Of course." I paused. "But you may want to give the dragon time to search the nearby areas. It wouldn't work out so well if she found you outside."

"I'll take my chances." He folded his arms across his chest.

"It's your choice. I'd suggest taking the northern route." I stepped outside and pointed. "We're dead center of the Blasted Lands, so either way is a long journey. But the north route will take you closer toward Incarnadine, at least a little bit." I paused. "Assuming that's where you want to go."

"Can't really be seen anywhere else," he said, pointing at his chromark.

"You could stay with us," Caedan suggested. "We can always use more fighters."

He looked at Caedan for a moment, as if he were seriously considering it. Then he shook his head. "Nah, you people are crazy. The dragons are going to catch you eventually."

"Maybe. But we're having a great time until they do." Caedan uncocked the crossbow.

"Like I said: crazy."

"All right," I said. "Caedan, can you help him get down? I'll go let everyone know what happened."

I headed downstairs to find the others. They were assembling their packs and equipment in the hall outside Kelly's room. I sent Lovat back up to the screen room, telling him to let me know if he saw Amaranth return to her city.

"Then it worked?" Kelly asked, struggling with Chance. He clearly wanted to get down and wander on his own two feet.

"Yeah. The dragon is gone searching for us. I figure once she gives up and heads back home, we can actually leave."

"Doesn't that start the whole discussion over again?" Fern wanted to know. "Is there anywhere safer than this?"

"We can head back to the Asylum first," I explained. "They won't know we're there, unless we make it obvious. From what Royal has told Caedan, no one's come to bother them while we've been here. The workshop, at least, is a secure hiding place. From there, we can decide whether to set up in a new city, whether we go back to Viridia, or Caesious, or Amaranth."

Lainey gave me an odd look, but I kept going. "As long as we stay here, we're trapped. They know where we are, and we can't accomplish anything at all. I'm kind of worried about what's been happening in the cities while we've been here."

"Then it is settled," Hunter said. "I guess we should finish packing."

I turned to Kelly. "Will you be all right?"

She gave in to Chance and set him down. He toddled over to the backpacks and pulled on the straps. "I've been walking up and down the stairs every day for the past week or more. I think I can handle it." She pointed at the infant. "We'll have to take turns carrying Chance, though. He'll get tired pretty quick."

For a moment, an utterly bizarre image popped into my head of somehow fashioning a saddle for Glacier and letting her carry Chance around. The sheer bizarreness of the thought made me chuckle. "Yeah, uh, we'll do that."

Caedan joined us, reporting that Carmine was down and on his way home. "So we're going soon too?"

I caught him up. He scratched behind his ear and grinned. "So… should we leave some surprises for Onyx?"

"What did you have in mind?"

He shrugged. "I don't know. Just some sabotage here and there. Turn on the faucets and leave the water running. Brace the door open on the landing pad to let cold air in. You know."

It felt petty, but… "Knock yourself out. You do know Mazarine and his pal downstairs will be the ones who find all that first, right?"

"Even more reason."

I laughed, and he made for the stairs. "I'll start at the top and work my way down."

"I'll join Lovat for now," I said, following him.

Over the past two months, I'd grown awfully tired of the stairs. But it felt weird to think this would be the last time I climbed them. On my way,

I picked up the sledge hammer.

"Any sign of her, Lovat?"

"Nope," he reported from the chair. "Atramentous stuck his head out, but that's all. Gone now."

"Really?" Huh. We never saw him after months of watching, and now that we were leaving, he sticks his head out? I seriously would never understand the movements and motivations of the dragons. No use trying to figure it out, I guess.

I hefted the sledge hammer. It would be a shame to smash all of this, but if we couldn't stay and use it, I didn't want Onyx to have this resource any more.

"There she is!" Lovat exclaimed, pointing at the Amaranth image.

"And now we go," I said. "Head downstairs, Lovat. I'll be with you in a minute."

I boosted my arm and swung the hammer.

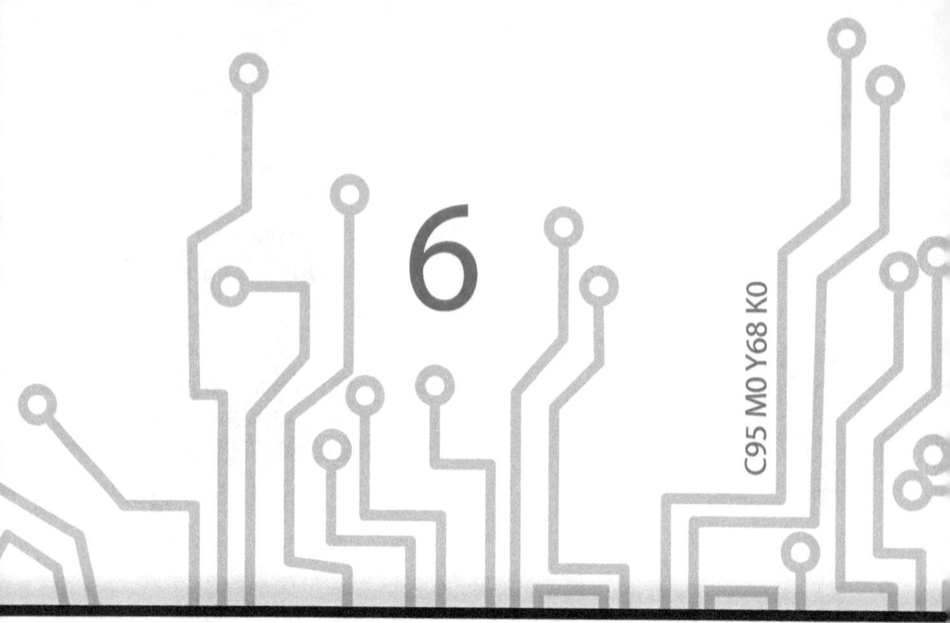

Getting out of the tower was a huge process. Onyx had it built without a door for ordinary humans, or at least not one we'd been able to find. Maybe he'd just had it walled up once construction was completed. He flew all of his people in, I assumed.

So we had to descend via rope from the tower's main balcony. This proved especially problematic with Glacier. She'd grown in the two months we'd been here… grown a lot. No one would be able to hold her in their lap or any other way. We had to secure the rope to her and lower her down alone. Needless to say, she wasn't happy about the situation. Lainey went first and waited at the bottom, calling out to her during the entire descent. The minute her feet touched solid ground, she tried to scramble away. Lainey had to grab on to her and hold her while untying the rope. I don't know how she did it.

We also had to lower Kelly and Chance down together. Though she was much stronger, there was no way she could handle a rope climb. Once on the ground, she set Chance down. He immediately began to wander about, in awe of his surroundings.

I descended last, which was no small task. I couldn't hold the rope with my left hand, so I had to slide down, using boosts to my gloved right hand to slow the fall. I landed hard, with a short boost to my legs to soften the impact.

"You okay?" Caedan asked.

"Yeah." I looked up. "Guess we have to leave the rope."

"Eh, there's more back at the workshop."

"Right. Let's get moving."

Glacier bounded across the rocks. Her growth in the past two months made her movements even more amazing. Watching this huge cat land on tiny outcroppings, then leap across open air to another smaller landing spot… it defied understanding.

As Caedan led the way down the mountainside, I paused to take one last look at the dark tower where we'd lived for weeks. If I zoomed my eye a little bit, I could make out the broken corner of the platform where I'd hammered pieces off. I smiled and let my vision return to normal… only to catch a glimpse of someone standing on the platform. When I looked again, I saw no one.

Had Mazarine or the other guard already left the basement and wandered that high? Or had I just imagined it? One other possibility remained: the purple robes. I hadn't seen one of them since the day I almost killed Onyx. Of all the mysteries of The Circle, this one puzzled me the most, and they weren't even from The Circle.

I hurried to catch up to the others. Hunter brought up the rear, ready to help Kelly if needed. For the moment, she seemed all right. Lainey carried Chance.

"You said there are more cybernetic eyes in Loden's workshop?" Hunter asked me.

"Yeah. Assuming the acid didn't damage the connections inside, I should be able to just pop a new one in." I stumbled a little. "And it'll be nice to have depth perception again."

He chuckled. "I am sure." He glanced back at my face. "I doubt I can do anything for the rest of your burns while we are there, but if we ever gain access to a hospital…"

"I appreciate that," I told him. "Not sure when or if that'll happen, but it's something to look forward to."

"How long will this take?" Kelly asked. "I know you've told me, but I can't remember. Plus, I flew the last time."

"It took us almost three days to get to the tower, but we were going up for much of it, and it was snowing." I looked around at the clear weather now. I could see hints of snow further up the mountains, but nothing nearby. It was still cold, but winter would soon be leaving us.

"So… two days, even with taking it easy for me?"

"Yeah." I smiled at her. "We'll still have to spend two nights outside, since we got such a late start, but it shouldn't be that hard."

We walked on, working our way down, sometimes over very steep areas. Descending was far easier than ascending, but we still struggled through a few places. Kelly, Lainey, and I took turns carrying Chance. He would have loved to walk on his own, but his little legs couldn't move as fast as ours, and we couldn't trust him to stay with us. Glacier, of course, did whatever she wanted.

At our first rest stop, I looked around at the team. Despite some misgivings at the start, everyone now appeared fully dedicated to this trip. The cold air made the Lovat and the women's faces look cheerier with their red cheeks. Caedan's olive skin and Hunter's dark brown didn't show as much. But I don't think Caedan had lost his grin since we set out. Being cooped up inside the tower for so long had been torture for him.

Chance toddled about, investigating everything he could find. We watched him for a while, not speaking. When Chance tried to climb a rock, and fell back in a heels-over-head roll, I think I even saw the hint of a smile on Fern's face. The infant draconic growled and tried again.

We didn't reach Royal's old watch station before dark, and had to make camp under a sharply-angled cliff. It didn't provide much shelter, but with all of our clothing and blankets, at least we could stay warm. I didn't dare light a fire now. In this clear weather, a dragon could probably see it from many miles away.

As the others prepared for bed, Caedan sat down beside me. "How long do you think it'll be safe at the Asylum?" he asked in a low voice.

"I have no clue," I admitted. "But I don't think we should stay more than a few days."

He glanced over his shoulder at the others. "Do you think Kelly and Chance can handle a walk across The Circle? I mean, we have a four-wheeler, but just the one now. Might be complicated."

"We'll figure it out. Look, we know Loden's workshop stood firm when Onyx attacked, so at the worst, we hide in there. It saved Bice and Don, after all." I looked out over The Circle. We weren't high enough for me to see all the way to one of the cities from here. Only the Blasted Lands lay below us now. "I'm worried about Viridia," I said. "I think we should check in with Stacy before we do anything else."

"Sounds like a good first step. You won't go alone, will you?"

"No, I'll take Lovat. And probably Lainey, if she insists on it." I remembered the rest of the team. "Maybe Basil, if he's still around."

"And after that? We look for Bice and Don again?"

"We can try." I pulled the collar of my coat up around my neck. "We have so many possible directions we could go, Caedan. I'm feeling a little lost, honestly."

He ticked off on his fingers. "You're worried about Viridia. We think Bice and Don might be in Auric. What else?"

I held up two of my own fingers. "The other half of Loden's notes are in Incarnadine. We might need to run a mission there. Or we could head right for Amaranth, and… finish Onyx off before he fully recovers."

"That sounds crazy and risky. I love it. But… I don't know if we have the right team for that kind of risk any more. This group…" He looked back at them. "Not exactly a warrior tribe, not even including my gang."

I agreed with his logic, but… "I think we can do all right, between you, me, and Lainey. And Glacier."

"The rate that cat is growing terrifies me," he muttered.

"You didn't see its mother," I countered. "I know what to expect. And she's going to be more dangerous than any of us."

"Good thing she's on our side." He paused. "And maybe one day we'll have a draconic on our side too."

"We can hope."

We sat in silence for a while. "I just don't know," I said at last. "I have no clear direction. I'm hoping whatever news Stacy has will point me somewhere."

"What will advance our cause the best?"

I nodded. "Good thought. I'll have to think about that. The dragons have almost certainly given up on their war, so where does that leave us? How can we get rid of the remaining five?"

"Trick them all into turning human and then killing them?"

"If only."

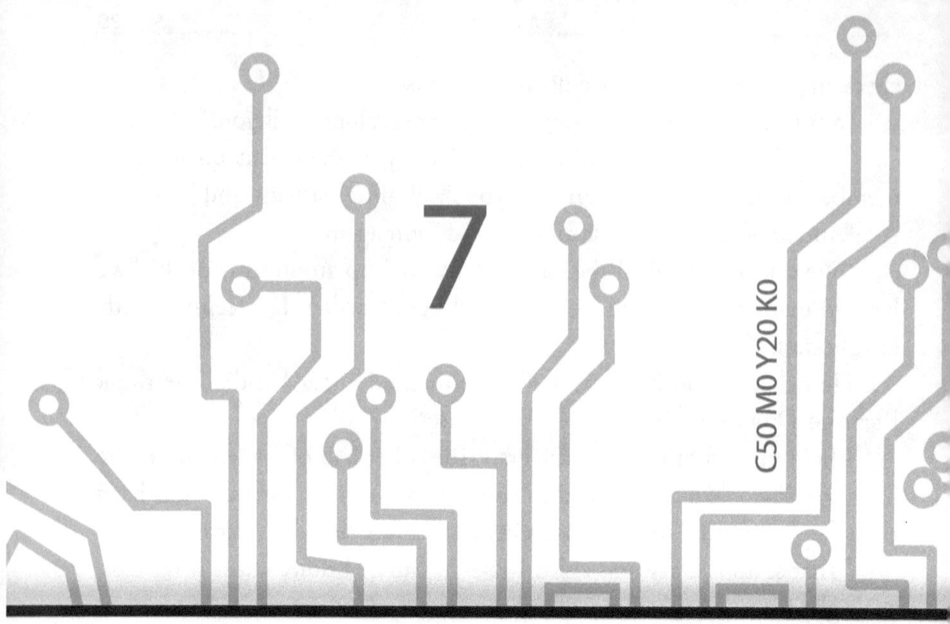

We spent the next night out in the open, only a few miles from our destination. On the next day, we reached the Achromatic Asylum. A lot of news and excitement awaited us.

Basil and Caedan's crew had done extensive work in our absence. Rather than try to re-create things as they'd been before Onyx's attack, they'd chosen instead to dig out a series of tunnels through the ruins and hills. They used a lot of Don's old construction pieces to shore up the tunnels. Altogether, they'd built a home base with enough sleeping quarters for a couple dozen people.

"This is fantastic!" I told them all. "You've done a lot in two months!"

"It was Basil," Saxe said. "We wouldn't have gotten much of anything accomplished without him."

Basil only shrugged. "Work is work," he said. "I did my part."

Caedan slapped his guys on the back and praised their work. "Where's Sapphire?" he asked, looking around.

"She went back to Caesious," Cobalt said. "She, uh, said she didn't feel comfortable here."

"You let her go alone?"

Cobalt's eyes widened. "No, no! Turq went with her."

"She's safe," Turq confirmed.

Caedan frowned. He probably thought losing one of his team, just for not feeling comfortable, didn't say much to their dedication. It didn't make much sense to me either. Sapphire had appeared completely on board for our cause.

Needless to say, all of the Asylum dwellers were astonished to see Chance, and repulsed to see my face. I fixed a little of that by going straight to Loden's workshop and changing out my eye. To my relief, the new one worked perfectly. Depth perception. Gotta love it.

Once the excitement of being back died down, I showed Hunter the cybernetic hands in the workshop. "Do you think one of these would work for me?"

Hunter took the nicest-looking of the bunch off the shelf and looked it over. "I have not had much experience in attaching cybernetic limbs…"

"You ran cybernetics through my entire body!"

He chuckled. "Not quite the same thing, but…" He turned the hand over and looked at the connections on the wrist. "I think this could be done. The problem is that we'd have to cut off your existing hand—what's left of it."

"I'm guessing that will hurt."

He glanced at my face. "No question. But we would knock you out for it, obviously."

"Do we have what you need here, or would this require a hospital or something?"

"Ordinarily, I would not even consider it without a fully equipped operating room, a backup surgeon, multiple nurses… but it does not seem likely that we will have those kind of resources any time soon."

"Not until we liberate an entire city."

"Then I suppose we will have to make do with what we have." He sighed. "It would not do to keep our leader short-handed."

Was that a joke? If so, I ignored it. "How soon? I need to go to Viridia within the next few days."

"If you want to do it tomorrow, we can," Hunter said. "You have to understand, though: I cannot guarantee anything."

"I know." I held up the ruins of my left hand. "But it can't possibly be any worse, now can it?"

He was about to answer when we both heard a distant but familiar noise. "Is that—?"

"Hard to tell from in here." We both hurried out through the tunnels to join everyone else still sitting around talking. Outside, we distinctly heard the sound again: a train whistle.

Kelly realized it at the same time. "The trains are running again?"

"Oh, right," Saxe said. "They've been going back and forth for the past week."

Caedan turned to Royal. "And you didn't think to report this?"

"It started after my last report to you!"

"It just means what I already suspected," I said. "The dragons aren't at war any more."

"Anyone else forgetting to tell us something important?" Caedan demanded.

"Well, um…" Cobalt began.

"What now?"

"We were going to tell you! It's just… everyone was running around all excited and looking at everything and—"

"Cobalt," I interrupted. "It's all right. Just tell us."

"While you were gone—for weeks, you know—we got a little bored sometimes," he explained.

"So we went exploring," Turq put in. "The two of us, that is."

"And one day, we were way up northwest—no, northeast—of here," Cobalt went on, "and we found this place that could almost be a secret base on its own."

"Right. We built that place to be a temporary fake headquarters," I told him. "We needed a place to hold the gold draconic while I went to visit Auric."

"Oh. I didn't know that."

"This is your news?" Caedan asked.

"No, we found something there."

"Do we have to drag it out of you?" Kelly growled.

"Just tell them!" Turq shouted.

"We found a message!" Cobalt blurted. "From Auric, I think. It's addressed to you, Beryl!"

Turq ran to a pile of supplies in the mouth of the tunnel. He searched for a moment, then returned holding a golden tube.

"That looks familiar," Kelly observed. From her lap, Chance wiggled and reached toward the shiny object.

I took the tube and unscrewed the lid. It was identical to the last message we'd received from Auric. "Could you tell how long it had been there?" I asked.

"It had been a while," Turq said. "No way to know for sure, I guess, but it had dirt on it."

"I cleaned it off," Cobalt added.

I slid out the rolled piece of parchment, and read the familiar opening lines: "To Beryl, once of Viridia, now seeking his own name. From Auric, first child of Chroma, creator of The Circle, and immortal god of gods. Greeting.'"

Lainey looked up at that.

"'Your actions in Viridia came as a surprise to me,'" I continued to read. "'Although I suspect you also were surprised. The return of Onyx is an event that will shape the ongoing future of The Circle. I do hope to discover that you have somehow survived this momentous occurrence; though at present, none of my spies have located you. Should this message reach you, I hope to invite you for another discussion.'"

"Without a hostage, can you even trust him?" Kelly asked.

"'I expect you will want to come, as I have something that belongs to you. While scouting the region following the reappearance of Onyx, my agents discovered two strays.'"

"Bice and Don!" Lovat exclaimed before anyone else could.

"'Rest assured that they are safe, and being kept in comfort. When you come to discuss, you can be reunited with them. I look forward to this occasion.'" I rolled the message back up.

"Well, it was the next logical possibility," Caedan said. "Now what?"

I rubbed my new eye. It felt a little dry. "I still want to check in with Stacy first. She's our best source of information."

"After that?"

"I may have to go to Auric."

"How can you trust him?" Kelly asked. "Last time, he at least promised your safety. He didn't do that this time."

I'd noticed that. "He feels like he has all the advantages this time. He has our friends and knows I want them back. He also knows we're both opposed to Onyx."

"But he wants your cybernetics, like they all do," Kelly argued. "He'll have no reason to let you go."

"I don't know," Lainey broke in. "Auric seems... more honorable than the other dragons."

"Honorable? They're dragons!"

I smiled. "Kelly, I can't tell you how good this feels."

"What?"

"You. Chiming in with your opinion. Trying to be a voice of reason. I've missed that."

"Are you saying the rest of us are unreasonable?" Caedan asked.

I held out my hands—well, one hand and one bandaged and broken thing. "Let's just say that if Kelly is at this end of reasonableness"—I waved my right hand—"You're at the other." I waved my left.

Half of the group laughed, including most of Caedan's crew. "But seriously," I said, "I need different counselors. Your perspective is one, and Kelly's is another. But the one I miss most is Bice. I need him back."

"We all want him back," Kelly said. "But is that chance enough to risk your life that way?" In her lap, Chance looked up at the sound of his name.

"I'll go get him!" Lovat offered, his face unusually hard.

"I wish it worked that way, buddy," I told him. "We don't know much of anything about the city of Auric. Even if we did, they're sure to have plenty of guards."

"It might be worth scouting," Caedan suggested.

"Maybe." I wasn't convinced. "But none of us have the right chromarks to get around there."

"So get some makeup from Stacy," Kelly said. "We've done it before."

"Good point." I put the lid back on the tube. "We're not deciding any of this right now, though. First things first. We visit Stacy."

"As long as Amaranth does not find us here first," Hunter noted.

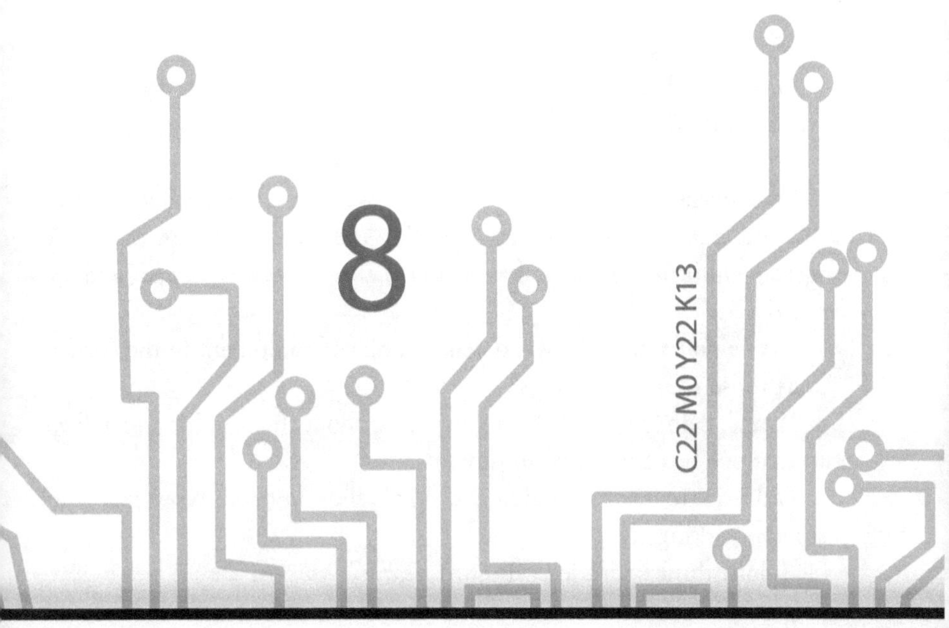

Hunter performed the surgery the next morning. He kept me asleep for it and got assistance from Fern. I didn't wake up until mid-afternoon. When I did, the pain in my left hand didn't surprise me, but the other odd sensations did.

"Easy, easy," Hunter's voice said as I started to sit up.

"What happened?" I asked groggily. "It feels… weird."

"I think it worked," he said. "But you are going to have to be patient."

"What does that mean?" I lifted my hand. The arm looked the same as always, with a thick bandage wrapped around the base of the wrist. The hand itself gleamed of freshly cleaned metal. I tried to flex the fingers, but something didn't work. They moved, but a full second or two later than I meant for them to. And I had no sensation of actual movement.

"Give it time. Your brain is trying to establish and understand the new connections we've made."

I touched the metal hand with my right fingers. "I guess it wouldn't make sense for me to feel that," I said.

"No, that was how your old hand worked. This one… well, you should be able to control it, once your brain understands it. But you'll never feel anything through it." He paused. "Of course, the trade-off here is that it'll be stronger than your old hand, especially with your boosts."

I tried flexing again, but the mental effort made me woozy. "Whoa."

"You should rest some more," Hunter said. "Your Viridia trip will have to wait until tomorrow."

"Yeah… okay…" And I was out.

I woke again a couple of hours later. Whatever Hunter had used to knock me out was still working. Ignoring the pain, I tried to move my fingers. I think it worked a little better. Lainey checked on me, and we chatted a little.

At one point, my eyes wandered to a pile of equipment in the corner. "Aren't those your dad's things?"

"Yeah," Lainey said. "I don't know a lot about them. I think he talked into that one box from time to time."

"Talked into it? Did it talk back?" My eyelids drooped. Wow, that stuff just kept working, didn't it?

"I don't think so. At least, I didn't hear it."

I wondered if it worked something like our talkers, and if Carl had been making reports to the purples robes. Then why had they taken him away? My mind sorted through various theories, but I couldn't hold on to any of them before fading out again.

After slipping in and out of unconsciousness all night, I got up the next morning ready to move on. My hand still didn't always behave the way I wanted it to, but I couldn't wait. Too much was happening, and we'd been out of it all.

As expected, Lainey insisted on coming along. Together with Lovat, we set out, leaving Caedan in charge of the Asylum. Kelly sent a letter along for Stacy. And Glacier tagged along, of course.

Traveling through the open lands reminded me of our early days, almost a year ago. We couldn't stay near the tracks now, with the trains running again. And now we had to deal with the possibility of encountering farmers out in the fields, evaluating what they'd lost during the war, and preparing for a new season.

We talked a lot as we hiked. To my surprise, Lovat kept the conversations going much more than usual. He wanted to talk about our time in the tower, whether Chance would turn evil someday, what might be happening in Viridia, and more.

"Are you two going to get married?" he asked abruptly, right in the middle of a conversation about which dragons were left.

"Um…" I glanced at Lainey. "It's a little soon to be talking about that kind of thing, Lovat."

"Why?"

"Well, because marriage is something you have to think about for a while. Lainey, help me out here."

"But it's fun to listen to you try to answer it." She giggled.

"Why do you have to think about it?" Lovat wanted to know.

"Marriage is a serious thing," Lainey explained. "People shouldn't jump into it unless they're sure."

"Sure of what?"

"Sure that the person they're marrying is who they want to spend their life with."

That was a good enough explanation. I didn't want to try to tell him about how we shouldn't make any major decisions while in the midst of a crazy rebellion against our dragon rulers. He wouldn't understand just yet. Then again, what did a kid his age understand about marriage, anyway? For that matter, what did I understand about marriage? Not much, if I were honest. I still wasn't sure I understood love.

These kind of thoughts made me wish we'd left Lovat behind, so Lainey and I could talk about stuff in private. But maybe it was for the best for now. So much going on…

I was pleased to discover our usual barn hiding place for the night remained unused and unoccupied. At least that hadn't changed.

The next morning, as we approached the city, I recommended we take it slow and careful. "We don't know how the city's changed," I said, "so maybe we don't march down the middle of the street. Lovat, take us through the back ways."

"Got it."

Lovat excelled at this. We entered Viridia about a mile from the train station, in an area where most of the buildings were empty. From there, Lovat led us through back alleys and side streets, watching for problems at every corner and intersection.

And we saw many. A new melancholy seemed to have settled on the city, as if everything had gone back to the way it was before we started anything. More than that, we saw far more Viridian Guard patrolling the streets than ever before. Troilus Green was cracking down on the people. If any of them saw us, it would cause problems I'd rather avoid.

By lunchtime, we'd arrived at the back door of the Citrine, the theater where Stacy spent most of her time. Lovat slipped inside to be sure the coast was clear. He returned a few moments later, and let us in. Somehow, Lainey convinced Glacier to stay hidden behind a trash bin and wait for us. I don't know how she did that. In my experience, cats didn't obey anyone.

Inside, Lovat led us to Stacy's private room. She sat in front of her mirror and didn't get up when we entered.

"I suppose I should be surprised to see you still alive," she observed. "But this is getting to be a habit, Beryl. You disappear for a couple of months at a time then show up like nothing has changed." She turned to look at us, and her eyes widened at the sight of my face. "I take it back. What's happened to you?"

"A lot has changed this time."

"Including your face."

"Turns out Onyx can spit acid, even in human form."

"That's freaky. Did you… did you kill him?"

"Almost. But he got away, with some help."

"Bleaking traitor."

I offered her the letter. "Kelly has a message for you."

"You found her?" Stacy jumped to her feet and took the letter. She tore it open and read the whole thing. "Oh. My. Gods." She looked up. "This is all true? The baby draconic?"

"His name's Chance, and he's so cute!" Lainey put in.

"Really?" Stacy shook her head. "I didn't see that one coming. What are you going to do when it grows up?"

"We're taking it one day at a time," I said. "What's happened while we were trapped? We saw the trains running again."

"Yeah, the war's over, or so they tell us. But things are not well here in the city." She folded the letter and placed it on her makeup stand. "Troilus Green has been proclaiming himself to be Viridia reborn, the dragon in a new body. He even claims it was done to be closer to his people."

"Judging from the number of Viridian Guard we saw in the streets, it doesn't look all that rosy."

"It's not. He's cracking down hard. They've already arrested a huge number of the prisoners you busted free. I don't know for sure, but at least one of my contacts claims the Pit is open again."

I winced. I hated to think of any of the prisoners being sent back to that place. How devastating would that be?

"But it's more than that," she went on. "He's actively trying to convince people now. In person. He sets himself up and lets people come to him and ask questions. Reportedly, he tells them things only a god could know about them."

"He lets people come to him?" That was unlike any of the dragons. "Where does he do this? At the Emerald Ascendancy?"

"No. That's the other thing. He says it's about getting close to the people, right? So he does it at the shrine."

"Our shrine?"

She nodded. "Every other day. At the same place where he supposedly defeated you, and where you used to have your base. He's erasing every good thing you did in this city."

I paced and fumed. Troilus Green, or Viridia, or whatever he was, definitely had it in for me, personally. I guess it made sense, after our previous battles, and our connection with the accident and Loden. Yet if he really was the dragon, he was behaving most unlike one. They never seemed to have much feelings about individual humans, one way or another. Maybe he was some weird mixture of the two. Or maybe… he wasn't really Viridia at all.

Lovat disappeared from my view, digging through some of Stacy's costume racks.

A thought occurred to me. "Where is Troilus Green getting all these soldiers? Wasn't the Viridian Guard having trouble keeping enough people?"

"Good thinking." Stacy pointed at me. "See, you can use that brain sometimes. The truth is: we don't know for sure. But if I had to guess… I suspect that a fair number of them came from Atramentous. If you watch them around the city, you'll notice most of them keep their helmets on."

"So you can't see their chromarks."

"Right."

"This is so sad," Lainey said. "It's like he's undone everything we've done."

"We'll set it right," I declared. "Eventually."

"You never give up, do you?" Stacy shook her head. "But considering how unbelievably lucky you are, I guess you can afford to show some optimism."

Lucky? I didn't feel lucky. Right now, it felt like Lainey said: like everything was being undone.

Stacy tapped the letter. "Kelly doesn't say everything, obviously. Did you ever find Bice?"

"Not yet. But we got a message from Auric. He claims to have Bice and Don, and wants me to come talk." I exaggerated the last word.

"You're just full of good news, aren't you?"

"Back at ya."

She laughed. "That's fair. But I do have some news that might be good. Cerise hopes to see you sometime soon, whenever possible."

"Really? Why is that?"

"She and Marcus have made contact with another group of rebels… in Amaranth."

Another group of rebels? I'd always hoped we would inspire people throughout The Circle to rise up against the dragons, but hearing that some existed still surprised me. And in Amaranth, of all places. I knew we needed to go there!

"Did they tell you anything else? About their numbers, maybe?"

"No, but she thinks you should come find out for yourself. Says this group has someone rich and powerful backing them up. A patron, I guess."

"That could come in handy."

"Patrons always come in handy."

"What about the other cities? What have you heard from them?"

"I've been to a couple of them," Stacy answered. "Things are mostly returning to the way they were. Except in Caesious, of course, which is still mixed up. As usual, I have no idea what's going on in Auric."

"Are you doing performances in other cities now?" Lainey asked.

"Not yet. But I've been traveling, helping prepare for upcoming shows. The commerce between the cities is only just getting started again. The arts are the last priority, sadly."

Lovat chose that moment to stick his head out from behind a row of costumes, wearing a red mask with horns. "Lovat! Put that back!" Stacy scolded. "I need that one intact for Thursday night!"

"How about other allies?" I asked. "How is Jaden?"

Stacy shook her head. "He's scared, that one. He doesn't want to be seen at all, with all the new security measures. He does his work and keeps hidden. I don't think we can count on him for much."

Jaden had been nervous about our work from the very beginning. I guess I couldn't blame him.

I sat down on a props trunk and considered all these factors. I squeezed my left hand into a fist. I could still tell a little bit of lag time between my thoughts and the actions, but it wasn't much now. A strong part of me wanted to just find a way to kill Troilus Green during one of his little gatherings. But he was probably prepared for something like that. It didn't stop me from imagining it. Maybe Lainey could shoot him with her rifle. Blow his head off, right in the middle of a speech. I smiled at the thought.

"What is that look for?" Stacy asked. "Whatever it is, don't do it again, at least until you get plastic surgery or something. It's kind of creepy."

"He can't help how his face looks," Lainey said.

"Oh ho, you're quick to defend him. Something going on here?"

Lainey blushed.

"And there's the confirmation!" Stacy crowed. "Beryl, you dog. Tell me more."

I rolled my eyes. "Why do you always want to talk about… relationships?"

"Part of my charm, love. I deal in information and gossip. You want me to keep getting it for you, you gotta dish some to me."

"I don't like dishing."

"But do you like spooning?"

"What?"

Stacy laughed, rocking back in her chair. "Oh, Beryl. Never change."

"You do this every time I'm here!"

Stacy composed herself. "Fine. I'll get Lainey to dish after you leave the room. We can go back to being all super serious and stuff for you."

"I'm not—ugh. Whatever."

"So what are your plans now? Are you all going to stay at the Asylum again?"

"I don't know. Onyx knows where it is. If we can find another place, it would probably be better." I shrugged. "I just don't know where we could hide. None of the cities are safe at the moment, at least not for long."

"Definitely not here."

"We'll search for something, but for now, Loden's workshop is the safest place to be."

"What are your next plans, then?"

I took a breath. "I need to go to Auric. And visit Incarnadine and Amaranth. After that… maybe we'll come back here and deal with Troilus Green. We'll have to play it by ear. There is a lot going on. So many enemies…" I paused. "Here's a weird question for you: have you ever heard of some people who wear purple robes?"

Lainey shot me a look, but I ignored her.

Stacy sat back. "Wow. Funny you should mention that."

"Why?"

She tossed a makeup brush from one hand to the other. "In the past couple of weeks, I've heard two rumors involving someone in a purple robe. After the first one, I thought someone just didn't see the color right. But then another one popped up. And now you ask."

"What were the rumors?"

She held up a finger. "First, Cerise told me that a co-worker claimed she saw someone in a purple robe in the Flame, talking with one of the draconics. That's the one I thought must be just a color problem. Maybe there were too many shadows and it made a red robe look purple."

"And the other?"

"It was here." She lowered her hand. "I had two different people see it. On the steps of the Emerald Ascendancy. One of them even claimed he appeared out of nowhere."

"Someone in a purple robe?"

She nodded. "Talking with Troilus Green."

I clenched my jaw. And Lainey wouldn't tell me anything. Who were these people? She said they were from outside, but it was starting to sound like they were working with the dragons!

"I didn't think much of it," Stacy went on. "You hear weird stories crop up from time to time, but two of them that close together… have you seen them?"

"Yes. I don't know anything about them, but they keep showing up." I got to my feet. "Thanks as always, Stacy. Maybe once we get things figured out, we can set up a regular information exchange again."

"Be happy to, as long as we're more careful. The streets aren't as safe as they used to be." She waved me away. "Now get on out of here and let me have my girl talk with Lainey."

I sighed and motioned for Lovat to come with me. "We'll be outside. Please don't take too long."

Lainey giggled. "I won't. I don't have that much to say, anyway."

"Oh, you have more to say than you realize," Stacy countered. "I'll get it out of you."

I shook my head and left the room, followed by Lovat.

"Girls like to talk," he observed as we exited the building.

"You don't know the half of it, buddy."

He looked around. "Where's Glacier?"

"I don't know. She's not where Lainey left her?"

Lovat bent down to look into the shadows behind the garbage bin. "I can't see…"

A hand grabbed his arm, and a Viridian Guard stepped out from the side of the building. A second Guard appeared behind him, shockspear at the ready.

"You can stop right there, rebel."

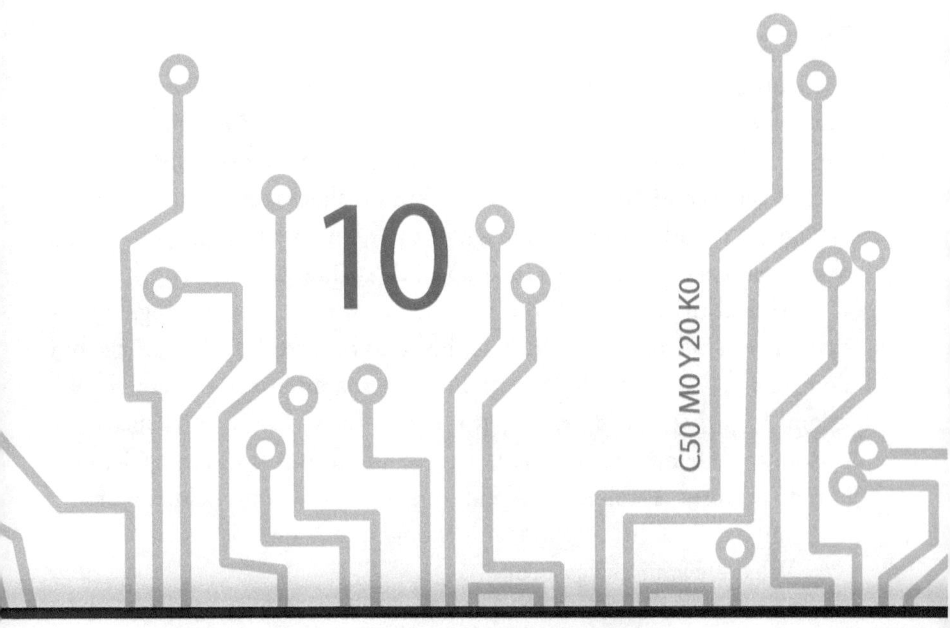

"Let him go," I ordered. "You don't know who you're dealing with."

The helmeted figure tilted his head. "A freak, obviously. What happened to your face?"

I widened my stance and channeled some boosts into my limbs in preparation. "My name is Beryl. Maybe you've heard of me."

"They say Beryl has a multi-colored chromark," said the guard holding Lovat, "but nothing about scars." The boy struggled, but had no chance against the armored soldier.

"I got burned." I held up my cyb hand, palm outward. "Now let my friend go, and you won't be embarrassed when you tell your superior how you got stomped."

"You? You're going to stomp both of us? By yourself?"

"Last warning." A growl came from the garbage bin. I glanced at it and smiled. "I'm also not alone, by the way."

The second guard looked and saw what I saw: Glacier crouched on top of the bin, ready to pounce. Her mouth was open, showing off her growing saber fangs. "Holy Viridia! What is that?"

"Let the boy go," I repeated.

"Char, maybe we should listen to him," the one holding Lovat said.

The other one shook his head. "Idiot. You're wearing armor in the places that matter. We've got weapons. That guy is—"

I lunged forward with boost-enhanced speed. With my cyb hand, I seized the forearm of the Guard holding Lovat, and squeezed. He screamed, letting Lovat pull loose. I yanked him around and shoved him into the path of the second Guard. That one jerked his shockspear up to keep from hitting his friend. I took advantage of the moment, and let loose with a palm heel strike at his chest. The impact threw him back against the wall.

I ripped the helmet off the first Guard, who kept screaming. I must have broken his forearm. Slamming his head back against the garbage bin shut him up. As he slid to the ground, I spun around and reached for the second Guard again. He swung at me with his shockspear. I deflected it with my cyb hand. Seizing the Guard by the front of his armor, I threw him up against the wall for a second time. I grabbed at his helmet with my left hand, but it didn't respond with enough precision.

"What are you?" he gasped.

"Death to the dragons!" And yes, I actually said it, rather than thinking it up five minutes later.

I pulled the shockspear out of his hand and jabbed the tip up under his helmet. His body shook with the electrical charge and slumped down.

Glacier complained at me from the garbage bin. "Try helping out next time," I grumbled. "Stupid cat."

Lainey burst out of the theater door. Stacy peeked out to be sure no one was watching before joining us.

"Oh, great. Did they see you come out of the theater?" Stacy asked, looking over the unconscious Guards.

"No, they showed up after. You should be in the clear." I gave Lovat a side hug. "You okay, buddy?"

"Yah. That was hue."

"Right. See you sometime. Back inside before anyone else shows up." Stacy darted back through the door.

I smiled at Lainey. "Done with the girl talk?"

Our return trek to the Asylum was faster and simpler. I decided to take a risk. We waited until nightfall not far from the train station. Once it grew dark, we watched for a train to pass by. At the slow starting speed, it was easy to hop on to one of the freight cars. We rode until I recognized the place where we'd killed Caesious. From there, it was a short hike over the hills to home.

Along the way, I practiced some more with my new hand. It sort of worked during the battle with the Viridian Guard, but not completely. I compared its motion with my other hand. It moved slower, but only by a little bit. Maybe it would clear up in time.

We found Basil sitting outside, watching the stars. Everyone else appeared to be in bed, even Chance. We exchanged a few words, then went to bed ourselves.

In the morning, we gathered the whole team to discuss what we'd learned and our next moves. I detailed everything Stacy had told us, then let everyone else talk.

"It feels… convenient that we discover this anti-dragon group in Amaranth just now," Kelly said.

"Why there and none in the other cities?" Turq wondered.

"Who says there aren't any in the other cities?" I asked. "Maybe we just haven't met them yet."

"If they exist, they aren't doing much," Caedan said. "Even this one. We've never heard of anything they've done."

"We never hear about anything happening in the other cities," Saxe countered. "How would we?"

"It's just odd," Kelly said.

I didn't argue with her. I wasn't sure what to think about that, but I knew we had to check it out. In the meantime…

"I'm going to Auric first," I announced.

"You can't!" Kelly exclaimed. "You'll never come back!"

"I'm with Kelly on this one," Caedan said. "Why do you think you can trust a dragon?"

"I know that's not like me," I admitted. "But I owe Bice and Don. I have to try."

"Why don't we scout the city, see if we can find them and attempt a rescue?"

"We've been to the city." I gestured at Lainey. "It's… different. I don't see how we could sneak around in it the way we do in Viridia, or even Incarnadine."

"Did you get some gold makeup from Stacy?" Kelly asked.

"No. I, uh, forgot to ask…"

She snorted. Chance, asleep in her lap, stirred.

"How about this?" I suggested. "I'll go to the outskirts of the city and make my presence known. You all can be in position to help out, if I get attacked. I won't enter the city itself without some guarantees."

Caedan rubbed the back of his neck. "Well, if Lainey has the rifle, I guess it might work… as long as they don't march an entire army out to get you."

"He'd probably try to take them all on," Kelly said.

I looked around at the rest of the room. "This is not just about what Kelly and Caedan say, you know. I'm happy to hear any other opinions."

"After you went down into that pit, I don't question anything you want to do," Cobalt said.

"He's not a god," Caedan muttered.

"It sounds risky," Hunter said, "but risk is part of everything you do, is it not?"

"What happens to us if you don't come back?" Fern wanted to know.

"I would hope that at least some of you would keep up the fight. It's not just about me. I'm only one man."

"But you have become a symbol of the rebellion," Hunter pointed out, "at least in Viridia."

"It doesn't matter. It's bigger than me. Look, if I don't come back from Auric in a day or two, you should—"

"Come find you," Lovat said.

"No. You should go meet with Cerise and Marcus. Caedan can handle that."

"Or I can," Kelly said. "I know them better than anyone else here."

"Sure. I was just assuming you would be here with Chance."

"If I wrap him up well, no one will know he's not a human baby."

Toddler, more like, at his rate of growth. "I don't know. I don't like the idea of him being that close to Onyx."

"It doesn't matter," Caedan said, "because you're coming back, even if we have to come get you, like Lovat said."

"No, you can't do that!"

"Oh, so now you're giving us orders? What happened to hearing other opinions?"

"Other opinions are fine, as long as they don't involve suicide missions!"

"Like the one you're about to go on?"

"I have a question," Royal said, raising his hand.

"What?" Caedan asked, a little too sharp.

Royal lowered his hand and looked down.

"Seriously, what is it?" I asked him.

"Well, um, Auric sends you messages. Why can't you send him one?" He bent down and picked something up, then he held it aloft: the golden tube.

I suddenly felt very stupid.

"Where would we send it?" Caedan asked.

"Anywhere they're likely to find it," I said. "We could get close to the city and dump it off in a public location. I don't know why we didn't think of it before. Royal, you're promoted."

"I am?"

"Yes. Caedan, double his salary."

"Done." Caedan grinned.

"Now let's figure out the exact words to write. Also…" I looked around at everyone. "Who here has good handwriting?"

My first inclination was to ask Hunter… and then I remembered he was a doctor. Maybe not.

"Mom, your handwriting is the best," Kelly said.

Fern mumbled something I couldn't hear.

"Great," I said. "Let's write something."

We worked together on a draft, then Fern wrote it out in much nicer script than anyone's I'd seen, besides Bice. I told Auric I was willing to meet with him—but only under another promise of safety. I suggested he send Taizong Gold out of the city with his reply, and we'd be watching for him.

"Can you believe we're dictating terms to a dragon?" Saxe asked. "This is crazy."

"We've been crazy for at least a year," I told him. "You haven't seen anything yet."

After it was ready, we headed north to the gold city early the next morning. I took along Lainey, Caedan, and Turq. Kelly would have come if I'd let her, I know. But it didn't feel right to drag little Chance along with us. Maybe in a few months, if he kept growing.

We spent the night out under the stars again. At least this far away from the mountains, the night was only cool, not frigid. Traveling to Auric took longer than our regular walk to Viridia. We finally drew within sight of it after midday.

The city loomed large as we approached. I don't know if I'd noticed how high it sat the last time we'd been there. We'd ridden a train in that time. But it looked like the whole city had been built on higher ground than the others.

"All right. I will run to within sight of those in the city and wait until I'm noticed," I told the others. "When someone approaches, I'll leave the message and run back."

"We'll watch the whole time," Lainey promised.

I jogged toward the city. The ground definitely sloped up. In a few minutes, I could feel the burn. At least running back would be easier. Once I thought I was close enough, I began to wave the golden tube in the air. Eventually, someone would notice me. I kept moving closer for a while but stopped when I got within about a hundred yards from the first buildings.

I waited. If it took this long to attract attention, maybe we should have just snuck into the city. I'm not sure how long I stood there, but it was long enough to lose any patience I had left.

Finally, a trio of golden armored soldiers appeared, walking toward me. One carried the massive two-handed bladed weapon favored by some, while the others held swords. I waited until they were in hearing range.

"It's about time!" I called. I held up the tube. "I have a message for your dragon!"

"We'll take you to him!" the leader shouted back.

I set the tube on the ground. "Not today, boys."

"Wait—" he began, but I took off. Boosting my legs, I ran back the way I'd come, far faster than any ordinary human could pursue. After I'd covered enough ground, I turned back to see their reactions. Two of them stood watching me, while the third went to retrieve the tube. At least it got into the right hands. I hoped.

I rejoined my friends to find they hadn't been idle while I waited. Caedan and Turq had gathered a large number of tree branches and rocks to form a barrier of sorts. It wasn't a perfect hiding place, but it was enough to camouflage us from distant viewers. I crouched down to join them.

"They took it back into the city," Caedan reported.

"How long do you think it'll take?" Turq asked.

"Well…" I made myself more comfortable. "I don't think it'll be very fast. They'll probably look it over themselves, then take it to a superior, who will take it to his superior, then maybe to a draconic, before finally getting all the way to the dragon. And then he has to decide how to answer."

"What if his answer is to fly out here himself?" Turq wondered.

"Then you'll get to see a dragon up close, at least for a few seconds."

We settled in to wait. Lainey broke out some dried meat strips for a late lunch. As I took a bite, a thought occurred to me. "How are our food supplies at the Asylum? I haven't even thought about that."

"You have too many things to think about already," Lainey said.

"Yeah, leave that to us," Turq chimed in. "Saxe and I have that under control."

"You do?" Caedan asked.

"Sure. Sapphire is helping too, when she can. We've got arrangements to pick up food from Caesious every ten days." He glanced at me. "Uh, we'll have to use the four-wheeler to fetch it, if that's okay."

"Are you kidding? Of course it's okay. As long as we have fuel, let's use that thing as much as we need to."

We discussed other things while we waited, speculating on the rebels in Amaranth, what to do if Onyx showed up again, and whether to make any moves in Viridia. It was all just talk, throwing out ideas. We didn't make any decisions without the others. Throughout the conversations, I couldn't keep my eyes from straying to Lainey. I wished we'd left the other two guys behind. We hadn't had a moment to ourselves since leaving the tower.

Time passed. The sun began to move down toward the mountains.

"How long do we wait?" Caiden asked.

"I've about had enough," I admitted. "If we don't hear something in the next hour or two, we need to do something different."

"Like what?"

"Knowing me, probably something stupid."

Caedan groaned. "Do I have to be the voice of reason again? I hate that job."

"Don't worry about it," Lainey said. "I think we've got our answer." She lowered binoculars and pointed toward the city.

We all turned to look. I zoomed my eyes and saw a gold draconic with a cybernetic left hand and forearm walking out from the city. Taizong Gold. He walked alone, but I could make out other figures waiting at the city's edges. They would be watching just as we were.

"All right. I'll go meet him and see what he has to say." I started to get up.

"And if he offers you safe passage?" Lainey asked.

"Then I'll take it. And I'll bring Bice and Don back."

"And if he doesn't offer it, you're not going, right?" Caedan caught my arm.

"Why would I?"

"You're not answering."

"No, I won't go to meet the dragon without at least some kind of promise of safe passage." I sighed. "I'm not suicidal."

"Since when?"

I ignored him and turned to Lainey. "I will come back," I told her.

She smiled. "I'm starting to believe that."

I leaned in and gave her a kiss, feeling a bit awkward in front of the other guys. When I pulled away, I spun around before Caedan could say anything. "Let's do this."

I hopped over the barrier and jogged toward the city again. The draconic saw me coming and stopped to wait around the same distance from the city where I'd delivered the message. Unlike Troilus Green and his ridiculous robe, Taizong Gold wore only a pair of loose-fitting gray-green pants. I wondered at that. The draconics really didn't need to wear any kind of clothes. Did they think it made them fit in with humans better?

"Ah, Beryl," it observed as I drew near. "I see you have experienced some… difficulties since last we met."

I waved my left hand. "Trying to look more like you. Did Auric get my message?"

"Yes. We expected you weeks ago, but I suspect you've had your… hands full."

Was that a joke? Draconics didn't make jokes, did they?

"The almighty Auric welcomes the opportunity to renew dialogue with you. Will you come with me?"

"Not so fast. I need assurances."

The draconic's smile broadened. "We have something you want this time. We have kept your friends safe and will continue to do so… as long as you come with me. Should you reject this offer, you reject their safekeeping as well. That is the only assurance I am authorized to offer you."

"So if I come with you… you'll let them go?"

"You have my word."

"But no promise for me."

"None."

In essence, I was being asked to sacrifice myself for Bice and Don, and Auric knew it. Was this another of his strange tests? He seemed very interested in how I behaved in difficult situations. I glanced back at my friends. They were watching through binoculars, but they couldn't hear our conversation. I'd promised Caedan I wouldn't go without safe passage... but I didn't say safe passage for me. And I couldn't leave Bice and Don at the mercy of the dragon.

"All right. Let's go."

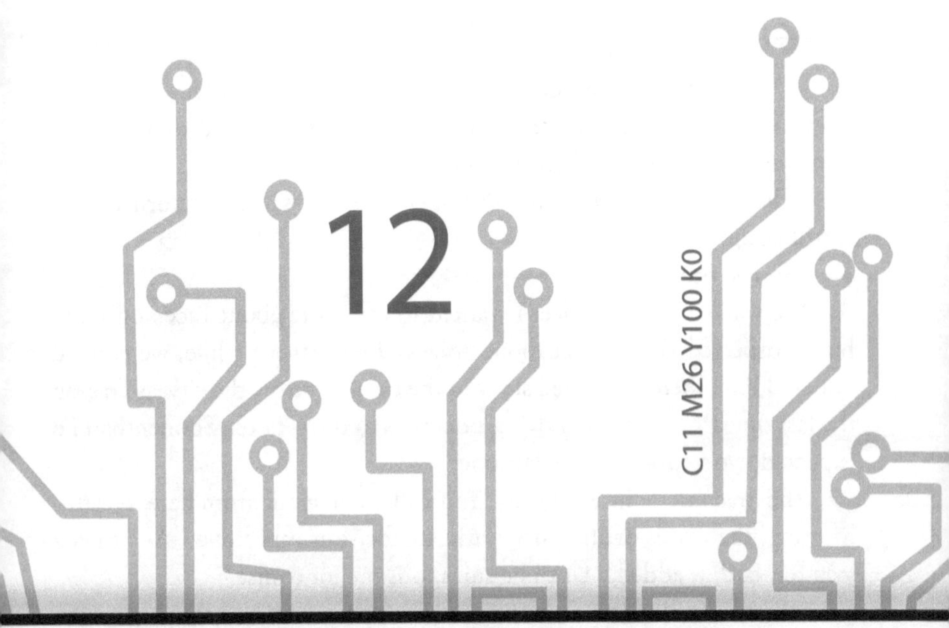

Taizong Gold led the way back into the city. Gold-armored soldiers fell into a circle around us as we entered. No turning back now.

Since I had nothing better to do, I admired the architecture while we walked. During my last visit, I'd been more obsessed with talking with people. Our guide had tried to tell us about the architecture, but I'd ignored most of it at the time. Many of the buildings had pointed roofs with rounded corners leading to strange tips. I saw a lot of wrap-around roofed decks or balconies. As before, no one color, dominated, not even gold.

I made sure to observe the citizens of Auric along the streets again. They didn't walk with heads down like the people of Viridia. They didn't flinch and cower at the sight of the draconic and soldiers. Some even waved. It made me want to talk with some of them to see if this was real or if it had all been staged for my benefit. But how would I know? My last such attempt had brought mixed results.

"When will I get to see my friends?" I asked.

"We have made no such agreement," Taizong Gold answered.

"You knew that's what I wanted!"

"Your wants are irrelevant. Only the will of Auric matters."

I shook my head. "I guess you learned nothing from Protogonus Blue."

After a moment of silence, the draconic asked, "How is my cousin now? Did Onyx spare him?"

"Onyx did not. He's dead. I buried him myself." Interesting. They knew about Onyx. Did all the dragons know? How would they react to knowing Amaranth was sheltering him?

"That is very sad to hear. Without a sire, he will not return to this world again."

"So I've been told."

We walked on in silence. I wanted to ask more about Bice and Don, but I suspected I'd only get more stonewalling. After a while, we entered one building, then descended stairs to the tunnels below the city, as I'd seen the last time. We used the moving sidewalks to travel faster. Sooner than I'd expected, we stepped off the last one.

The draconic pointed ahead. "You will go on alone from here. For this meeting, the words of almighty Auric are for your ears alone." As I took a step forward, it added, "Until he summons me, of course."

"Right." I walked on. I remembered this part. I entered the gargantuan cavern full of floating lanterns. The golden dragon, curled up in the middle around his orb, lifted his head as I approached.

"Ah, there you are, human," his voice boomed. "I was pleasantly surprised to receive your message. We had long since assumed you were dead, destroyed by the second coming of Onyx."

"Auric. I'm here for my friends."

"And they will be released following our conversation, as promised. You need have no worries on that front."

"Yet you gave no promise for my safety. Will you be killing me and stripping out my cybernetics for your scientists to study?" I saw no reason to dance around the issues.

The dragon cocked his head. "I suppose that depends on what you say to me in the next few minutes. Are you still the angry child who appeared before me months ago? Or has time and pain matured you?"

I considered my words before I answered. "I am… a different man than the one who spoke to you before. In some ways."

"And what does Onyx have to do with this?" Auric uncurled his body and stretched his limbs. The orb pulsed with multicolored lights. "I am curious to know your part in his… revelation."

"He betrayed me," I said, seeing no reason to hide it. "He was with me all along, disguised as a human. I didn't know, of course." I spread my hands. "But you told me where to find Viridia's source. That was what he needed to restore himself to dragon form. Did you know that would happen?"

"Of course not. We believed Onyx dead for all these years."

"Then why did you tell me about Viridia's source?"

"I wanted to see how you used the knowledge. I will admit: I did not expect you to have the capability of destroying it."

"That was Onyx. I wouldn't have known what to do without him. And then he killed Viridia."

"Yet he did not kill you."

"No."

"And why is that? Are you still doing his bidding?"

I pointed to my face. "He spit acid in my eye. He betrayed me, destroyed my home, killed one friend and kidnapped another. The last time I saw him, I drove my sword through his chest."

"Indeed?" The scales on the dragon's face moved, perhaps something similar to our raising eyebrows. "He returned to human form again?"

"He did."

"Then where is he now?"

I hesitated. Auric obviously did not know the answer himself, or he'd be taking action. They all would. Is that what I wanted right now? Auric, Atramentous, and Incarnadine ganging up against Amaranth and Onyx? It would be an all-new dragon war, only this time: the dragons themselves would fight. The city of Amaranth would be destroyed in the carnage. Hundreds or maybe thousands of humans could die. No. I couldn't tell him just yet. I would need to make contact with this rebel group in the city first. Maybe with their help, we could orchestrate something to get the fight outside the city.

"I'm not positive," I said. "And if I did know, why should I tell you?"

"Hmm. There is the issue of your safety, as we already mentioned."

"So you say. From my point of view, that means I have nothing to lose."

"You seek revenge against Onyx. Would it not be better to allow me to execute it for you?" He scraped the claws of one foot along the ground. "I do possess… a bit more power than you."

At his words, I felt my energy drain away, part of the gold dragon's power. I took a step backward. "I cannot deny that. But your way would result in the deaths of too many innocent human lives. That's where I draw the line."

"And yet, you worked to prolong the war between the cities, in which a large number of humans died."

Ouch. "My goal has remained the same throughout."

"What is that goal? You would not tell me the last time, though it is not hard to deduce."

"I want all of you dead. I want humanity free to make our own choices. That's all."

"If that is the case, you have not been very effective as of yet."

"Two dragons are dead." I clenched my fists. I didn't even notice my cyb hand now. It felt real.

"Are you claiming responsibility for that?" The dragon's wings rose from his body.

I needed to tread carefully. Losing my temper with him last time had not been wise. And if I claimed responsibility for the deaths of Caesious and Viridia, it would be even... less wise. I probably wouldn't leave the cave.

"No. I'm just saying that my goals are happening."

"And yet another dragon has returned from the dead. And one of those who died now possesses the body of one of his children."

"Is that really what happened?" I asked. "Is that really Viridia?"

"Tell me where to find Onyx, and I will answer any questions."

I shut my mouth.

He sighed. "You have lost some of your anger, but not your obstinance."

"Why should I trust you?"

"Have I not always kept my word to you?"

"I don't know. I haven't seen my friends yet."

"They will be released. And you may yet see them yourself. You are wholly at my mercy."

"So I noticed." One of the floating lanterns passed close enough to make me take a step back. "I can't trust you, though. You tried to kill the entire city of Caesious."

"Which you prevented."

"But you tried! You had no problem with killing hundreds of thousands of people!"

"Everything I do is for the greater good. It is a lesson you should learn. There are reasons beyond your understanding."

I tried to push down my rising frustration. "Everyone keeps on telling me things like that, implying all this stuff about larger battles and things outside The Circle." I waved in the direction of the mountains. "But no one will tell me all of it. Only hints. If you're truly acting for the greater good, then explain it. How could the deaths of hundreds of thousands produce a greater good?"

"If it prevents the deaths of millions."

I squinted at him, trying to understand his facial expression. Millions? Only a million or so people lived within The Circle. How could… oh. Did he mean people outside The Circle? Were there really that many? And how could our war in here affect them?

"For the sake of all those lives," Auric went on, "Onyx must be stopped. I will ask you again." He spread his wings wide. "Where is he?"

"I don't know for sure. If he's in dragon form, it should be easy to find him, shouldn't it? And if he's in human form… how could we find him? He could be anywhere." It was much easier to ask more questions rather than outright lie.

"This is true. And since I have not located him, he must be in human form again. It is an effective method of hiding, but it leaves him more vulnerable." Auric shifted, his lengthy neck gyrating.

"I don't know about that," I said. "I stabbed him through the chest, and he still escaped."

"Assuming you speak the truth, it was a stroke of luck on his behalf." Auric lowered his head. "When we are in human form, we have human bodies. We can be killed like any other human."

"But you still have some of your dragon powers. My face is proof of that."

"True. But we have no accelerated healing, in either form. I would presume that Onyx is now recovering somewhere from this grave injury. He may never be the same."

That was good to know. But… "Why are you telling me all of this? I don't understand your motives here."

"And that is intentional. I have no desire or need to explain myself to you. Save for this: the verified death of Onyx benefits all of us."

I frowned. "Last time, you challenged me to save Caesious. Are you challenging me again? Is this another one of your tests?"

"It is not. But…" The dragon paused and tilted his head as if listening for something. "Should you continue to be of service, in the long run, you will understand more. And perhaps… perhaps we will end up on the same side."

"I don't see that happening. I told you I want humanity free."

"What makes you think I could not accept that?"

I blinked. He couldn't be serious. "Uh, one thousand years of history."

"Tell me: did you finish reading the Cerulean Books of Lore?"

"Not personally. Onyx took them." And we never found them in the tower. I assumed Onyx took them to Amaranth for some reason.

"A pity. Perhaps then you would understand more, especially from the beginning."

It probably wasn't the time to tell him we didn't get the first book. I almost told him Bice had read the rest of the books, but I didn't want to do anything that might jeopardize his chances of leaving the city.

"Enough of this." Auric shook his wings and folded them back against his body. "This audience draws to a close."

"And what happens when it does?" I took a quick glance around, watching for soldiers or draconics.

Again, the dragon watched me. I almost channeled a boost then and there to prepare to run, but I held back, waiting.

"As I said, you may yet be of service. To that end, I have a gift for you." Auric patted the ground, probably as a signal to someone.

A lone man approached from the distant left. With the floating lights, I couldn't tell if he'd been there all along, or just entered through a doorway beyond my vision. There was nothing unusual or memorable about the man. If I had to guess, based on his frame and body language, I would guess him to be a scientist. He drew near without speaking and held out a small box.

I took the box with some trepidation and opened it. I half expected to find an orb like the dragon always had with him. Instead, sitting on a foam cushion, I saw a metallic disk about three inches in circumference. It was covered in tiny details, but I couldn't make out much of anything. It looked cyb to me. "What is this?"

"Leave us now," Auric ordered. At first, I thought he was addressing me, but the scientist spun on his heel and hurried away. The dragon watched him go, then turned back to me. "Even the scientists who worked on it do not know its full purpose. Should they learn, I will have to remove them."

"But you're telling me?"

"I am telling you because I believe you may have opportunity to use it. You are also the least likely person to be able to duplicate the technology."

That much was probably true, though not if Loden were still alive.

"Even so, there are precautions," Auric went on. "Should you, or anyone else, attempt to pry open the device, it will destroy itself. I advise against doing so."

The box felt a little heavier in my hands.

Auric lowered his head all the way to the floor and spoke in a very low voice. "When activated, the disk will attach itself to human skin, so be careful about touching it, until you are ready to use it. Your goal is to attach it to the skin of Onyx."

"What will it do?"

"It will lock him into his human form. He will not be able to transform into a dragon, nor will he be able to remove the disk himself. However…" Every word the dragon spoke sent a wave of heat washing over me from this close. Combined with the weakness I already felt from his power, it made me want to fall to my knees. I sent a boost into my legs to keep upright.

"The effectiveness of the disk is dependent on its location. Should you place it on an arm or leg, for example, he may be able to transform before it becomes effective, if he realizes what is happening."

"So… the head then?"

"The neck would be best. Back of the neck, if possible, to allow it a direct connection to the brain stem."

I stared down at the small disk. What kind of technology could do something like that? A dragon's transformation seemed more magical than anything else. Yet here was a piece of metal that could counter it. If Auric's scientists could do something like this… I couldn't even imagine what else they might be capable of doing.

My mind also raced through the different possibilities. If I could slap this thing on to Rick, prevent him from transforming, it would be a massive advantage. But only if I could get him away from Amaranth. Again, I considered telling Auric about them. But the potential lives in jeopardy held my tongue again.

"Thank you," I said at last. "I sincerely hope to be able to use this gift."

"It can only be used once," Auric cautioned, lifting his head again. "Once it locks onto a dragon's identity, it cannot be used on another."

A dragon. He said "a dragon," not "Onyx." This hadn't been designed specifically for him alone. I could use it against any other dragon if I caught them in human form. Interesting. Of course, Onyx was my primary target, but it was always good to have more options.

"How is it activated? Is there a button to push or something?"

"When you touch it with your bare skin, it will activate, locking onto your identity as its user. You must then apply it within a minute's time, or it will lose its effectiveness."

"It locks on to my identity?"

"And then the target's identity when placed. Thus, you will be the only person who can also remove it. Although… I hope you will not have cause to remove it until the target is dead. And then there will be no reason."

I picked up the disk with my cyb hand and slid it into my pocket. As long as I only handled it with that hand, I could keep from activating it.

"Any other words of wisdom?" I asked.

"You made it through the entire conversation without anger. That is good." Auric looked away as if he were bored. "It shows that perhaps you have grown beyond the angry child. If you continue this growth, combining wisdom with your… unique abilities, you may yet prove of great service to… The Circle."

The Circle? Not Auric?

"For now, I would continue in your quest for revenge against Onyx. In doing so, you help us all. Farewell, Beryl of Viridia. I wish you success in this mission."

I started to turn, but one more thought popped into my head. I looked back up. "What do you know of people in purple robes?" I asked.

A number of Auric's scales shifted at that question. Ha. He did know something.

"Why do you ask this?"

"Because I've encountered them multiple times now. I want to know who they are and what they're up to." I held out my hands. "If I'm serving The Circle, shouldn't I know its enemies?"

Another long silence followed. Auric closed his eyes and smoke trickled from his nostrils. *Uh-oh. Did I anger him?* I took a step back.

The eyes opened. "They are not to be trifled with," the dragon rumbled. "But yes, they are enemies of us all."

Ha. "I think Onyx may be dealing with them."

Auric froze. "Are you certain?"

"No, but one of his lackeys implied as much."

"Then it is even more imperative that we end Onyx's threat as soon as possible."

"Are the purple robes from outside The Circle?"

"Whatever you may think you know of them… you do not know enough. Do not attempt to engage them in any way. They are perhaps the most dangerous foes you will ever meet."

"More dangerous than you?"

"This audience is over. Leave my presence."

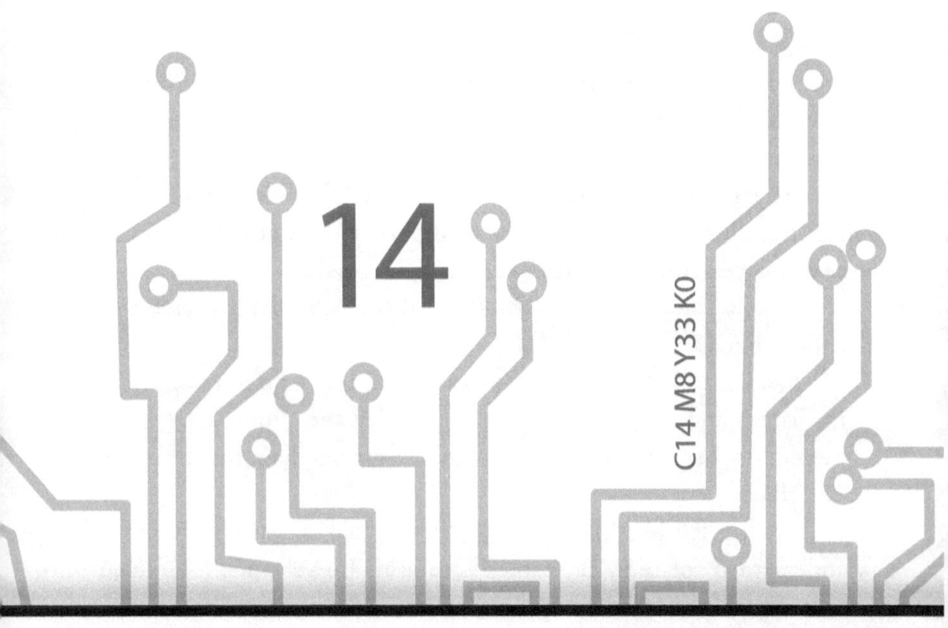

14

Wow. I got under a dragon's skin again, and without even trying. I hurried back into the tunnel and found Taizong Gold waiting for me. Now to find out if Auric had been serious.

"I'm ready to leave the city," I told him. "Have my friends been released?"

"They have," the draconic answered, watching me with an odd expression. Curiosity, maybe. "I understand that almighty Auric wishes you to leave, as well. These soldiers will escort you."

"Well. I'd like to say it's been nice seeing you again, Taizong… but that would be lying. Goodbye."

"Farewell. You are a most unusual human."

"I'll take that as a compliment."

Together with the soldiers, I stepped on to the moving sidewalk again. I tried engaging them in a conversation, but got only one word responses. I gave up and went along until we reached the edge of the city.

"Should you return, do not attempt to approach the city without an escort," their leader warned.

"Wouldn't dream of it." I gave him a wave and started walking away. I almost expected an arrow or something to hit my back, but nothing happened.

I jogged toward where I knew the others were hiding. The metal disk in my pocket slapped against my thigh with every stride, reminding me of its presence. What an amazing gift from Auric, but what a set of complicated thoughts came with it.

As I got closer to the makeshift barrier, I could see heads moving around, illuminated by the setting sun. They did not appear to have noticed me yet. And then I realized: I saw five heads.

I broke into a run. Was it really them? Already? It made sense, of course, but…

I was only a couple dozen yards away when one person stepped around the barrier and walked toward me. I stumbled and almost fell. I recognized the slightly bent stance, the dark skin, the graying hair, the soft smile.

"Bice."

My legs felt like jelly all of a sudden. I held myself together somehow and reached for him. Bice spread his arms in welcome. I tumbled into them, unable to speak, wrapping my own arms around him, tears springing into my eyes. He held me tight, rubbing one hand in circles on my back. "My boy," he whispered.

"Bice," I managed to say again, choking on the word. I wanted to say so much more, to tell him how important he was to me, and how much I'd missed and needed him. But my throat wouldn't let me form the words. I couldn't get anything out.

At last, he pulled back, holding my shoulders. "Let me look at you," he said, his voice as soothing as ever. His eyes filled with concern. "You've been through a lot of pain, son. I'm so sorry I wasn't there to help you through it." He reached up and brushed his hand against my cheek, not far from the acid-ravaged scars.

"I looked—" I wanted to say I looked everywhere for him, but again, the words just wouldn't come out.

The others came out to meet us, and with them came Don. I broke away from Bice long enough to give him a quick hug as well. The craggy-faced miner, not one for showing emotion, mumbled something and looked down.

Lainey threw her arms around me next. "When the other two came out, I was worried! I couldn't help wondering if you'd traded yourself for them."

"I told you I'd come back."

"I see there have been more changes," Bice observed.

I laughed and turned back to him, Lainey's arms still around my neck. "You have no idea."

Caedan stepped in and held up his hand. "Yeah, there's a lot to tell, but how about if we move further away from that city before we do it. You guys may be ready to trust Auric, but I'm not. Not yet."

I took a deep breath and let it out. "Yeah. Okay. Let's… head back. Bice, Don, are you two all right with walking?"

"We've been well treated," Bice said. "We're both as healthy as the day we last saw you."

We started walking, letting Caedan lead the way. Turq walked beside him, glancing back at us from time to time. He'd never met Bice or Don, but I assumed they'd been introduced before I arrived. Lainey walked beside me on one side, with Bice on the other. Don walked to Bice's left, speaking as little as he always did.

I insisted they tell their story first. Bice told about the black dragon descending on the Asylum. They ran for the cave, but Mazarine stopped Kelly. "I tried to go after her, but Protogonus Blue stopped me," he said, shaking his head. "He forced me into the workshop, then went back. The tunnel caved in a few moments later."

"We shut the door," Don added.

"And then you dug out!" I exclaimed. "We found the tunnel you made."

Don shrugged. "Had to do it."

"When we got out, we started to go back to the Asylum, but spotted the gold warriors approaching," Bice went on. "They'd already seen us, so we went to meet them, rather than leading them to the base."

He didn't have much to say about their stay in the city of Auric. They'd been interrogated by a draconic, then left to themselves in a nice set of rooms, like the ones Lainey and I stayed in. And there they'd stayed until today.

"The draconic would show up every week or two, ask a few questions, and then leave us again. Every day was the same as the one before. I didn't know why they were keeping us alive, but I'm grateful for that much."

"They were waiting for me," I said. "They left a message for me, but we didn't find it until a few days ago."

"You turn. What's happened to you in the past six months?" Bice took a look around him at everything else. "And the rest of the world, as well.

We know nothing."

"Do you… do you even know who attacked the Asylum?" I asked.

"Atramentous, weren't it?" Don said.

"Definitely black," Bice agreed.

I stopped walking and bowed my head. It still hurt to admit the truth. Everyone else came to a halt as well.

"It was Rick," Caedan said when I didn't. "He's been Onyx, the missing dragon, all this time."

Don wrinkled his brow. Bice took a step back. "Gods above," he whispered. He looked like he might fall over, so I caught his arm with my left hand. His eyes noticed it for the first time. He looked up at me with such sadness, I thought I might fall over too.

"He betrayed us," I said. "He killed Viridia, destroyed our home, killed Protogonus Blue, and took Kelly prisoner because she was pregnant with his draconic child."

Bice put a hand to his mouth. This time, I let him sink to the ground. I knelt down with him. "It took me weeks just to recover enough to go on," I told him. "If not for Lainey and her father, I think I'd probably have just curled up and died."

"You would have pulled out of it eventually," Lainey said.

"I don't think so."

"Tell me the rest!" Bice insisted. "Kelly? Mazarine?"

I told him of Mazarine's betrayal as well, then gave a quick summary of our time in Viridia, with the prison break. I talked about Caedan's return with his team and then our trip to the tower.

"We were trapped there for two months because of the weather," I explained, "and Kelly's health. We just got back to the Asylum, found the message from Auric, and came for you."

"Then… the draconic child still lives?" Bice asked.

I nodded. "Chance. It's… a hard thing, Bice. It might grow up to betray all of us."

"Or he might not. We can save him, Beryl." He gripped my arm again. "So your newest injuries? They come from Rick? Onyx?"

"Yes." I flexed the hand. "It's not that big a change. Except my face, of course. Although Hunter says he can repair it, if we ever get medical facilities."

"I look forward to meeting this Hunter." Bice got back to his feet, waving off my help. "Or meeting him again, I should say. I have a vague memory of Loden introducing me to his assistant one day when you were in the hospital."

"He reminds me a little bit of you," I said. "In appearance, anyway."

Bice wrinkled his brow. "What do you mean?"

"You don't look all—"

"The assistant I met was a tall, skinny guy with pale skin," Bice said. "What does this Hunter look like?"

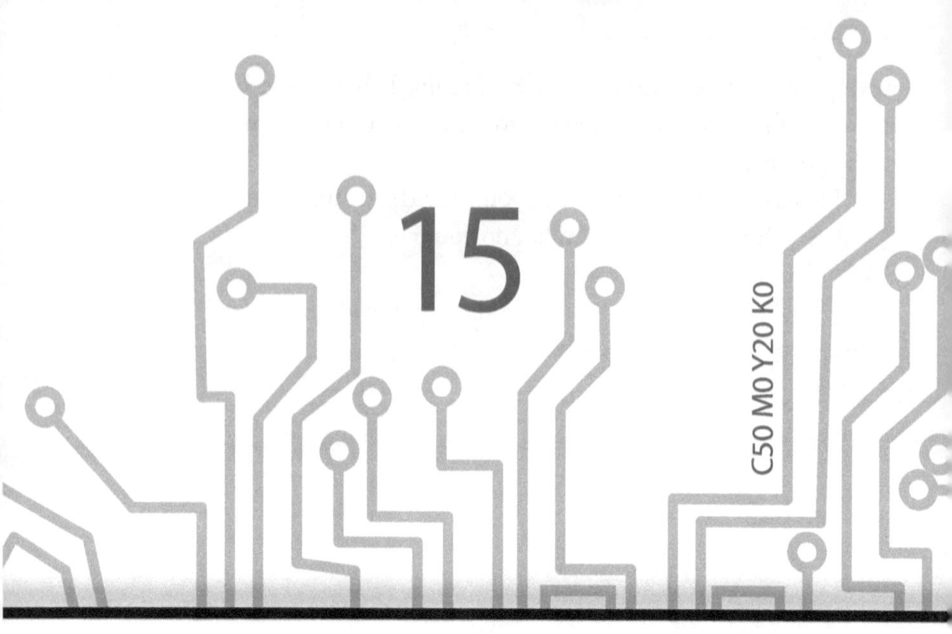

15

Could Hunter have been lying to us all this time? No. That made no sense. He knew too much: about me, about Loden, about the process I went through…

"Loden had another assistant," I said. "Someone else is out there."

"Hunter wasn't an assistant," Lainey put in. "They were partners, really."

"But if Loden had an assistant, why hasn't Hunter mentioned him?" I wondered.

Caedan groaned. "Why can't anything in our lives be simple?"

"The world is not simple," Bice said.

I laughed. "See? That right there. That's one of the things I've missed so much." I pointed at Bice. "Wise statements like that one. You are so good at that." I laughed again. "I am so happy you're back."

"Shouldn't we keep moving?" Bice asked. "I want to meet all these new people."

"Yeah," Caedan said. "And Beryl hasn't even told us about his talk with the dragon yet."

"Oh, that…" I reached into my pocket to feel for the disk, but with my cyb hand, I felt nothing. Kind of ruined the point of handling it.

"Well?" Lainey asked.

"Let's wait until we get back, so I only have to tell it once."

Caedan grumbled, but we kept going until it grew too dark. Our camp that night was the most upbeat and jovial it had been in… maybe half a year. I couldn't remember enjoying a night outside more than that one, anyway. Someone had remembered to bring two extra sleeping bags (probably Caedan), so everyone slept comfortably, or as comfortable as we could be on the ground.

Before I fell asleep, my thoughts wandered around the puzzle of the assistant. Hunter was a genius medical scientist, who worked with Loden's cybernetic science to install all of the enhancements in my body. But that didn't mean that Loden never had an assistant with his regular work, another mechanical or cybernetic engineer. If we could find him, he could be a great asset to our team. But where would we look? If he'd been in the Virescent Pit when we freed the prisoners, he hadn't approached us, even after I name-dropped Loden. Could he have remained in the dragon's service? Or kept his connection to Loden secret? He might still be employed at the Emerald Ascendancy, even. I could have Stacy ask around. Speculations chased around in my head until I finally fell asleep.

It took all of the next day to reach the Asylum again. We arrived an hour or more after sunset, far too late for a meeting. We found sleeping space for everyone, which took a little doing. It was amazing how much our organization had grown. In addition to the fourteen people (and one baby draconic) here at the Asylum, we now had people in three different cities, at least. I wondered how big the group in Amaranth would be.

At last we gathered as a group the next morning. The workshop wasn't big enough for a meeting this size, so we sat outside under the morning sun. We chose the side of a hill so I could sit at an angle high enough to see everyone else. I looked over the group. Bice sat beside Kelly, holding the sleeping Chance, staring down at the infant with wide eyes. Don and Lovat, reunited to great joy the night before, sat together on the outer edge of the group. Basil also sat slightly apart. The rest gathered around and in front of me. Glacier stretched out in the sun on the hill above me. I couldn't help feeling that every time the others were looking at me, they were actually looking at the cat.

"Well, as should be obvious, our trip to Auric was a great success," I began. "I can't tell you all how thrilled I am to have Bice and Don back with us." Several people cheered, only to be hushed by Kelly. "Annnd… looks like our meeting will have to be low-key until Chance wakes up,"

I added. "We'll do our best, Kelly."

I took a deep breath. "I spent some time talking with the gold dragon again. He had some… interesting things to say."

"I don't understand," Cobalt said. "We're fighting against the dragons. Why does he talk to you?"

"I don't understand it all myself. Auric has always been the… most mysterious of the dragons. His motives confuse me. This time, he even claimed to be acting on behalf of the greater good."

"The greater good of the dragons," Royal muttered.

"The point, as far as I could tell, is that he knows about Onyx and is just as interested in seeing him dead as we are. We have a mutual enemy for the moment. And that's why he gave me this." I took the disk from my pocket and held it up. "I slap this on the back of Rick's neck, and he's trapped in human form. For good."

"Whoa." Cobalt squinted through his glasses. "That kind of tech in that small a device? That's crazy."

"I agree." I explained what Auric had told me about the disk and its use. "So we have to be very careful and deliberate about when we use this. We'll only get one shot."

"That one shot can make a world of difference," Bice said quietly. "If it's taken at the right time."

"So is that our next move?" Caedan asked. "To go find Onyx?"

"Let's… walk through our possibilities," I said with a glance at Bice. I wanted him to see that I'd matured enough to think things through more than I used to.

"We have possibilities?" Fern asked.

"Let's start with Viridia. The dragon is dead, but Troilus Green claims to be the dragon. He's even meeting with people at the old shrine to prove himself."

Bice looked taken aback at that one. I hadn't gotten around to telling him that part.

"In my mind, this makes him an easy target. Our goal is to get rid of the dragons, and he's acting like one. And… he's a lot easier to kill than any of the others."

"We already did it once, and he got better," Caedan said.

"We'll make sure he's dead the next time." I had to admit: I really wanted to take that mission. "This would be a big step forward in our goals. If we have two cities without any kind of dragon rule, then it'll be harder for the other dragons to keep control over the populace."

"But is it a priority?" Hunter asked. "I want Viridia freed as much as anyone, but is that the next, best step we can take?"

"That's the question," I agreed. "The other option is to head to the red cities. Cerise and Marcus have made contact with a rebel group in Amaranth. If we connect with them, maybe they can help us get close to Onyx." Oddly, I found I wanted to take that mission just as much, if not more. And not just because of Onyx.

"So…" Bice handed the baby back to Kelly. "Both of your proposed missions have an element of revenge to them, it seems."

"I can't deny that. But both of them advance our cause either way. Dead dragons."

"If we do what Auric wants us to do," Turq said, "do you think he'll help us after that?"

"I don't know. Like I said: I can't understand his motivations."

"There's the other option," Kelly said.

"What's that?" Fern asked.

"Auric wants Onyx dead? Why don't we just tell him where he is? Let them fight it out?"

A couple of Caedan's team murmured agreement.

"I've thought of that. In fact, Amaranth is betraying the other dragons by hiding Onyx. So if we spread the information wide… we could see Auric, Incarnadine, and Atramentous all come down on the two of them. Three dragons versus two."

"That would be a sight to see," Saxe said.

"A devastating sight." I pointed behind me. "The Blasted Lands are right over there, remember? How will the city of Amaranth look after a battle like that? How many humans would die while the dragons fought? I can't justify that."

"Even if two or three dragons die too?" Kelly asked. "I'm not saying it's good. I'm just wondering where we draw the line."

"We defend life," Bice said.

"But we started a war," Caedan pointed out.

"And maybe that was a mistake," I said quickly. "It only got humans killed. It almost got Caesious destroyed."

"Are you saying we shouldn't have killed the blue dragon?"

"No! I don't know what I'm saying. I just… I can't justify it. I can't agree to put that many human lives in danger again."

"So… green or red?" Basil asked.

"I can't believe I'm saying this, but…" I hesitated, then went on. "I say red. The opportunity to expand our network is too good to put off. I want Troilus Green dead, but the Amaranth mission fulfills multiple goals and opens up new possibilities."

"It sounds sneakier, which I'm not so good at," Caedan said. "I'd rather go green, but you know I'll follow whatever you decide."

"I'd want to go back to Viridia," Fern said.

"But even if you kill this draconic who claims to be the dragon," Hunter said, "what is to stop another one from claiming the same thing?"

"Good point. We need to get rid of all of them."

"Red," Kelly voted.

"Do we all get a vote?" Saxe asked.

"I'm interested in opinions," I said. "We're not actually voting, necessarily. And I have a different mission in mind for you guys." I turned to the ones whose opinions mattered to me. "Lainey? Bice?"

"I'm kind of still a guest." Lainey shrugged. "I don't know enough."

"You've been with us for almost six months!" Caedan exclaimed. "You're not a guest."

"Then I'd suggest red," she said. "More allies are good."

Bice steepled his fingers back and forth. "I have to say red as well," he said after a moment. "I would dearly love to return to Viridia, but as Hunter pointed out, killing one draconic won't solve the problems there."

"Sounds like we're going red." Caedan sighed. "I'd just gotten warm too."

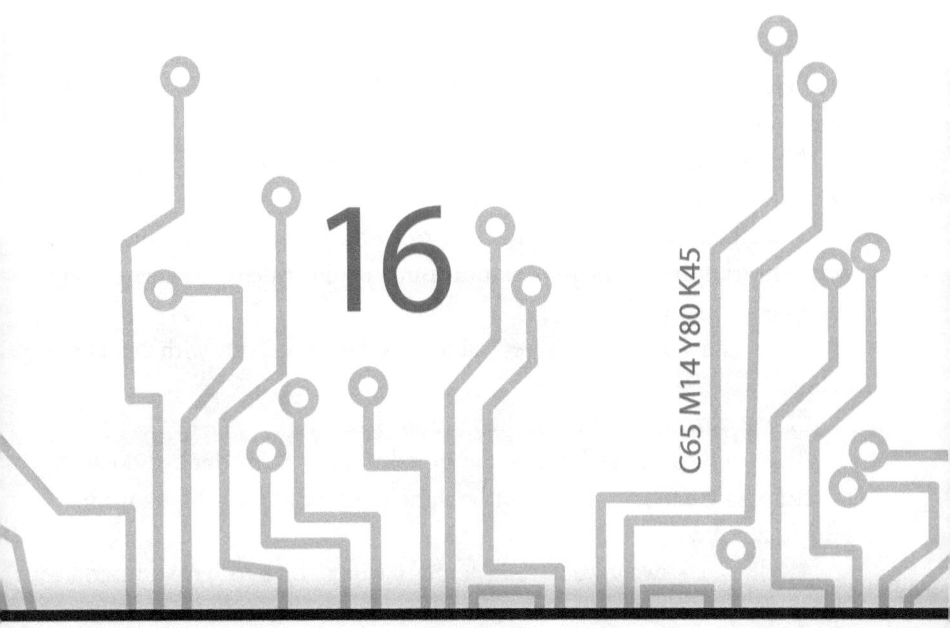

"What's the other mission?" Saxe asked.

I took a glance at the sky. "As much as we love this place… it's not completely safe. Onyx knows about it. I don't know if he's told Amaranth, but if so… she could show up here at any time."

Several of the others looked up at the sky too, worried they might see a red shape descending.

"Since she hasn't come yet, I don't think it's likely," I added quickly. "I suspect Onyx doesn't want her to know about the workshop. But once he's recovered from his injuries, he might come himself. So… we need a new base."

"You want us to find one?" Turq asked, his eyes lighting up.

"Exactly." I nodded. "We've been close to the Blasted Lands long enough. I want you to scout the area between Auric and Amaranth. See if you can find a place for us, whether it's a cave system near the mountains, or a small valley we could work to conceal, or… I don't know."

The blue team looked at each other. "We got this," Cobalt declared.

"All right, but at least one of you should stay here and be the go-between, in case we need one."

"We'll alternate," Turq said. "We need to make a food run soon, anyway."

"Good. Then we just need to decide who stays here and who goes to Incarnadine with me."

"Lovat and I would like to join the search for a new home," Don spoke up.

"Oh. Uh, okay." I had intended to bring Lovat along to the cities, where his skills could help us all out. But I couldn't deny Don, especially since he just got back.

"You know I'm in," Lainey said. "Caedan too, even with his complaints."

"I just don't like the cold," he grumbled.

"I would love to go," Kelly said quietly, "but…" She looked down at the sleeping Chance. "You might be right about not taking him anywhere near Rick. Onyx."

"Kelly…" I swallowed. "You know I would love to have you come along. You're important to this team. But… it's a long walk. We only have one four-wheeler, so it needs to stay here."

"I know." She sighed. "It's bleaking annoying, is what it is. But I guess I'll have to stay here."

The three ex-prisoners all expressed their desire to stay behind as well. I hadn't expected any of them to come along. They weren't the mission type. I did still need to talk with Hunter, though.

"You'll need to keep a watch out," I told them all. "If you see even a hint of a dragon in the air, get into the workshop and close the door. It should keep you safe."

That only left…

"Bice? You ready to get back into things?"

He stirred, as if he'd been thinking about something else. His smile grew. "You know what? I think I am. Before, I thought my well-known face would be a detriment to your work, but now…" He chuckled. "You've got me beat on that front."

I threw up my hands. "So because I got acid in my face, you'll go on missions now?"

"I think it suits you," Caedan said. "Makes your face even more distinctive than the multi-colored chromark."

"Makes you look more rugged. Anyone who sees that face knows they're looking at a serious person," Kelly teased.

I shook my head. "Nobody even looks at my face any more."

"I do," Lainey said softly.

"The others make a good point," Bice said. "You stand out now. People will remember you. That's both a good and bad thing, depending on how you use it."

"I know. Even so, as soon as we have access to the right equipment, Hunter…"

"I will fix it," he promised. "I can even change your chromark, if you like… or get rid of it altogether."

That idea hadn't occurred to me. I thought my multi-colored chromark created a symbol for people to recognize, but… I looked at Lainey's clean face. The chromark had always indicated ownership. Without one… no dragon owned me. Maybe it was time to get rid of it.

"All right." I got to my feet. "I think my team can leave right after lunch. We've got a long way to go."

"We could try to catch a ride on a train again," Lainey suggested.

"We'll keep an eye out. We might be able to shorten the trip a little bit that way."

Everyone else got to their feet and started moving around, talking to one another. "Hunter," I called. "Can Bice and I speak with you?"

As the others moved away, he joined us where Bice remained sitting. "What do you need?"

"Bice remembers Loden having another assistant," I said, pointing at him. "A tall, skinny guy. Sound familiar?"

He wrinkled his brow. "Loden often had other people with him when we met, but… I think I remember the one you describe."

"Why didn't you mention him before?"

"I had no reason to." Hunter looked genuinely perplexed. "I told you I helped Loden with your operations. I did not spend time in his lab, otherwise. Other people came and went."

"Other people?" I couldn't believe this.

"Two or three, at least."

"Did they know what was happening to me?"

He scratched the back of his neck. "I don't… I don't know. They might have? I mean, they knew we were operating on you. And the draconic. But I don't know if they knew how much."

"But you remember the assistant?" Bice asked.

Hunter nodded. "Yes, yes. I do remember him. He had an odd thing with his voice. Cracked like a young teenager." He laughed a little. His eyes drifted away from us, like he was seeing Loden's lab in his mind. "I think… I do not know. Maybe he was in on all of it. I can't be sure."

"You don't remember a name?"

He shook his head.

"Ugh. If we could find this guy, who knows how much he could help us!" I flexed my cyb hand a few times. "He might have more of Loden's notes, or know stuff about all the junk in the workshop."

"He might not even be in Viridia," Hunter said. "Loden traveled to other cities, even during your operations a couple of times. Maybe his assistant did too."

"Or he might be dead," Bice said. "I'm sorry, Beryl, but we have to consider that. The simple fact that we haven't heard anything about him in the past year suggests he's either not around, or…"

"Or he might be working for the dragon. I know, I know." I thought for a moment. "Do either of you think you would recognize him if you saw him again?"

"It has been a few years, but maybe," Hunter said. "I do not know if he would have changed that much since then."

"I barely remember," Bice said. "The description I gave you is the best I can do."

"Okay. When we do get back to Viridia, this gives us something else to do, if he's even there." I stretched. "Seems like our potential missions keep multiplying."

"Growing pains," Bice said. "As the movement grows, so do the possibilities. And problems." He got to his feet with a helping hand from Hunter. "Could you have foreseen all this a year ago?"

"A year ago, I had no idea what I was doing!"

"Exactly. Imagine what it'll be like in another year."

I tried for a moment, then let it go. Imagining only led me to picture either amazing victories or stunning defeats. Which, I suppose, is exactly what had happened over the past year.

"Right. Let's get ready to go."

I headed to the workshop and met Kelly coming out. She handed me an envelope for Cerise. "You already wrote her a letter?"

"I wrote her two months ago, while in the tower," she answered. "I just needed to finish updating it."

"All right." I tucked the envelope into my pocket. "Are you going to be okay?"

She shrugged. "I have to be. I guess I just have to accept that my role is changed for a while, at least until Chance grows up a little."

"He's doing that awfully fast."

"Yeah."

"Listen." I put my hand on her shoulder. "If you need us, you know, if something happens with Chance, or, or whatever, send one of the blue team on the four-wheeler. I will drop whatever is going on and rush back."

Kelly smiled. "I know you mean that. I won't do that unless it's a desperate situation."

"You know… you're kind of my best friend," I admitted. "I can't fathom the thought of losing you again."

"So since Rick turned out to be an evil dragon in disguise, now I'm your best friend?"

My shoulders slumped. That hurt.

"I'm kidding," she said in a hurry. "I know what you mean. We're… well, we're the Viridian ones, aren't we? I mean, we've got Bice and Don and Lovat, but you and I were the first."

"And we knew each other before that."

"At the bike shop. I wonder how Mr. Brunswick is doing by now?"

"I, uh, checked on him a few months ago while we were in the city." I laughed. "Nothing looked like it had changed. He had a new assistant he was bossing around."

"It's good to know some things don't change."

I gave her a hug. "Yes. Yes, it is. Don't change, Kelly."

"I have to grow up, Beryl. I'm a mother now."

"You know what I mean."

She smiled and gave a little nod. "Yeah. I guess I do."

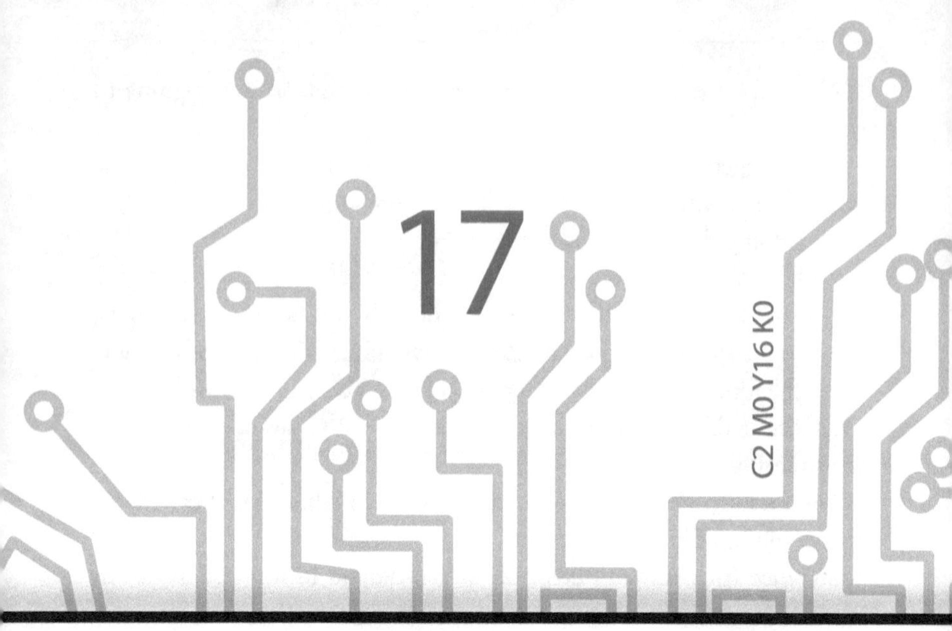

We set out after lunch. We all carried our usual camping supplies while Caedan, Lainey, and I took our weapons. Bice didn't want or need a weapon. If we got into trouble inside the cities, he might be able to call on the resomancy, or whatever the strange power beneath the cities was called. We also packed the last two talkers. Never knew when they might come in handy.

Glacier bounded past us from time to time. She would race ahead, then circle around behind us or something. I couldn't keep track of her movements.

I kept the pace a little slower than our usual trekking. Bice insisted he was in perfect health, but he'd been cooped up in a city for six months, and he was old enough to be my father. Or older. I never did ask him his age.

"Sure hope I can remember how to find the apartment," I said. "I'm the only one here who's been."

"What happens if we knock on the wrong door?" Caedan asked.

"We tell them we're selling books of lore."

Caedan snorted. "As long as I don't get left outside in the cold again, I'll be happy."

We followed the tracks for a little while. One train went by, but was moving far too fast for us to attempt to board it. Our best bet for something like that would probably be after the Hub. We would need to circle around it from the south. But that would take a couple of days, at least.

"I hope we're doing the right thing," I muttered to myself.

Lainey overheard me. "About what?"

"Leaving Kelly and the others at the Asylum. It's not really safe."

"It's a little late to second-guess now. Don't waste time on worry; it doesn't help anything."

Easy for her to say. I could turn worry into an art form. I needed something to replace the rage I used to obsess over, didn't I? I wondered if that's what defined me: obsessions over negative emotions. If anyone ever told my story, is that how they would define me? "Beryl's life was marked by rage, anger, despair, and worry." Ouch. I needed more joy in my life.

My knees ran into something big, and I almost fell over before Lainey grabbed my arm. Glacier looked up at me. "Fewmets. Stupid cat!" Why would it run in front of me and just stop like that?

"She likes you," Lainey said. "She just has weird ways of showing it."

"I think I could do without any showing from her." I gave the ever-growing cat a push, and she moved on, as if nothing had happened.

"Hm. Maybe I should stop showing too," Lainey said with an up-turned nose.

"Please don't. I like the way you show it." I reached out with my right hand and caught hers. We walked on that way for a while.

When we stopped for a lunch break, Bice commented on it. "Lainey, I barely got to know you for a handful of days before we were torn apart, but it seems you've been by Beryl's side ever since."

"She has," I said. "I wouldn't be here. None of us would be here if it weren't for her."

"I wouldn't go that far," she protested.

"When I knelt in the ruins of the Asylum beside the dead body of Protogonus Blue, I believed everything was over," I said slowly. I hadn't tried to express to her how much I owed her. May as well do it in front of the others. "If you hadn't been there… I would have given up."

"You're exaggerating. What would you have done? Turn yourself in?"

"No. I wouldn't have given the dragons the satisfaction, at least. I probably would have just gone for a walk in the Blasted Lands." The thought had occurred to me. Just walk into the toxic region until I couldn't take it any more. My body would fall and decay faster than the digger we'd left there.

"That's bleaking dark," Caedan muttered.

"My point," Bice said in a loud voice to redirect the conversation. "My point is: I'm very, very happy you stuck around. And that the two of you are together."

"They are?" Caedan asked. "When did that happen?"

"I'm going to need you to move a little closer," I told him. "So I can slap you."

"Depends on which hand you want to use."

After the laughter, Bice leaned in. "I'm serious. We've experienced so much loss and disaster over the past year, it helps my heart to see someone embracing love and joy."

What had I just been thinking? I glanced at Lainey as she took my hand again. I didn't know if I was ready to use the word "love," necessarily, but joy? Yeah. She brought me joy.

"Thanks, Bice," I said at last. "That means a lot to me."

"Is the whole trip going to be like this?" Caedan asked. "Because I'm starting to regret not going with the blue team."

I lifted my cyb hand. "It's this hand now."

We finished up our lunch and set off walking again. I reminded myself again, that this is what we were fighting for. Human companionship, community, family. All of these were ruined or at least strained under the rule of the dragons. If only all of life could be like this, enjoying each others' company.

But I had thought the same thing back when Rick had been with us. I thought he would be by my side to the end. I clenched my fist. Even then, a dragon had been conspiring to ruin it all. They all needed to die. If joy and love were going to win, violence had to succeed first. Or something like that.

That night, as we all snuggled into our sleeping bags, I found myself staring through the dark to where I knew Lainey lay. We still hadn't had any real time alone since the tower. Would we ever? I thought back of all the alone times we'd had before that, back when I didn't want to commit, when I was worried about Kelly… the time we sheltered together from the rain… Even in our breakneck-paced lives, I wasted so much of it.

I was an idiot. No question.

Another day passed, and we made our way around the southern side of the Hub, keeping out of sight. We crossed the tracks leading to Caesious. I looked at Caedan and we both stopped and looked down the track, honoring Peri with a few moments of silence. I would never forget that day.

Glacier disappeared for most of the afternoon. She trotted up at our supper break, carrying something in her blood-stained mouth.

"Do I want to know what that is?" Caedan asked.

"Looks like the leg of a goat," I said. "Glacier's been hunting."

"Good for her," Lainey said. "She needs to learn to feed herself more often."

"As long as she doesn't get a taste for human meat," Caedan mumbled.

By the time twilight came, we reached the track leading toward Incarnadine. We backtracked it closer to the Hub and found a good place to attempt boarding. The trains would not be moving very fast as they emerged from the Hub and started the second half of their journey to the red cities.

We were in luck. A train appeared no more than half an hour later. The gathering darkness would help disguise us, but it wasn't too dark to see our way.

"Caedan, go first," I instructed. "Lainey, follow him. Then I'll get Bice to you."

"You'll do what with me?" Bice asked.

Caedan ran from our hiding spot and jumped on to a half-empty flatbed. He positioned himself, then motioned for us to follow. Lainey jumped next, catching Caedan's hand and easily gaining her footing.

"Hands around my neck, priest," I instructed.

"I didn't think—"

"Now!"

He grabbed me and I ran with a boost to my legs. My enhanced strength let me jump with him clinging. We both landed a little rough, but Caedan and Lainey helped steady us.

A few seconds later, Glacier leaped past me and landed on top of a crate on the flatcar. She yowled a complaint, then stretched out.

"That was… something else," Bice said. He shook his head and lowered himself onto the flatbed.

"This will take us straight to Incarnadine, right?" I asked.

"Maybe," Caedan said. "The tracks split when we get close. North side goes to Amaranth, south to Incarnadine. If the train turns north, we'll have to get off and walk the rest of the way."

"Either way, it's saving us hours." I joined Bice.

Caedan shivered. "Couldn't we have found a boxcar, instead? That wind is only going to get colder."

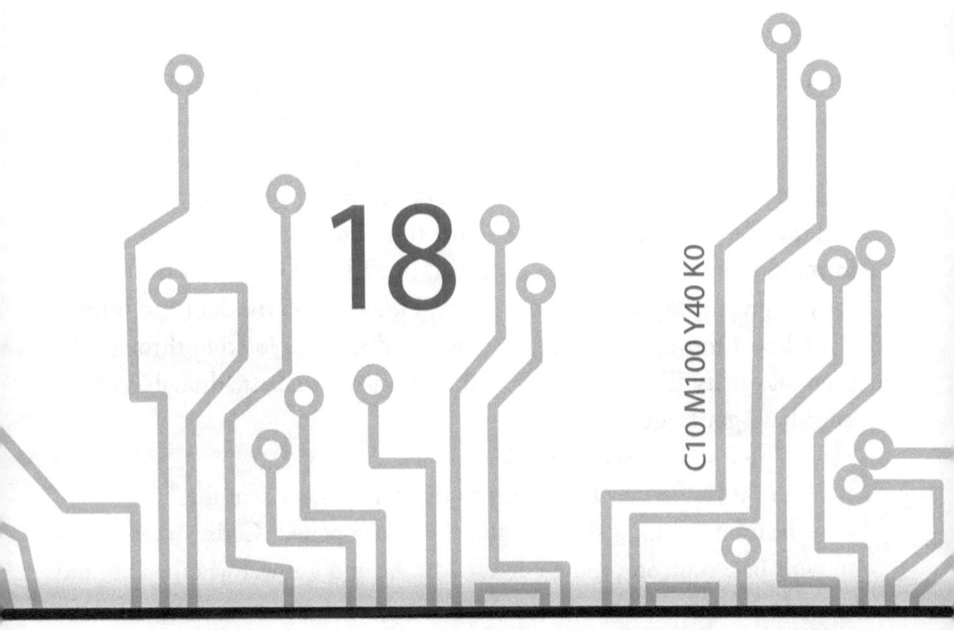

18

We lucked out again, as the train took the southern turn toward Incarnadine. We waited until it was fairly close to the city before disembarking. In a couple of hours, we'd covered a distance that would take us over a day to walk.

Caedan put his hands on his hips and looked toward the city. "Well, this view is familiar." He turned to us. "But this is as far as I got the last time. Hope Beryl knows the rest."

"I walked it enough times," I answered. "We'll get there."

Morning was still several hours away. A good time to sneak through the city streets. I led the way, trying to remember everything I'd learned from following Lovat around, as well as the directions to the apartment building where the Vermeils lived. We hid from the Crimson Elite four different times, slowing our movements. I lost my way only once, but it cost us another half an hour in figuring out where I took the wrong turn.

The others hadn't seen the architecture of this city before. As we drew near the center, I did pause a time or two to let them stare at the glass and metal buildings, and, of course, the biggest attraction: the Flame, home to the red dragon. Looking at it reminded me of all we'd done the last time we were here. I had no desire to enter that building ever again.

I expected the city to be even colder than the last time we were here, but it felt about the same. It still wasn't comfortable, especially in the dark. Maybe Caedan had a point.

At last, I found the right apartment building, situated atop a series of small shops. I couldn't forget those fancy red roofs. I located the entrance and the elevator. After ascending to the third floor, I walked down the hall to room 326. The sun hadn't risen yet, but I knew Cerise, at least, woke early to prepare for her job at the Flame. I knocked on the door and waited.

I heard movement inside, and assumed she was looking through the peephole at us. The light in the hallway wasn't the best, though. A bulb must have gone out.

"Who is that?" asked a familiar voice.

"It's Beryl, Cerise," I said next to the door. "Stacy sent me."

I heard a deadbolt thrown, and the door opened. Cerise, a tall woman with pale skin, stood there in a bathrobe and a towel wrapped around her hair. "Beryl? We expected to hear from you months ago!" She glanced down the hall. "Come in! Come in!"

We moved inside and relaxed at the warmth of the heated air. I glanced around at the familiar furnishings. Nothing had changed here. Cerise moved past us toward the bedroom, but stopped when Glacier pushed in and jumped onto the couch. "What is that thing?"

"Ah, yeah. Um, that's Glacier. She's a, uh, big cat. I hope you're not allergic. We couldn't really leave her outside."

Cerise shook her head. "Let me get Marcus before you start explaining anything," she said. A moment later, she re-emerged, trailed by her husband. He yawned and ran his fingers through his curly black hair. "Beryl? What happened to you? You look… horrible."

"Thanks for noticing." I stepped up and gave him a firm handshake. "And thanks again for all your help last time we were here."

"It was fun," he said. "We all thought you were dead, of course. I almost didn't believe Stacy when she told us you survived." He gestured at my face. "Is that from… Incarnadine?"

"No. This is from Onyx. I'll tell you everything. But first…" I introduced my team. None of them had met the Vermeils before, but everyone had heard about each other. They couldn't help staring at Lainey's bare face, and Marcus almost jumped out of his skin when he finally noticed Glacier on his couch.

Cerise unwrapped the towel from her head, squeezing her hair dry. "I have to get ready for work, so I don't have time for all the stories. I assume you're here about the Amaranth group?"

"Right. Stacy gave me your message. They're an actual rebel organization?"

"They are. And they seem to know what they're doing. They've caused a few problems for the ruling elites over there. Nothing as crazy as you've done, as far as I can tell, but they're active."

"We need to meet them. I'm assuming you can set that up?"

"I can take you later today," Marcus offered. "We have a meeting spot set up."

"Later is good," I said. "We're all quite a bit tired."

"That's what happens when you do your traveling at night," Cerise scolded. "You always show up here and want to sleep on my couch again."

I grinned. "Is that okay?"

She laughed. "Of course it's okay. We're low on breakfast foods, though."

"I can make some oatmeal," Marcus offered.

"Oatmeal would be wonderful," Bice said. "Thank you."

"What about the, uh, cat?" Cerise asked.

"Oh, she just ate before we entered the city," Lainey said. "She'll be fine for a few hours, at least."

"Right…" Cerise folded the towel over her arm. "I'll go get dressed for work. Make yourselves at home."

I thought I might fall right asleep, but the smell of Marcus's cooking perked me up again. Despite Cerise's comments, he fried some sausage to go with the oatmeal. We all enjoyed having hot food again. Cerise returned, putting in her earrings. In the time before she had to leave, I told them both as much as I could about the past few months. Somewhere along the way, I finally remembered Kelly's letter, and gave it to Cerise.

"So Onyx is apparently hiding out with Amaranth," I concluded. "Which gives us even more reason to contact this group you discovered."

"We haven't heard anything about that," Marcus said, exchanging looks with Cerise. "It's definitely not public knowledge."

"No, it wouldn't be. The other dragons want Onyx dead, dead, dead. Auric even let me go so I could do that for him."

"Why is Amaranth helping him?" Cerise wanted to know.

I shrugged. "They worked together in the past, before the destruction of his city. Maybe he's just convinced her again."

"Maybe she loves him," Lainey suggested.

"I have a hard time thinking of dragons being in love," Caedan said. I agreed completely. How could they even have a concept of love with the way they treated people?

"Well," Cerise said, rinsing out her coffee cup, "it sounds like, once we connect you with the other gang, you won't be needing us on this one."

"I don't think so," I said. "In fact, if they have a place we can hide out, we won't even need to use your couch beyond today."

Cerise looked toward the couch. "That cat isn't going to rip up my cushions, is she?"

"I'll make sure she doesn't," Lainey said. "She's usually very well behaved."

"If she weren't, she'd probably eat us all," Caedan muttered between bites of oatmeal.

"What kind of cat is it?" Marcus asked, baffled.

"Some kind of big… mountain cat with giant teeth," I said.

"Saber teeth," Lainey said. "They're like sabers."

"What are sabers?" Caedan asked.

"A curved sword."

"Then why not say sword teeth? Or curved sword teeth?"

"Because saber teeth is more descriptive."

"Not if you don't know what sabers are."

I took the last bite of oatmeal and chuckled. "Whatever they are, she's scary. I'm glad she's on our side."

"Yeah." Marcus eyed the cat, not looking convinced.

"Well, I'm off to work," Cerise said. "It was good seeing you all, if you're not here when I get back tonight."

Glacier lifted her head and growled, staring down the entry. At the same moment, someone knocked at the door.

"You don't have any other team members showing up, do you?" Cerise asked.

"No." I got to my feet and moved to the side as Marcus headed for the door.

"Since that light went out, I can't see a thing out there," he complained. He took a quick look back at us. We all moved out of sight from the door except Glacier, whose tail twitched as she watched.

"Who is—oh." Marcus opened the door. "You're the last person I expected to see."

"I know they're here, Marcus. Just stand aside. Good man." Oh no. I knew that voice too well.

He walked into the living room, looked around, and spread his arms wide.

"Here we are again!" Rick announced.

My hand slipped into my pocket to grab the disk from Auric. I triggered a boost to my legs, about to spring forward. He'd walked right in! I could take him right now…

"The building is surrounded by Crimson Elite," Rick said quickly. "If I don't emerge at the time I've designated, they have orders to burn the whole place down."

Cerise, her face pale, pulled aside the kitchen window's curtain to look out. She looked to me and nodded. "They have the fire launchers." He wasn't bluffing.

Rick turned his eyes on each of us, one by one. He sported a red chromark now. Makeup probably. "Beryl. I see I improved your looks. Caedan! You came back after all. How nice. Lainey, always a pleasure. Please keep a good hold on that cat. And Bice the heretic. I guess you did survive that day."

"How did you know we were here?" I asked, moving a little closer. I could still put the disk on him. We could still find a way out of this. I shifted the disk to my right hand, but kept my fingers on the edge so as not to activate it just yet.

"I've been here, remember? I've had this apartment under surveillance since I left you. I figured you or someone else would show up eventually." He tapped his own head with a cybernetic finger. "As soon as you did, word came to me and I came straight over, to join the reunion." He waved at Marcus and Cerise, who'd moved together behind the couch. "You two don't need to worry. Reporting you to Incarnadine wouldn't serve any purpose of mine."

"Yeah, we might tell him about you," Cerise shot back.

"Exactly. We can't have that."

I shot forward as fast as I could move and reached out to grab him with my cyb hand. Rick moved with blinding speed to catch my hand with his own. I gasped.

"Look at that! You decided to imitate me!" He pointed to our cybernetic hands clasped together, then narrowed his eyes. "While I was imitating you."

I didn't grasp what he meant at first. Then his hand began to twist mine back, pushing against it with incredible strength. "Addicting stuff, this boost energy, isn't it?"

I broke free and stepped back, keeping the disk hidden. "What are you talking about?" I had a sick feeling I already knew the answer.

Rick pulled up his sleeve, revealing large scars running down his arm. "I will admit: I didn't know the procedure would hurt so much, and I'm a little bit baffled that you don't have these kind of scars. But… anything you can do, I can do now." He grinned. "Well, with my arms, anyway. I haven't done the legs yet."

My worst fear. A dragon with the same cybernetic enhancements I possessed. If he were able to complete the procedure, he would be more powerful than any of the others. Maybe more powerful than two of them at once. All the more reason to use the disk on him as soon as possible.

Rick ran a finger along one of the scars. "I'm not very pleased with this aspect of it, but I do like the results. It wasn't easy, you know."

"You haven't been recovering from Beryl's attack all this time!" Caedan realized. "You've been having surgery on yourself!"

Rick looked at me. "Was he always this smart? I thought of him more as the dumb muscle."

"I'll give you—"

Bice put a hand on Caedan's arm. "Not now," he said quietly.

Rick looked past us toward the bedroom. "Kelly's not hiding back there, is she? The spies reported four of you, but I was hoping they were wrong."

"You'll never get near her again," I said, fighting to control the rage building up within.

"Then she is alive. Thank you for letting me know." He folded his hands together and put them near his mouth. "Of course, I know the child lives. I can sense his existence. He will come to me, when the time is right. Are you seriously thinking to raise him as a human?"

"He won't ever come to you!" Lainey declared.

Rick gave a short shake of his head. "Lainey! You're not usually so forceful. I guess you've been around Beryl too long."

My brain ran through different scenarios. If I could get behind him, I could uses boosts to move fast enough to get the disk onto his neck. He might not even realize what I'd done, but he'd be unable to remove it. He'd probably take us all off to some kind of prison, but he was probably going to do that anyway. It would be worth it. But maybe the disk would also weaken him long enough to kill him. Then we just had to deal with the Crimson Elite outside. I could take some of them, Lainey could shoot them from the window, Caedan and Glacier…

"The child will be mine," Rick repeated. "But that's not why I'm here now."

"Hey, if you're with Amaranth, how is the Crimson Elite working for you?" Marcus asked.

"As far as they're concerned, I'm just a high-level officer working for Amaranth," Rick said. "The two dragons and cities work fairly well together. But you know that."

"If you're not here for the child, why are you here?" Bice asked.

Rick pointed at him. "You always were the really smart one, Bice. Beryl's actions have been much more predictable without you around to advise him."

"Answer the question," I growled. I stepped a little to the side to get a better angle at him.

"You might want to advise him now," Rick said. "If he attacks me, things will not end well for all of you."

"It might be worth it," Caedan said, moving around the breakfast table to back me up.

Rick rolled his eyes. "Let me put it this way. You won't win. You'll all die. And I'll go after Kelly and the child. But…" He raised a finger. "Do what I ask, and none of that happens."

"You want something from us?" Bice asked.

"Yes, believe it or not… I need your help."

"Why would we help you?" I growled.

"Marcus, how many apartments are in this building?"

"I, uh, over a hundred," he answered.

Rick locked eyes with me. "And this early in the morning, how many people do you think are in them? And working to open the shops downstairs?"

"I don't know. At least a couple hundred. Maybe three."

"Let's be conservative and say two hundred." Rick took a short step toward me. "You might be able to kill me, Beryl. But the conflagration that follows would kill two hundred humans. Am I worth that much to you?"

I glared at him. He knew he had me. I couldn't risk that many deaths.

"Two hundred humans," he whispered. "I know you, Beryl. That's why you haven't told the other dragons where I am. You can't risk them killing humans. It makes you predictable."

He couldn't predict that Auric would be helping me. But it wouldn't work this particular moment. I would need to get him somewhere more private. Maybe after we did whatever he wanted.

"If that's not enough motivation, I'll give you something as well," he went on. "How would you like the other half of Loden's notes?"

I flinched. I couldn't help it. He'd given the other half of the notes to Incarnadine scientists. He'd probably had no trouble getting them back now, and obviously, he'd benefited from their research.

"You'll love them," he told me. "I only wish I could be there to see your face when you read the last bit."

"What does that mean?"

"You'll find out. Now." He motioned to Caedan and me. "You two move over there by the couch so I can see all of you together."

We complied without arguing any further. I let the disk fall back into my pocket.

"Very good. See? We can work together."

"Cut to the chase," Caedan growled. "What is it you want us to do?"

"It's something you would want to do, anyway. And it will benefit all of us."

We waited. He was trying to be dramatic, but I didn't satisfy him with any more questions.

Richard Onyx smiled his largest smile yet. "I want you to kill Incarnadine."

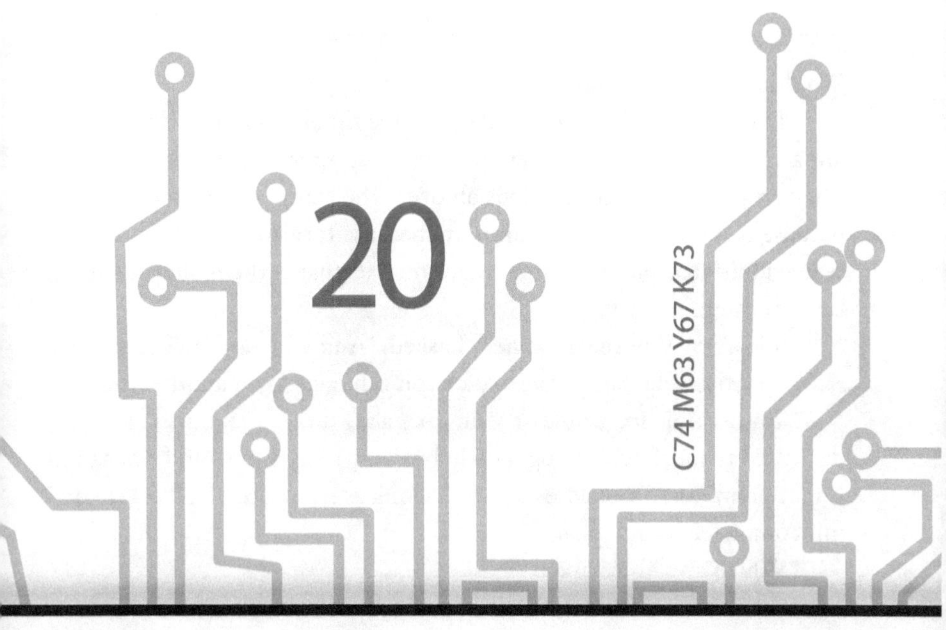

20

"Obviously, we want to kill Incarnadine," I said. "And you. And the rest of the dragons."

"But you can't," Rick said. "Even with all your enhancements, as amazing as they are, you can't kill a dragon. It's impossible."

"We killed one already," Caedan said.

Rick raised a finger. "Correction. A fantastic invention from Loden mortally wounded a dragon. And then I finished the job, remember? Since then, you haven't had a clue about how to actually kill another one."

"I wouldn't go that far," I countered. "I almost killed you."

"Almost doesn't count. And good luck catching any of the others in human form. Some of them haven't done that transformation in centuries. They may have forgotten how to do it."

"Dragons forget things? I thought you were gods."

"Debating is not helping any of us," Bice put in. "Let's get into specifics. I assume you have a plan, Rick?"

"Of course I have a plan. I've had plans for centuries, you know." Rick scratched the scars on his arm. "I actually have plans to kill all of the dragons, but I couldn't do it while stuck in this form. I got lucky with Viridia, since Auric told you the location of his source."

"All this time, and you haven't found the sources of the other dragons?"

"Yeah," Caedan said. "Seems like you could just follow the cold here.

Wouldn't the coldest spot be it?"

"Do you think I haven't tried that?" He shook his head. "The dragons are a thousand years old. They protect these spots. They disguise them. They create fake source locations all over. The reason it's so cold here isn't because of a single source location; it's because Incarnadine has built six or seven additional phony source locations. He guards them all as if they're the real thing."

"All right. Why Incarnadine?" I asked. "And why us? You've got Amaranth on your side. Surely the two of you can take down another dragon."

"You'd think so, wouldn't you? But alas, dear Amaranth is not that dedicated to me. She's willing to help but only to a point. And Incarnadine is that point. She's too close to him. As long as he's there, she'll never commit completely to my plans."

"Which are?" Bice asked.

Rick raised a finger. "Ah, ah. Nice try. You know enough already."

"All right," I said. "So humans kill Incarnadine. In her grief, Amaranth sides with you, and the two of you defeat the other two dragons and rule all of The Circle together."

"Something like that."

"Fine. Tell us how to kill Incarnadine." I didn't hate the concept. One more dead dragon would be a big step forward. Rick knew I wanted that, of course. But if we actually could kill one… it was worth the attempt, at least.

Rick paced in front of the entry hall. "The basic idea is quite simple. Incarnadine, unlike every one of the rest of us, has built a huge trap on top of himself." He waited for our reaction.

"What?" Caedan asked.

He rolled his eyes. "The Flame, you idiot! Even Viridia, with his vaunted Emerald Ascendancy, left a huge open space in the middle. Incarnadine has only a narrow shaft through the Flame, a very long one at that."

I wrinkled my brow, which actually hurt a little bit from the scar tissue. "You want to seal the shaft?"

"No, you're not thinking big enough. I want to bring down the entire Flame on top of him!"

"Several hundred people work in the Flame!" Cerise exclaimed. "You're back to threatening human lives again."

He waved dismissively. "Whatever. I'm sure this 'team' can find a way to get the humans out. You're quite good at that kind of thing."

"I don't see it." I shook my head. "You think we'll bury him under the ruins of the Flame? Viridia also had another exit, a tunnel that led to his source. You don't think Incarnadine has an escape route?"

"I know he doesn't. I've been down there, you know."

"How?"

"Three. Hundred. Years. You seem to keep forgetting that. I've been a human for that long. I traveled through all of the cities, learning everything I could. And one day, I got into Incarnadine's lair." He chuckled. "He only has the one way out. He's arrogant enough to think he's invincible, so the thought of an escape route has never even occurred to him."

I could believe that. Arrogance was a trait all the dragons shared. And based on what we'd read from the Books of Lore, that arrogance had only grown throughout the centuries.

"So we use explosives, then? Bring the Flame crashing down on top of him?"

"Exactly. I'll supply you with those, as well as a full set of blueprints for the building, so you'll know where to plant them."

"What about the last Cerulean Book of Lore?" I asked. "We should try to get it out before we blow it."

Rick cocked his head and lowered his brows at me. "Seriously, Beryl? Do you really think that dusty old tome will help you out now? Forget it. It's not worth it."

"Forgive me if I don't take your word for that."

He shrugged. "Whatever. If you want to risk your life to retrieve a single book as the entire building collapses, it's your life to risk."

"I don't buy it," Bice said, folding his arms across his chest. "The dragons are not gods, but they are immensely powerful creatures. I don't think a collapsing building, even one as big as the Flame, will kill one."

"Probably not," Rick admitted. "But at the very least, it will leave him badly wounded and weakened."

"And then you'll sweep in and finish him off?"

"No, haven't you been listening? I can't act against him directly, or Amaranth would never forgive me. I'd have to kill her sooner than planned."

"Go ahead," I said. "What's the rest of your brilliant plan?"

"I won't finish him off," Rick repeated. He looked around and spotted our supplies against the wall. He strode over and took my sword from the pile. He held it up and grinned at me. "You will. With this."

"You can't be serious. We agreed those stories of a lone warrior killing a dragon were ridiculous."

"But you're not just any warrior, are you?" Rick drew the sword and sighted down its length at me. "You're Beryl Godslayer, defender of humanity! And this is your chance to prove it."

"How?"

Rick tossed the sword and caught it with his other hand. "With Incarnadine wounded and weak, you can get in close enough and drive this sword straight into his heart!"

"You're crazy. That sword won't penetrate a dragon's hide!"

"Lainey, I believe you witnessed something a few months back. What happened in Caesious after Incarnadine attacked the peace summit?"

"The black dragon came, and they fought."

"Exactly. And guess where Incarnadine took the most damage?" Rick patted his own chest. "Right here. Tore off almost all of his outer scales. That's why he's been in hiding ever since, recovering. But... those outer scales take a very, very long time to grow back to a good size. He's still vulnerable right now."

"By now, they'll have replaced it with some kind of cyb scales or shielding," I argued. "The green dragon replaced scales all the time."

"Don't you think I know my own siblings?" Rick asked. "Incarnadine's not like that. He begrudges even that eye of his. No, no. He's vulnerable. He hasn't healed yet." Rick grew more animated, waving the sword in the air. "Picture it! You set off the explosives, and the entire Flame comes crashing down, burying the dragon under tons of steel and concrete. As the dust settles, he fights his way toward the open air, pushing rubble aside, blasting some of it with his flames, until at last, beaten, wounded and exhausted, he pushes his way into the light and open air. Dust clouds are everywhere, of course, but they're settling. And as they do, just as Incarnadine takes a moment to catch his breath, who appears out of the dust?" He pointed the sword at me. "Beryl! He charges forward, boosted by his cyb implants, and drives this sword deep into the red dragon's evil, evil heart."

Rick tossed the sword back with our other supplies. "Now I ask you: what could possibly go wrong with a plan like that?"

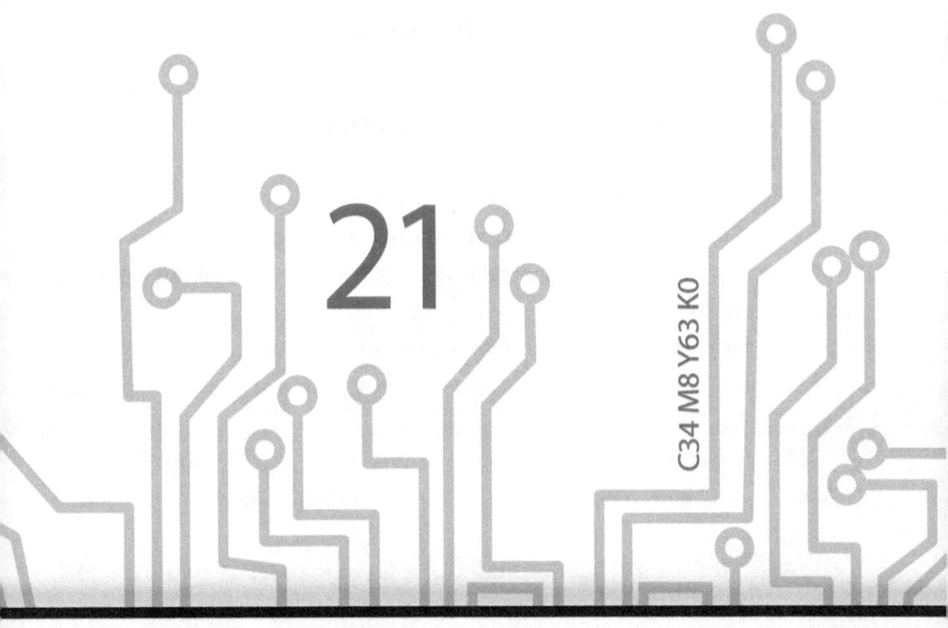

"You don't care if it works or not," I said with sudden realization. "Either way, you can't lose. If it works, one of your rivals is dead. And if it doesn't, I'm dead."

"And Incarnadine is weakened to the point of irrelevancy," Rick acknowledged. "You can be clever when you have time to think, Beryl."

He turned his back on us and walked into the entry hall. "Let's sum up, shall we? I've given you an offer you can't refuse, which will bring about results that will enormously benefit me, no matter what happens." He grinned over his shoulder. "And you say I'm not a god."

Rick opened the door. "I'll have the explosives delivered to your workplace, Marcus. You can load them on that truck you drive so well." He gave us one last wave. "May the grace of Onyx be upon you!"

The door closed. We sat in silence. At last, Cerise moved to the window and looked out. "They're leaving." She sighed and looked back at us. "You guys work this out. I've got to get to work." She hurried to the door. "At least I still have a job."

I picked up the dropped sword and put it back in its sheath. I rubbed my eyes. "Now what do we do?"

Caedan waved at the door. "You heard the dragon. We don't have a choice."

"We always have a choice," Bice said.

"Really, Bice?" I slapped my hand against the wall. "What is our choice here? Because he didn't seem to leave us with much of one."

"We could just run away," Lainey suggested.

"He's got people watching this apartment," I reminded her. "He'll know if we do that. And we can't abandon Marcus and Cerise, anyway."

"I appreciate that," Marcus said. He sat down at the breakfast table and put his head in his hands.

"We have time," Bice said. "We can think of something."

"Maybe." I sighed. "I don't know. I mean… right now, I don't see a way out of it."

Lainey got up and put her hand on my arm. "I won't let you die, Beryl. Maybe if I'm there too, I can shoot the dragon with my rifle and make it easier for you."

"And then what? Do you think Onyx is going to let us go once we kill the red dragon? We know we can't trust him."

"Look, we're all very tired right now," Bice said. "Let's get some rest and then take our next step."

"If we connect with the Amaranth rebels, maybe they can help us out," Caedan pointed out. "That is our next step, right?"

"Yeah," I agreed. "But we need to make sure we aren't followed to that meeting. We can't let Onyx know about them."

"Again: let's rest," Bice said. "We'll think clearer after some sleep." He walked over to Marcus and patted him on the back. "I'm sorry this happened, Marcus. We'll do everything we can to keep you and your wife safe."

"I know." He sighed and lifted his head. "It's not your fault." He got to his feet. "You, uh, make yourselves at home for a few hours at least. I have to check in at the theater, and probably run some errands. When I get back, I'll take you to the meet site."

We all thanked him before he left us. Afterwards, we spread out the sleeping bags on the floor and tried to get some rest. The others fell asleep one by one, but I stayed awake, staring at the ceiling, thinking. Bice was right, of course. I would think better after sleep, but my brain wouldn't shut up. I ran through as many different scenarios as I could imagine.

None of them turned out well.

I think I might have dozed off for an hour, at most. When I heard the others getting up, I joined them. We cleaned things up so the Vermeils wouldn't have a disaster area in their living room.

"Anyone dream any ideas?" Caedan asked.

"Maybe," Bice said. "For the moment, anyway. Beryl is the one who needs to meet with the rebels. But we need to make sure he isn't followed. Let's split up."

"You mean go in different directions to confuse the followers?" I asked.

"No," Caedan said. "We let you go on ahead with Marcus and maybe Bice, and then we come after. We'll spot anyone following you, and get them busy doing something else."

"Like what?"

"Like chasing a wild creature wandering the streets," Lainey said, patting Glacier.

"Or being chased by one," Caedan added.

"This depends on you being able to spot the followers," I said. "What if you can't?"

"We brought the talkers for a reason," Bice said. "We can report to each other."

Why didn't I think of that?

"All right." I sat down in the easy chair. "Bice coming along is a good idea. He's the most diplomatic among us."

"And let's be honest," Caedan added, "Lainey's face would require too much explanation. You might want to save that for later in the relationship."

"That's fair," Lainey said.

They were right. My first inclination had been to take Lainey with me, but telling these new rebels about people outside The Circle would be an added complication. Better to keep things simple.

"All right," I agreed. "But I don't want you doing anything too risky. If stopping the followers would put you in danger, we'll call off the meet for today."

"But—" Caedan began.

"No," I cut him off. "Neither of you can blend in with the local populace, let alone with that cat. You've got to be extra careful."

"We will," Lainey promised. "Don't worry about us."

"I can't help it. I'm always going to worry. I'm worried about Kelly back at the Asylum. I'm worried about Don and Lovat wandering in the wild. I'm worried about what's going to happen with Onyx." I waved my hands. "I'm worried about what will happen to all of you after I get killed."

Lainey got up, walked over to me, and wrapped her arms around me. "You can't protect us all. And it's not your job."

"Then whose is it?" I hugged her back.

"Our own," Bice said. "Let your friends do what they do best. You do what you do best. And trust that it'll all work out." He smiled. "I'll be praying for us every step of the way."

I shifted Lainey to my side. "You don't even know who you're praying to."

"It's simple faith," he pointed out. "I have to believe."

I didn't feel like arguing the point with him.

A sound at the door was followed by Marcus coming in. "Are we still doing this?"

We explained the plan to him. "All right, let's do this," I concluded. "Caedan, take my sword. You'll need it more than I will. Marcus, Bice, let's head out."

The three of us left the apartment building and turned in the opposite direction from which we'd entered that morning. "It's going to be a long walk," Marcus warned.

Bice chuckled. "We walk across the entire Circle," he pointed out. "Going across a city is nothing."

Bice and I kept our heads down, hiding his chromark and my scarred face from everyone as best we could. Marcus led the way at an easy stride, trying not to appear suspicious. I did notice him doubling back a couple of times on our path, to confuse anyone behind.

About an hour into the walk, the talker on my belt squawked. I grabbed it and stepped into the nook of a doorway. "What's happening?"

"Two reds tried to follow you," Caedan reported. "Now they're not. Glacier had some fun."

"Not too much fun, I hope."

"Nah, they're alive."

"All right. Head back to the apartment. We'll meet you there as soon as we're done with this."

"Good luck."

I put the talker away and reported the news to Marcus and Bice. "That's a relief," Marcus said. "I guess we can stop being so sneaky now."

"We were being sneaky?" Bice asked.

"Sneaky enough," I said. "Let's move on."

We moved a little faster, with no more tangents, that I could tell. The buildings continued to look all the same to me, but I did notice that the Flame was getting further behind.

"How will we know when we cross from one city to the other?" I asked.

"Oh, you'll know," Marcus said. "Not far now."

We turned a corner, and then I saw. The road led to a bridge a few hundred yards ahead.

"There's a river between the cities?" Bice asked.

"More of a canal," Marcus said. "Sometimes it has water in it, sometimes it doesn't."

As we drew nearer, I noticed people moving about on the bridge itself. I did a quick zoom with my eyes and saw: they were all guards.

"We can't just walk past those guards," I pointed out.

"We won't have to," Marcus said. "We're not crossing the bridge." He turned another corner and led us down an alley to a doorway. He took a quick look around, then opened the door and walked in. Bice and I followed.

We entered a hall with a single dim bulb hanging from a loose socket in the ceiling. Marcus walked to the end of the hall, then turned right into a set of stairs leading down into a dark basement. He took out a small flashlight to illuminate just ahead of him.

"Seems like anyone could walk in here," Bice observed when we reached the bottom of the stairs.

"They could, but why would they bother?" Marcus answered. "And if they did, they would find… nothing." He turned in a circle with the flashlight, revealing concrete floors and walls. A few pieces of rotten wood, and other unidentifiable trash items lay here and there. One ragged step-stool in the corner looked mostly intact.

Marcus pulled the step-stool to the far wall. He stepped up on it and felt around at the juncture with the ceiling. "It's here somewhere," he muttered. "Ah. Got it." He stepped off the stool and back, as a grinding noise filled the small basement.

I glanced up at the dim light coming from the stairs above. No one poked their head down to see where the noise came from.

An entrance opened up in the wall. More accurately, a hole opened. I couldn't tell where the concrete slid away in the darkness. "We have to crawl?" I asked.

"Yep." Marcus got down and wiggled in. "Only a couple of feet. Come on."

I let Bice go ahead of me, and then I came last. I couldn't quite get up on my hands and knees, so had to scrunch-crawl through. As promised, it opened up a couple of feet later, and I got to my feet in a dark tunnel lit only by the small flashlight. Marcus pushed a button on the wall, and the crawl-hole ground itself shut again.

"How did you find all this?" Bice wanted to know.

"I didn't," Marcus admitted. "The rebels showed it to me so I could come through and meet them without arousing suspicion from crossing the bridges all the time. The guards keep records of your crossings."

"Did they build this?" I asked, putting my hands to the walls. The tunnel was about three feet wide and seven feet tall. I couldn't tell how far it extended.

"No. Nobody knows how old it is. Let's keep moving." Marcus started down the tunnel with the light. "Parts of these cities are a thousand years old, remember? I don't think this has been here that long, but who can tell? Maybe it was built by an earlier group of rebels. Or just smugglers transporting valuables from city to city and avoiding taxes."

The tunnel angled down for quite a while. When it leveled off, our steps began splashing. About an inch of water covered the floor. The walls felt damp to the touch.

"We're under the canal," I realized.

"Yeah, don't look down at the water. It's got stuff growing in it. Let's just get through and wipe our shoes."

I couldn't see anything in the water, anyway, not with our only light illuminating the way ahead. My shoes were not made for walking through water. After a few minutes, the unpleasant feeling of cold, wet socks added to my discomfort.

"I'm not doing very well with this," Bice admitted.

"Claustrophobia?" Marcus asked.

"I've never had trouble before, but I've never been in such a tight space for so long." Bice's voice trembled a little. I put my hand on his shoulder.

"Here's the way up," Marcus reported. A moment later, we stepped out of the water and began ascending. My wet socks squelched inside my shoes with every step.

"Our feet are going to freeze," I complained.

"I should have told everyone to bring spare socks. Sorry about that. The water was lower last time I came through. It comes and goes."

The ascent seemed longer than the descent, but maybe it only felt that way. Marcus found another button and pushed it. This time, an entire door swung open. We left the tunnel and entered another basement, but this one looked as if someone owned it. An old heating system crouched in one corner, while boxes were stacked in all the corners. A beat-up table filled the center of the room, surrounded by six chairs.

Marcus walked to the far wall beside the stairs going up and flipped on the lights. He pocketed his flashlight and took a seat at the table. "May as well relax," he told us. "It may be a little while."

"How will they know we're here?" I asked.

"When I flipped on the lights, it sent a signal," he said. "Someone will come as soon as they can. Until then, we have to wait. The door at the top of the stairs is securely locked."

Bice and I sat down as well, but not until after checking the stability of the chairs. I removed my shoes and pulled my socks off. I squeezed them as dry as I could, then spread them out on the floor. Bice joined me in the action. It might not solve the problem, especially since we would have to walk back through the water, but my feet felt better for it, anyway.

"Guess we're literally cooling our heels," Bice observed with a chuckle.

Marcus tapped his fingers on the table and fidgeted, casting repeated glances up the stairs. At last, he turned to me. "Tell me the truth, Beryl. Do you see a way out of this situation with Onyx?"

"No," I said. "I don't. But that doesn't mean there isn't one. Maybe this meeting will point us in the right direction."

"This is my home," he replied with emphasis. "Cerise's home. We're not ready to lose it."

"I lost my home one day after I got involved in all this," I said. "I can't promise you otherwise."

"We have family. Friends. Jobs."

I nodded. "I don't want you to lose any of that, Marcus."

"We'll do everything we can to prevent it," Bice added. "Sometimes, the truth requires sacrifice. We've all lost something." He pointed at my face. "Some of us more than others."

Marcus looked at me, then flicked his gaze away. "Yeah, yeah, I know. I just… I'm not ready for that part of it."

"No one ever is," Bice said softly.

The sound of a deadbolt being thrown echoed from above. We all looked up to watch the door open. A lone figure entered, shut the door behind him, and descended the stairs. He stopped at the final step and looked us over. He was almost ridiculously thin, but no taller than me. His red chromark stood out on his pale face like blood, running up into his almost white hair.

Marcus got to his feet. "I know we've met before," he began, "but I don't remember your name—"

"We don't use our real names," the man cut him off in a nasally tone. "You can call me Sangria."

"All right. You can call me Marc, I guess. And these are the men you've been wanting to meet." He gestured to us. Bice and I both stood. Only then did it cross my mind how silly we must look with our bare feet.

"Bice the Heretic," Sangria observed. "We know of you."

It continued to baffle me how far Bice's fame had spread. I guess when you're entrenched and the priesthood and leave, it's a huge event.

Sangria looked at me. "I do not know who you are."

"I'm Beryl. It's good to meet you."

He wrinkled his eyebrows. "You're Beryl the dragonslayer? That can't be right. What happened to your face?"

"Acid. What do you need for me to prove my identity?"

"This is Beryl," Bice put in. "I have known him for many years. He is the one you've heard about."

"I can confirm his identity as well," Marcus said. "We worked together in the raid on the Flame last year."

"That will be sufficient." Sangria swept his palm to the side in a gesture I didn't recognize. "I am very pleased to make your acquaintance, Beryl. Your reputation precedes you, and then some. Please. Be seated."

We all sat down again and Sangria took a chair at the head of the table. "I do not apologize for being wary," he began. "I am sure you well understand that secrecy is the shelter that guarantees our very lives in these times, since our goals are so antithetical to the continued authoritarian regimes."

"Yes, of course," I said, fighting to keep my eyebrows from going up. "Almost everything we do must be secret."

Sangria steepled his fingers with his elbows on the table. "Your actions, together with those of your allies, have altered a precarious balance of power, threatening the stability of the dictatorial dragons—the ones that remain, at any rate. We are pleased with the results, if not always the means."

I wasn't sure what to say to that.

"Which leads to the key question I must ask before this conversation proceeds any further: which dragon will you be slaying next?"

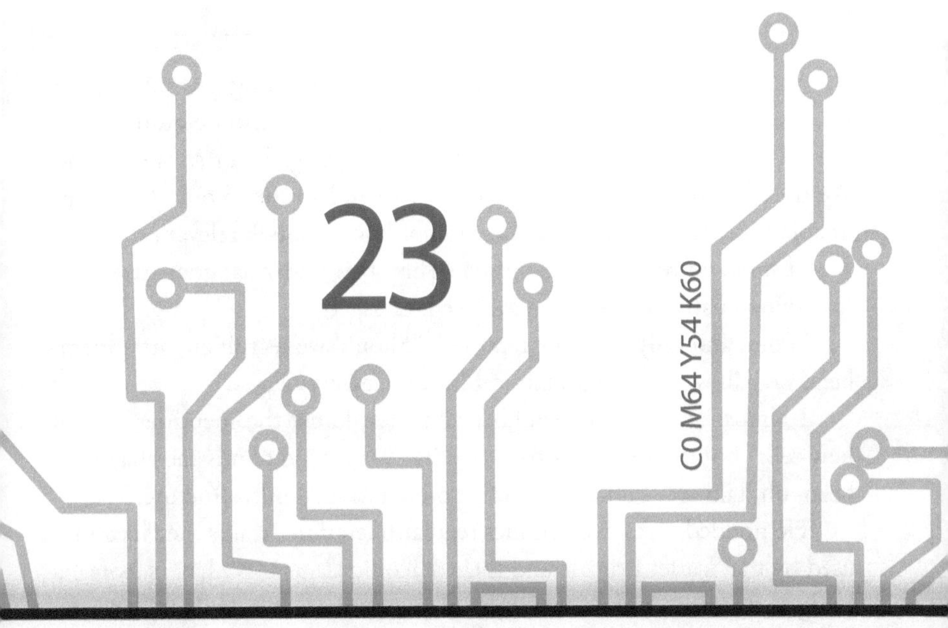

I glanced at Bice. "We wish to see all the dragons dead and freedom for all humans."

"Yes, yes, I realize that." Sangria pointed at me. "But which one will you target next?"

"Well, right now, we're considering plans to take down Incarnadine," I said.

Sangria folded his hands together with only his pointers extended together. He tapped his lips. "Should either of the red dragons fall, it would spread the remaining dragons' influence thin. Each would be forced to rule two cities; however, Auric would not be adjacent to a dragon-less city, thus complicating the process. Yes, yes. This would create significant chaos. We could coordinate our efforts with strategic strikes against valuable infrastructure, fomenting yet more instability."

"Uh, let's back up just a little bit," I suggested. "Tell us about your group. Are you the leader?"

"I am the coordinator for our cell," he explained. "Compartmentalization is another method of ensuring the survival of our movement. We have three separate autonomous cells, each with their own coordinator. None of us knows the names or locations of the other cells."

"That's a bit much," Bice said. "Do you really think that much security is necessary?"

Sangria leveled a stern gaze at him. "If this meeting had taken place two weeks ago, I would be informing you of four separate autonomous cells. The fourth was taken out by the Scarlet Brigade, or so we assume. We have heard nothing from them since then. But they would have been unable to inform on us, since they do not know enough relevant details."

"I stand corrected." Bice shifted in his chair under Sangria's gaze.

"How many people are in each cell?" I asked.

"Four, and only four," he reported. "Should we recruit any new members, we will work to split them off into their own cell."

I almost asked, "but wouldn't you then know the identities of that new cell?" but decided it wasn't worth it. "What kind of missions have you been, uh, taking?" I asked instead. "You mentioned infrastructure."

He nodded. "Yes, we conduct regular operations against key locations used by the Scarlet Brigade and their draconic leaders. We have sabotaged bridges, factories, and other targets of importance." He smiled. "I do not wish to boast, but my cell has undertaken the most successful operations during this past year."

Targets of importance. Hm.

"How long has your organization existed?" Bice asked.

"Long before my involvement," he admitted. "I cannot say for sure, but I am under the impression that the insurrection has been operating quietly for several decades now."

Several decades? And yet we never heard anything about them, not even through Stacy's network! Curious.

"So you have no central command?" Bice persisted.

"We have a patron," he answered. "While she does not 'command' us, she often gives us tips that lead to successful operations. That is in addition to the funding she provides, of course."

"Could we meet this patron?" Bice asked.

"That would be… inadvisable." Sangria's muscles clenched for a second. "The secret of her identity is our most important confidence."

"You admitted that you knew of our, uh, actions," I pointed out. "Are we not… significant enough to meet with this patron?"

"I. Well. Hm." Sangria didn't seem to know what to say.

"Let me explain a little further." I leaned across the table. "We have information about something happening with Amaranth. Something very significant. She has a guest staying with her. Are you aware of this?"

"A guest? What kind of guest would a dragon entertain?"

As I thought: most people didn't know about Onyx at all. "Exactly. Makes you wonder, doesn't it? The identity of this guest, and his goals, are a very big deal. It's enough to shake things up in The Circle even more than what we've done so far. So much so, that if the wrong people heard about it, the people of your city would be in grave danger. We may need to coordinate to prevent that from happening."

"And to do that," Bice added, "we need to start at the top."

Sangria harrumphed a bit, then nodded. "I will send an inquiry through the proper channels."

"And how long will that take?" I leaned back.

"I beg your pardon?"

"How long do we need to wait here?"

"Surely you cannot expect to meet with the Lady today!"

"Surely I can. Did you not just hear me? Your city is in danger. We don't have time to waste." Onyx might send over the explosives at any time and expect us to act as soon as possible. Also, I didn't relish the idea of coming back through that wet tunnel again.

Sangria's eyes looked about to pop out of their sockets. "I don't… that is…"

I stood up. With a quick boost, I punched my cyb fist through the table. "I am Beryl the dragonslayer, and I require a meeting with your Lady Patron at once. The lives of every citizen in your city may depend on it."

Sangria got to his feet. "If you will be pleased to wait here, then, I, I will attempt to ascertain if such a thing is even possible."

"Surely, someone with as many successful operations as you have had this past year should not have any difficulty in contacting the patron," Bice suggested.

Sangria's face turned a bit red. "Yes, yes, of course. I will return as soon as it is possible." He turned and hurried up the stairs and through the door, locking it behind him.

"Curious little man," Bice said.

"Not the word I was thinking of." I pulled my right foot into my lap and rubbed the toes to warm them up.

Marcus licked his lips. "Look, I, uh, will need to get back to work before the day is out. Can you two find your way back all right?"

"Show me where the button for this door is hidden," I said. Once he had done so, I looked to Bice. "I think we can do it. Once we're back in your city, we can use the talker to get directions back to the apartment."

"I don't see any problems with that," Bice agreed.

Marcus, looking relieved, said goodbye, and disappeared down the tunnel. Bice and I settled in to wait. I sat on the floor, pulling my feet in to sit on them cross-legged.

"Something is odd here," Bice said.

"Yeah. Several decades they've been at this?"

"And yet they're no closer to achieving anything… lasting." Bice rubbed one of his feet. "To me, that says they're either so ineffective that Amaranth doesn't care about their existence, or… I don't know. It seems like if they were truly accomplishing anything, they would have been wiped out by now, or at the least driven out of the city. I have a hard time believing such an organized resistance could exist for so long."

"Maybe they're not really trying?" I suggested. "Maybe they're satisfied with the little accomplishments, like he listed."

"Yet if they truly were taking down bridges and factories and such every year, they would be more than just a nuisance," Bice mused. "They would be something the dragon would have to deal with."

"Do you think Sangria was lying about all that?"

"I don't know. I don't think so. He seemed too proud of himself to be making stuff up."

"So maybe they did 'sabotage' a bridge, but all he means is they blocked it for an hour or something."

"Maybe. And did you catch his reference to not being pleased with our 'means'? He doesn't like the way we do things."

"What does that mean?"

"If I had to guess… I would say his group is in favor of incremental change, little by little. Big events, like killing a dragon, don't fit into that dynamic."

"But that's the whole point! To get rid of the dragons!" I waved my hands in frustration. "Why fight them if we're not going to get rid of them?"

Bice shook his head. "I don't know." He paused. "So… are we going to tell this patron of theirs about the dragon's guest?"

"Since I mentioned it, I guess we have to." I sighed. "I was hoping they'd be able to help us, but I'm not seeing much hope of that now."

"You never know. Maybe she'll surprise us."

I shifted my weight. I think my feet were finally warming up. "If we were to tell Auric—or Incarnadine or Atramentous, for that matter—about Onyx, then it might solve some of our problems. But the risk to the people here is too great. I was hoping this group might help with that somehow."

"I don't see how they could evacuate an entire city without—"

The door at the top of the stairs opened. Sangria descended halfway down and stopped.

"The Lady will see you."

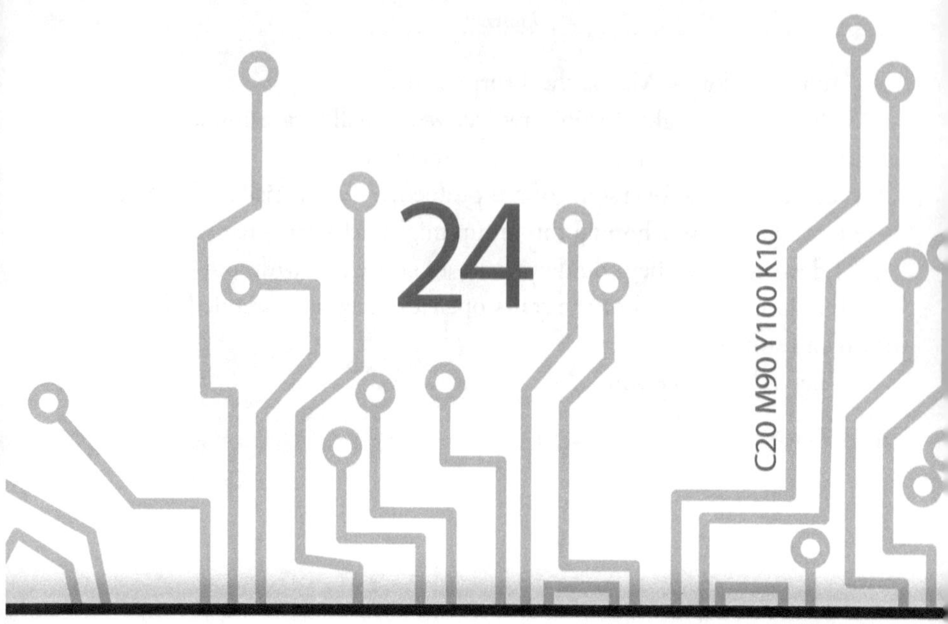

24

We had to put our wet socks and shoes back on before following Sangria up the stairs. I tried to resign myself to being uncomfortable, but every squishy step annoyed me. It didn't put me in the best frame of mind to be meeting someone important.

When we emerged through the door at the top of the stairs, I don't know what I expected to find. I know I didn't expect the back room of a grocery store. Yet that's exactly what we entered. Sangria paused to lock the door behind us, then led us out into the store, past aisles of food and a handful of shoppers, and through the front doors into the street.

I barely had a chance to glance at the buildings around us, which appeared not too different from the neighborhoods in Incarnadine, before Sangria gestured us toward the cobblestone road and my eyes locked on to something I'd only seen in history books.

"A carriage?" I asked. A literal horse-drawn carriage. I assumed the two creatures at the front were horses, though I'd never seen them before. I don't know that any other city possessed them. The carriage itself looked much like the old drawings I'd seen: four large wheels supporting a rectangular cab. Unlike the history books, this one looked brand new, with dark crimson decor and elaborate paneling. A driver sat at the front, studiously ignoring us.

Sangria cocked his head. "Though I suppose they are considered an ancient method of conveyance, they are still extremely useful for transportation purposes around the city." He opened the door. "They also provide a means of privacy." He gestured for me to enter.

I caught hold of a side handle and swung myself up inside. A fleeting thought crossed my mind that this could all be a trap, and we'd be carriaged—is that a word?—off to prison. But that thought vanished when I saw the other passenger waiting inside.

She sat with her back toward the front of the carriage, her head bent down, reading a book. With the illumination of a number of electric lights within, I took a quick look at our hostess. My first thought was: "How many different shades of red can there be?" My immediate second thought was: "You're looking at all of them." She wore a dark red dress in a decorative style I don't believe I'd ever seen before, with a pleated skirt, a very narrow belt at her very narrow waist, and a plunging neckline displaying an impressive amount of cleavage. She turned a page in her book with a hand wearing an elbow-length glove of a much lighter red. If that weren't enough, her own hair, flowing down past her shoulders toward the aforementioned cleavage, might be the reddest color of all. It shimmered with tiny sparks, as if she'd mixed some kind of reflective glitter into her hair.

"Will you be joining me today, Mister Beryl, or will you be gaping at me from the door for the next hour?" She lifted her eyes to mine, and I must admit I was relieved to see they were green, not red.

"I'm sorry," I stammered, scrambling into the opposite seat. "I just wasn't expecting…"

"What were you expecting?" she asked as Bice climbed in beside me. She lowered the book completely, revealing an unblemished face, perfectly proportioned, though perhaps her chin might be a little long.

I tried to smile. "Well, to be honest, from the way Sangria described his patron, I was expecting a much older woman." This lady couldn't be more than five years older than me.

"I see." Her voice, while a little severe, had a warmth to it. It also reminded me of something, though I couldn't place it. "And is my youthful appearance an advantage or detriment to my participation in our mutual goals?"

"What? Um, neither?"

Bice chuckled. "You caught my friend by surprise," he said. "All of this is very new to us." He gestured to the carriage itself. "We've never been inside one of these. My name is Bice, and this is Beryl, in case there was any doubt."

The Lady tapped on the ceiling. With a slight jerk, the carriage began moving. "I am aware of your identities," she said, setting the book aside. "You may call me Lady Amara Rust, should you need to address me by name."

"Where are we going?" I asked, trying to look through the window. The glass had a strange tint to it that did not allow a clear view of the outside.

"Nowhere in particular." The Lady adjusted her glove. "One of the advantages of this means of transportation is that we have leisure to discuss whatever we want for as long as we want. Now, I am told you have news for me."

"Yes," Bice said. "Before we share it, perhaps you could help us understand more about your relationship with these… resistance groups? We've been told you're their patron."

"Indeed. And it's an appropriate description for what I do." She made a fluttering gesture with her hand. "As you can observe, I am extraordinarily rich, thanks to wealth that has been passed down virtually since this city was founded. I do what I can to support numerous causes, from contributing to the city's defense during the war to funding an orphanage for those unfortunate children left without parents for whatever reason. And I also provide funds to the resistance, as you call it, in the hopes that one day the cause of these problems will be removed."

"Wait. You fund the city's defense, and those who fight against it?" I wondered.

She turned those eyes on me, and I have to admit, my heart fluttered. I swallowed and tried to think about Lainey. "As a prominent citizen of Amaranth, if I did not contribute to the war fund, it would have looked highly suspicious and unpatriotic," she explained. "And the dragon would only take it in new taxes if I didn't donate. It all balances out."

"Sangria said you do more than provide money," Bice said.

She nodded. "I also provide them with information, when I have any worthwhile. In my position, I often overhear news of importance, such as the movements of the Scarlet Brigade, or the opening of a new factory, and so on."

"So you help direct their attacks."

"If that is how you wish to phrase it. Now, I am well informed about the actions of you two. Your names are quite infamous by now, throughout the entire Circle, I would imagine."

"People get noticed when they stand up to the dragons," Bice said.

"Many have stood up to the dragons throughout the centuries, but you are the first to bring one down. Forgive me, bring two down."

"As much as I would like to claim the credit, we didn't kill Viridia," I said.

She raised her eyebrows. "I heard it was Atramentous who did the deed but that you were present when it happened."

"I was… but it wasn't Atramentous, either."

"I am confused."

I glanced at Bice. "This is the main reason we wanted to speak with you. The people of your city are in great danger."

"Please explain."

"Onyx, the lost dragon, has returned. He's the one who killed the green dragon. And right now, he's in hiding right here, with Amaranth."

To her credit, Lady Rust did not visibly react. She watched me for a moment, as if determining whether I was being serious. Then she nodded. "I can see you believe this. Do you have proof?"

"I watched someone I knew, someone I considered a friend, transform into the dragon in front of me," I said, my face hardening at the memory. "I watched him kill the green dragon. I fought with him when he returned to human form. He spit acid in my face and was rescued by Amaranth. She brought him back here. I saw him earlier today."

"He is in human form, then?"

"For now. It's how he's managing to stay hidden from the other dragons."

"Why would he do that?"

"There is much history to explain here," Bice put in. "You see, the other dragons once tried to kill Onyx. That's the true story of the Blasted Lands. He survived and has returned. If the others, besides Amaranth, knew he was here, they would come for him at once. It would be a horrific battle between dragons, and the city would be laid waste."

"We want to prevent that, naturally," I added. "I mean, if the dragons were to kill each other, I'm all for that. But not if human lives are placed in danger."

"Do you believe the other dragons will learn of this soon?"

"Only if we tell them."

"Then I must implore you not to do so."

"We won't… unless you can help us come up with a plan to get the humans out of the way."

She cocked her head. "How would we do that? We can't evacuate the entire city."

"No, I guess you can't. But we wanted to float the idea past you, at any rate."

"I see." She paused for a moment. "I must say, though: if this is the only reason you gentlemen have sought me out, you have wasted your time. I can do nothing for you."

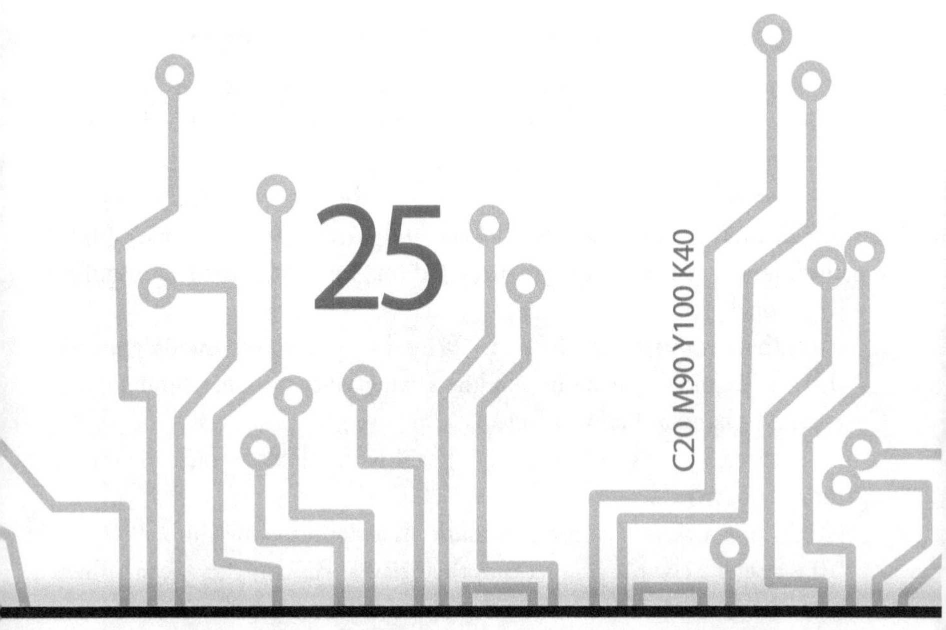

25

"Oh, I wouldn't say that," Bice said. "We are on the same side, so perhaps we can work together on other operations."

"Such as?"

Bice looked at me. "Do you want to tell her?"

"We already mentioned it to Sangria," I said. I turned to Lady Rust. "We are currently planning an operation against Incarnadine. If it is successful, it could change everything around here."

"I see. But I do not perceive how my own agents within this city can help you within that one."

"Maybe not," I admitted. "But we also want to go after Onyx. If your agents can help us locate him, maybe we can work together that way. While he's in human form, he's vulnerable."

The carriage jostled over an uneven spot in the road. Lady Rust put a hand on the seat beside her to steady herself. "This very concept amazes me. The idea that the dragons can turn into human form."

"It's how they spawn the draconics," I said. "While in human form, they, uh, get women pregnant with their children."

"And how does that work with Amaranth, since she is female?" the Lady asked with a slight smile.

"I honestly don't know," I admitted. "I'm not sure I want to think about it."

She let out a small chuckle. "I can understand your attitude there. Let's move on, then. I will tell my agents to be on the lookout for this Onyx. Can you describe his human appearance?"

I gave her as detailed a description of Rick as I could, including his predilection for black leather jackets and gloves. "And of course, a black chromark, but I've seen him with a red one too, so maybe he's disguising it," I concluded.

"That's interesting," she said. "Why do you suppose the dragons give themselves these ridiculous markings when they become human?" She brushed a hand at her own face.

"That's a very good question," I said with a look at Bice. "I've never thought of that."

"We've always seen the chromarks as a sign of ownership," Bice said. "The dragons claiming humans as their slaves. Perhaps they wear it themselves just to blend in? The better to disguise themselves?"

"I can't think of any other reason." Another jostle in the road threw me off balance. I put my hand against the door to keep from falling off my seat.

"Gentlemen, I appreciate this conversation so much." Lady Rust clasped her hands together. "You are so much different from the resistance fighters within this city. Not only do you dare the impossible tasks, but you think about the hard questions as well."

"We have sought as much knowledge as we can," Bice said.

"That's why we stole the Cerulean Books of Lore from the Flame," I added.

This time, her eyes widened. "You did what?"

"We infiltrated the Flame and stole the Books of Lore. Incarnadine chased me all the way to Caesious. It was a very close call."

"That was you? I must hear more of this." She glanced out one of the windows. "Unfortunately, this is all the time I have available today." She tapped on the ceiling with her knuckle again.

"I'm sorry to hear that," Bice said. "We were hoping to coordinate further, perhaps set up a permanent information exchange."

"This need not be our last meeting." She leaned across the carriage and put her hand on my knee, looking up into my face. I struggled to keep my eyes even with hers, and not look down at the opening in her dress. "We must speak again. I wish to hear all about your theft of the Lore Books.

Will you return tomorrow?"

"I suppose I can." I swallowed. "How would we set that up? Should I return to the place we met with Sangria?"

She leaned back and waved her hand dismissively. "Sangria has little imagination beyond his own fantasies of being a thorn in Amaranth's side. No, I want you to deal directly with me." She paused. "Do you know the Mahogany Birch Theater on the outskirts of Incarnadine?"

"I can find it." I had no idea where anything was in Incarnadine, but Marcus would certainly know a theater's location.

"Good. Be at the front doors at noon tomorrow, and my carriage will come for you." She turned to Bice. "I hope you don't mind. Should someone notice, it will be far easier for me to explain a young gentleman caller than a visit from two men at once."

Bice nodded. "Of course. Perfectly logical."

"Good, good." She smiled again. "As I said, this has been a fascinating conversation, gentlemen. Perhaps we can do more together than I first assumed."

The carriage came to a stop. "We've returned to where you boarded," the Lady said. "Please be discreet as you exit, so as not to allow your faces to be seen."

"Thank you, Lady Rust," Bice said, lowering his head in a sort of bow. "We are grateful for your time and attention."

"You're too kind."

Someone opened the door from outside. Bice got to his feet and stepped out. I got up to follow him, but Lady Rust caught my wrist. I looked down at her.

"I look forward to seeing you tomorrow," she said more quietly. "Alone."

I swallowed again, though my mouth felt dry. "I, uh, I'm looking forward to it also."

She let go of my wrist with a smile. Did I imagine it, or did she lick her lips? I clambered out of the carriage, keeping my head low as requested. Bice waited for me. Together, we entered the grocery store and made our way to the back room. I saw no sign of Sangria.

"Well, someone made an impression," Bice observed, opening the door.

"I don't, I, that is, I don't know what to think of that," I stammered.

He laughed. "I bet you don't."

We closed the door behind us and descended the stairs. "What's that supposed to mean?" I asked.

"She was quite taken with you," he said. "She rarely took her eyes off you."

"I didn't notice."

"Sure you didn't. And you didn't notice her eyes examining the rest of you either, I suppose."

"I didn't!"

"Uh-huh."

"Don't tell Lainey about this," I pleaded. "Everything is complicated enough as it is."

"Don't worry about it." Bice continued to chuckle. "I won't give you up."

I searched for the button that would open the secret door. "How does someone that young have so much money?" I wondered.

"She inherited it. She said it had been passed down since the city's founding. Her family's probably always been wealthy."

"Something must have happened to her parents then, if she's in charge of the family riches." Where was that button? I couldn't seem to find it.

"If so, that's something you have in common," Bice observed. "Don't be shy about sharing that with her, if it'll bring her more toward our side."

I looked back at him with mock horror. "Bice! Are you suggesting we manipulate that girl for our own ends? How does that fit with your moral code?"

"I didn't say manipulate. But… she could be a very important ally, and we need all the help we can get right now."

"Your time in Auric must have changed you. Ah, here it is!" I pressed the button, and the secret door slid open.

"Life experiences change us, Beryl. It's part of being human."

"Makes you wonder if the dragons' life experiences ever change them."

"They live so long, maybe it happens at a much slower rate." Bice looked down the secret passage and sighed. "I am not looking forward to walking through there again."

"Look on the bright side. Once we get back to the apartment, we can finally let our feet dry out and stay dry."

Pounding footsteps sounded above our heads, followed by loud voices.

"Go, go, go!" I shoved Bice into the tunnel. Once inside, I slammed the button to shut the door.

"Over there!" a voice yelled from the stairs.

I backed away from the sliding door, channeling boosts just in case. The footsteps and shouts came closer. A crossbow bolt ricocheted into the tunnel just before the door ground shut. Something pounded on the other side of the door.

"Bice?"

"I'm down here," he reported from further along the tunnel.

I turned toward his voice. Wherever he was, I couldn't see it. The shutting door closed off all the light. We were inside the tunnel, but also in complete darkness.

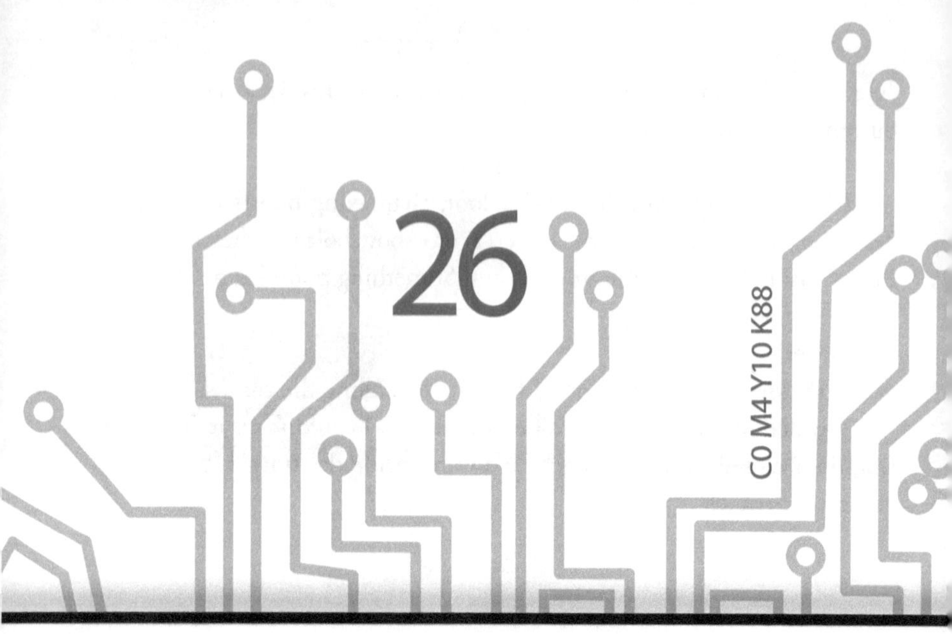

26

"We just have to follow the tunnel," Bice said, his voice echoing a little. "There aren't any side passages."

I put my hands out to either wall and moved in his direction. We could do this. It would be dark, wet, and annoying, but we could do it.

We made our way down the incline without slipping. I heard Bice's breathing long and loud. He'd had some trouble with the tunnel on our way through, with a flashlight. I felt a lot more stressed in the dark; I could only imagine how he felt.

A loud impact sounded behind us, echoing through the entire tunnel. "That door won't hold forever," I said.

"I'm going as fast as I can," Bice replied. A moment later, the tunnel leveled off and we stepped into the water again.

I caught up to him and put my right hand on his shoulder again. I kept my cyb hand touching the wall to keep myself oriented. More of the impacts sounded behind us. The secret door was thicker than any normal door, but it would give way eventually. Those soldiers would pour in, and they would have lights. They had ranged weapons, as well, and this tunnel ran completely straight.

My cyb fingers scraped something different from the concrete wall. From the brief scrape, it must have been metal. A panel of some kind? Another step later, and the concrete returned.

How had the soldiers found us? Surely, neither Lady Rust nor Sangria would have given us up. Had someone in the store reported strangers passing through?

Bice stopped. "I need a moment," he whispered. "I, I'm struggling here, Beryl."

"You can do this," I answered as another impact sounded. "We're at least halfway there. Let's get out of here!"

"I don't know. I don't know," he murmured.

I turned my head to look behind, knowing it was pointless. "If only Loden had put night vision in these eyes," I grumbled.

"How do you know he didn't?" Bice's voice perked up, as if thinking about my issues took his mind from the surroundings.

"If I send boosts to my eyes, all they do is zoom."

"Is there a way to send—I don't know—a different kind of boost? Maybe while you're squinting in the darkness?"

A different kind of boost? That was like asking if I could flex a muscle different. I didn't see… Wait. Maybe that was it. The first time I'd used the zoom had been when I was trying to see at a distance, so maybe… I stared into the darkness, and triggered a short boost to my eyes.

I gave a whoop, startling Bice. "What is it?" he demanded.

"You were right, priest! I can see!" I turned my head back and forth. It wasn't much, nothing like true vision, but maybe that was a result of just how little light was available down here. But I could make out the shape of the tunnel, Bice beside me, and even the water around our feet.

"Let me go first," I instructed, moving round him. "We can move faster now."

"If you say so."

I was so elated at the discovery, I didn't notice the change in the next impact sound. Bice did. He grabbed my arm. "Did you hear that?"

"Yes, they're still trying to break through."

"No! Listen!"

I stopped and obeyed. Another impact came from behind us. I opened my mouth to ask what difference it made, when the next impact came. From in front of us. They'd found the opposite door.

I groaned. Of course they would find it. It wouldn't take much to figure out the tunnel led under the canal. A quick search of the buildings on the opposite side would… but no, this was too fast. They couldn't have found it that fast. Unless someone really had given us away.

"We're trapped." Bice's breathing was accelerating.

"Wait, wait. We can get out of this."

"How?"

Only one thought occurred to me, and it was a preposterous one. I retraced my steps back a few yards. There. The metal panel. I examined it with my newfound night vision. It measured about three feet wide by two feet long. I felt around the edges and found moisture. It might be what I thought it was. I tried to ignore the continued hammering sounds, now coming from both directions.

"They're speeding up," Bice said. "They must be using two sledge hammers or something."

I used my cyb hand to twist the corner of the panel, trying to pull it away from the wall. I couldn't get a good grip. I took a deep breath and boosted my arm and hand. I managed to get one finger to squeeze under the edge. Immediately, a tiny but forceful spray of water erupted from the spot. I'd suspected as much.

"Bice, how good are you at swimming?"

"Who goes swimming?"

"Can you swim or not?" I demanded.

"I—yes, I can. When I was a young priest, we had—"

"Good," I interrupted. "We're both going to have to swim here." I didn't tell him that the last time I'd been swimming was when I was about ten years old. We didn't get much pool time in Viridia.

"I can't swim in the dark," he protested.

The latest impact sound came with an added noise of shattering. I looked back up the tunnel and saw a tiny bit more light. "They're breaking through. We don't have a choice now. You're going to have to hold on to me. I'll guide us out."

"Guide us out of where?"

"There's a panel here. I'm going to tear it off, and probably bring the entire canal in with it. When the water stops pouring in, we should be able to swim out through it."

"You don't know where that panel leads! It might—"

"Bice! There's no time! Here! Grab on to my belt and hold on for your life!"

I turned back to the panel and jammed my finger into the hole again.

I boosted the hand and succeeded in getting two more fingers under the lip of metal. More water shot out. "Here it comes!" I pulled a little further, then got a complete grip on the twisted panel. The water pressure exploded around my hand, some of it striking my face.

The sound of rock shattering came from behind us, followed by loud yells and more light. They were through!

I channeled every bit of energy I could into that arm and wrenched. With a scream of twisting metal, the panel tore away from the concrete and whatever else it had been attached to.

Water erupted into the tunnel. In two or three seconds, it was at our waists, and rising faster.

A light shone from the far end of the tunnel. "Hold it right—whoa!"

The water rose to our chests. I gasped. Even though I'd been anticipating it, it was still cold.

"Even with your boosts, we won't be able to swim for long at this temperature!" Bice shouted over the roar.

"We'll have to! Hold on to my belt!"

The water level surmounted the opening and the roar quieted abruptly. The light at the end of the tunnel wobbled and vanished. The Scarlet Brigade wasn't prepared for underwater operations, I'm guessing.

I held my face up above the water as long as I could. Then it grew too high to stand. We floated with it as it rose, treading water to keep in place. Just a few more inches…

"Now!" Bice grabbed my belt, and we both took in huge breaths. Then we ducked under.

The night vision, or whatever it was, worked under the water as well, much to my relief. I caught the edge of the opening and pulled myself to it. The water still flowed in, but at a slow rate, now that the tunnel was filling. I thrust myself into the opening, Bice following.

The opening led me into a long concrete tunnel of the same width. I pushed off with my hands and feet against the sides to propel myself along its length. Far ahead, I could see a lighter spot, which I hoped was sunlight on the canal itself. Over and over, I pushed myself along. My cyb hand was doing fine, but the skin on my right hand wore away and grew bloody as I kept shoving against concrete.

Would my cybernetic hand ever rust? What about the parts inside? Could water damage them? I wondered but didn't have time to dwell on it.

The tunnel turned upward, and I shot ahead with renewed hope. The light grew brighter. Already, I was having difficulty holding my breath. I'd never had to do it this long before.

I almost didn't see the iron grate blocking the tunnel until I slammed into it.

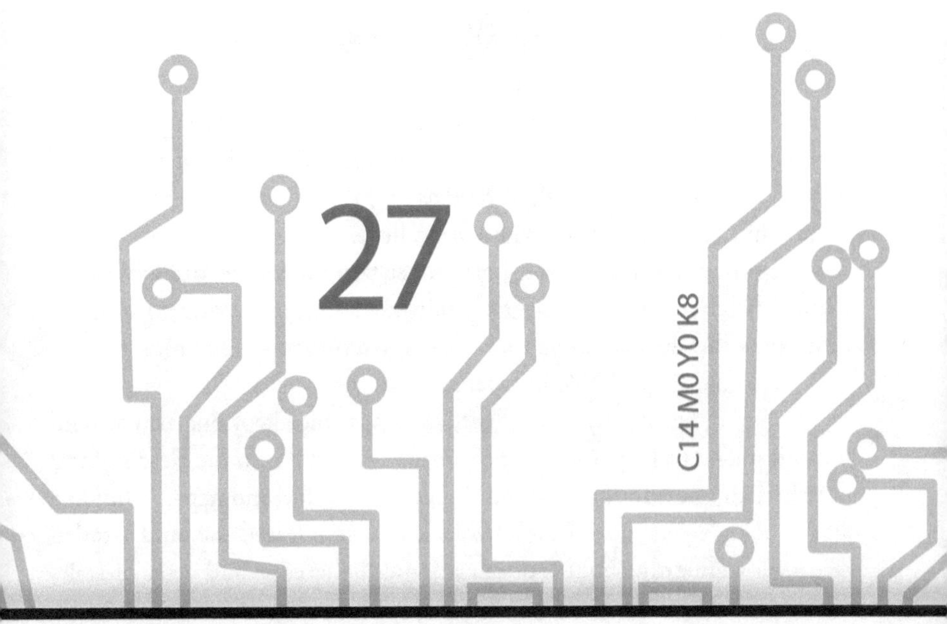

Sunlight definitely penetrated the water above our heads now. The night vision faded away, leaving things much darker. Air waited less than a dozen feet away. A few strokes and we could be there. Except we couldn't move past the grate.

I pushed at it with my cyb hand, but nothing happened. I couldn't get leverage. Bice started to swim up beside me, his eyes wide, but I motioned him back. He would be in the way of what I needed to try.

I positioned my back against the grate, then squeezed myself up against it, hands on one side of the tunnel and feet on the other. My lungs burned. I threw boosts into my entire body, as much as I could, and pushed with everything I had. The grate bit into my back, scraping against my backbone, but I kept going, channeling more and more boost energy. My head grew fuzzy, and my eyes blurred.

I gritted my teeth and pushed. My cyb fingers dug into the concrete. My knees felt like they were about to snap. My shirt and the skin on my back tore from the scraping. Darkness filled the edges of my vision.

And then the grate came loose. I popped out of the tunnel with it and floated. Bice glanced at me, then swam upward as fast as he could. I made a feeble attempt to follow him, but my arms no longer worked. The initial burst with the grate pushed me up, but now I began to drift back down, toward the floor of the canal. I released what little air remained in my mouth and watched the bubbles ascend.

Bice reappeared in my vision, right in front of me. He wrapped an arm around me and kicked off from the canal floor. We ascended toward the light. Bice stroked and kicked as hard as he could. I made another attempt to help him, moving my arms and legs a little.

We broke the surface, and I gasped, sucking in a huge drought of air. I immediately choked and gagged, spitting water and trying to bring in more air. I thrashed about as a bit of energy returned to my limbs.

"Hold on! Relax!" Bice instructed. "I've got you!"

I obeyed, letting my limbs drift free again. Bice kept one arm around me and pulled us both toward the shore. I stared up into the clear sky and breathed air, glorious air, into my lungs. After a few moments, I blinked and shook. "I can move now," I told Bice. He released me, and I rolled over. We were only about a dozen feet from the edge and a set of stairs carved into the concrete. We both swam with tired strokes until we made it. Bice insisted I climb out first. He followed right away, and we collapsed onto the concrete, shaking from the cold.

"We-we gotta find some warmth," Bice stammered, "or we're n-not going to make it."

I pushed up on my elbows and looked around. We lay on a concrete walkway running alongside the canal. About a dozen yards away, a set of stairs ran up to the street level. I staggered to my feet and pointed at it. "This way." As we hurried, I pulled off my wet shirt. Bice did the same. I don't know if it helped or not.

At the street level, we surveyed the nearest buildings. A row of expensive homes met our eyes. I pointed at one of the closest ones. "Chimney. We're going there."

We crossed the street and jogged to the house. "What if someone's home?" Bice asked.

"At this point, I don't care."

I shoved a wrought iron gate open and crossed a tiny yet immaculate yard. The back door was sliding glass. I broke the lock with my cyb hand and slid it open. No one came running. We might have lucked out. Bice joined me and closed the door behind us.

I breathed in the warm air, though I continued to shiver uncontrollably. Bice pointed. "The fireplace is over there. I'll try to get it going. You find some blankets."

We stripped off our socks and shoes first, then split up. I found a bedroom and tore the blanket and comforter off. When I returned, Bice had a few sparks glowing. "Almost there…" he muttered.

A few minutes later, we both sat wrapped up in the covers, our wet clothes spread out on the floor in front of the now-raging fire. It still took far too long for the shivering to stop.

"That was close," Bice said after a while.

"Yeah." I snorted. "We stare down dragons, and then die from drowning in a canal. What an epic end that would be, huh?"

"Seriously, when we met that, that iron grating, I almost let myself sink. But when you braced yourself in and started pushing, I knew we could do it."

"I didn't."

"Once we were out of the tunnel, I could handle it," he went on. "I told you I could swim."

"I wouldn't have made it without you."

"Good thing we were both there then."

We fell silent. Saying the obvious things seemed right, after what we'd been through, but once they were said, I didn't know what else to add. We were alive. That's all that mattered now.

"This house looks lived-in," Bice said after a while. "The owners are probably at work. We should try to leave before they get home. I'm guessing we've got at least an hour before we should really get out."

"An hour right here sounds good to me."

"Can you find our way back to the apartment?"

"I think so. It's easy to find the Flame, and when we get close to it, I can find the apartment building. It may be a roundabout route, but we can do it."

Bice grunted and extended his feet closer to the fire. A few more minutes ticked by.

"Someone gave us up, Bice," I said. "They couldn't have found both ends of the tunnel otherwise."

"I thought of that."

"It couldn't be Lady Rust. She could have just dropped us off at a police station. Sangria then?"

"Maybe he was jealous of us," Bice suggested. "He wasn't pleased that we demanded to meet his patron."

"Even so, to give away his secret tunnel under the canal? Did he dislike us that much?"

"It does seem a little extreme."

"But… he's the only other one who could have done it. Anyone else who saw us might follow us to the entrance and lead the soldiers there, but… the other side? He's the only one who knew where to find it."

"No, not the only one. Marcus knew."

"Marcus wouldn't betray us!"

"I'm not saying he would." Bice paused. "But he did express some doubts earlier."

My heart sank. I didn't want to think about Marcus that way, but after Rick, I suppose I shouldn't rule anything out. Hadn't we seen enough of betrayal?

"No." I shook my head. "If it were Marcus, the troops would have shown up on this side first, not the other side."

"Logically, yes."

"Then I'm sticking with logic. Still… I'm not going to use the talker, just in case the wrong person is listening."

That left Sangria as the most likely culprit. It was easy to imagine that uppity idiot turning traitor out of jealousy. It fit with his personality, after all. But I couldn't be sure. We would have to be extremely careful in further contacts. At least the next meeting would be bypassing him entirely.

After another half hour in which we both probably snoozed a little in front of the fire, we decided it was time to move on. Our clothes were mostly dry but still felt a bit clammy when we pulled them on. "Our hosts do have a shower, don't they?" Bice asked.

"Yeah." I glanced down the hall of the house we'd been occupying. "Maybe we should have used this one."

"The fire was better."

I couldn't argue with that. We slipped out the way we'd come, leaving the homeowners to wonder why someone had broken into their house and done nothing more than move blankets around and light a fire.

I spotted the Flame as soon as we rounded the corner. We worked our way across the city, aiming in that direction. Exhaustion dogged our steps. We would have stopped to rest more often, but stepping outside brought back the chill air. It didn't take long before we were both chilled again.

By the time I finally located the right apartment building, I was fully in agreement with Caedan: I'd had enough of the cold.

28

After a shower and a change of clothes, I began to feel human again. Or as close to human as I could ever get, I suppose, considering how much of me wasn't. Bice found some cocoa in the pantry and made us some hot chocolate.

Caedan and Lainey, dying of curiosity, demanded we tell them everything. Step by step, we told of our crazy day: the tunnel, Sangria, Lady Rust, and our escape back through the tunnel and the canal. The only part we left out was Lady Rust's appearance and Bice's idea that she was interested in me.

"So tomorrow, I have to meet with her again," I concluded.

"But only Beryl," Bice added. I shot him a look.

"Why?" Lainey asked.

"It's safer for her to only meet with one person," I explained. "And she's the one making the invitation, so I think we should stick to it."

"I didn't come along to sit in an apartment," Caedan grumbled.

"You got to do something this morning!"

"For a few minutes."

"You'll get plenty more to do when we get the stuff from Onyx," Bice said.

"Let's… save that problem for later," I said. "For now, I need—"

I was about to say "a nap," but the apartment door opened and Marcus entered in a hurry, carrying a long cardboard tube. He stopped on seeing us. "You're all right!" he exclaimed. "I heard there was a huge dust-up at the bridge with soldiers from both sides. I just knew it had to be you."

"It kind of was." So then we had to tell the story again. Marcus set the tube aside and started to prepare the evening meal while we talked. When we got to the possibility of a traitor, he frowned.

"I don't think Sangria gave you up," he declared. "He's a pompous jerk, yes, but he's totally dedicated to his cause. He wouldn't do anything to endanger it. And that tunnel was important to him."

"Then how do you explain soldiers on both sides?" I asked.

"I think you're underestimating how fast they can work together." Marcus lit the stovetop under a frying pan. "They each have guards stationed on the bridge itself, and there's a station close by on either side. From the moment you entered the tunnel, it probably took no more than five minutes before the Crimson Elite were searching buildings on our side for its exit."

I glanced at Bice. It probably would have been at least five or more minutes before we heard the pounding on the Incarnadine side. Even so, I didn't buy it. "It still seems too fast for them to actually find it."

"It's math," Lainey said.

"What?"

"Once they saw you enter the tunnel, and knew it existed, they could calculate its angle, which would take them straight to the building they needed," she explained. "Half a minute to calculate, and then the five minutes Marcus mentioned to get the news to the other side."

I ran my hand through my hair. "Maybe. I don't know."

"Our friend Rick delivered already," Marcus announced, adding oil to the frying pan.

"What do you mean?" Caedan asked.

Marcus pointed at the cardboard tube. "That was delivered to my theater this afternoon, along with a couple of crates full of what I can only assume are the explosive devices." He shook his head. "I can't imagine bringing down the entire Flame."

"Let's see what we've got then." I opened the tube and slid out some large papers. I unrolled one of them on the table.

"Looks like the building plans for the Flame," Bice observed.

Lainey pointed to some pen markings. "And he's marked where to place the explosives."

"So we've got to sneak in without being detected, place all these explosives, get all of the humans out of the entire building, and then blow it up." I shook my head. "That enough action for you, Caedan?"

"More than," he muttered, looking over the plans.

"I'm sorry. I'm having trouble with this." Marcus turned from the stove toward us. "Why are we even thinking of doing what the dragon wants?"

"He didn't give us much choice," Caedan said.

"When I meet with Lady Rust tomorrow, maybe we can come up with a way out of it," I added. "But until then, we have to at least consider potential plans. If we're trapped into doing it, we have to do it. Otherwise—"

"Otherwise, you and Cerise are dead," Bice said. "We might be able to sneak out and escape, but Onyx knows the two of you. He'll take his revenge on you, for starters."

"Besides, isn't this what we want, anyway?" Caedan asked. "It's a solid plan to kill a dragon. Shouldn't we take advantage of that?"

"It's just hard, that's all." Marcus waved a spatula. "It's all well and good to talk about stuff happening in the other cities. And even to pull off a heist, like we did before. But killing the dragon? Bringing down the Flame? It's scary stuff."

"Maybe that's why the rebels in Amaranth have never done much," I thought out loud. "They have high ideals, but when it comes to actually bringing about change…"

"Change can be frightening," Bice said. "But change is good for us. We stagnate otherwise. Sort of like that horrible water in the canal."

"Yes, we're all glad you took showers," Caedan said. "I didn't want to mention the smell, but there's a reason Glacier went to the corner when you got here and hasn't come back."

"Ha ha."

Lainey walked up beside Marcus. "We'll do everything we can to protect your family," she told him. "You have our promise."

He chuckled. "I know, I know. But being told that by a girl without a chromark is just another sign of how far away we are from 'normal.'" He shook his head. "Look, don't tell Cerise I asked these questions. She's all in with this, even though it means her job will be destroyed. But it's my job to think of her. And our future."

"My future has no dragons," I said. My hand started to close into a fist, but I forced it to relax. "My future has humanity set free. Nothing else matters."

"Cerise might be pregnant!" Marcus burst out. "How can we bring a baby into this world if it's in total chaos?"

No one spoke for a moment. "Congratulations," Lainey whispered.

"That's new life," Bice said. "It's what we're fighting for." He held out a hand toward me. "Beryl is always thinking of the death part of the story: killing the dragons. I'm here to remind him that it's about life. Life is what truly matters." He smiled. "If you are going to bring new life into this world, that is cause for rejoicing, regardless of what is happening everywhere else."

A noise at the door heralded the return of Cerise. She bustled in, pulling her scarf off. Everyone turned to look at her. She stopped, looked back at us, then to Marcus.

"You told them, didn't you?"

"It's what our life is about right now, babe. I had to let them know."

Cerise sighed and pointed to her stomach. "Everyone get a good look? Nothing showing yet. Let's move on." She hung her scarf and jacket up and joined us at the table. "So. How's everyone been today?"

Once again, we told the story of the day's exploits, now including the delivery to Marcus. Cerise absorbed it all, making occasional observations. She took a long look at the plans for the Flame.

"These are the original plans," she pointed out. "The first floor was redesigned about twenty years ago. I can mark the differences here."

"All right," I began, "so how can we get—"

"Ah, ah, ah!" Bice interrupted. "Enough plans for now. You and I are exhausted, Beryl. Let's eat this wonderful smelling meal that Marcus is preparing for us, and then get some sleep. Tomorrow, we can make plans."

"Onyx didn't give us a deadline," Caedan pointed out with a shrug.

"Fine." I held up my hands. "This can wait until tomorrow." But just saying it wouldn't take things out of my mind. Even while we enjoyed some light-hearted discussions around the table, I ran through various thoughts, trying to figure out a way to accomplish the goal without it benefiting Onyx. Nothing good came from it.

About an hour after the meal, I stretched out on my sleeping bag and felt my eyes growing heavy. My last thoughts were of the next day's meeting with Lady Rust. The dreams that followed were… disturbing.

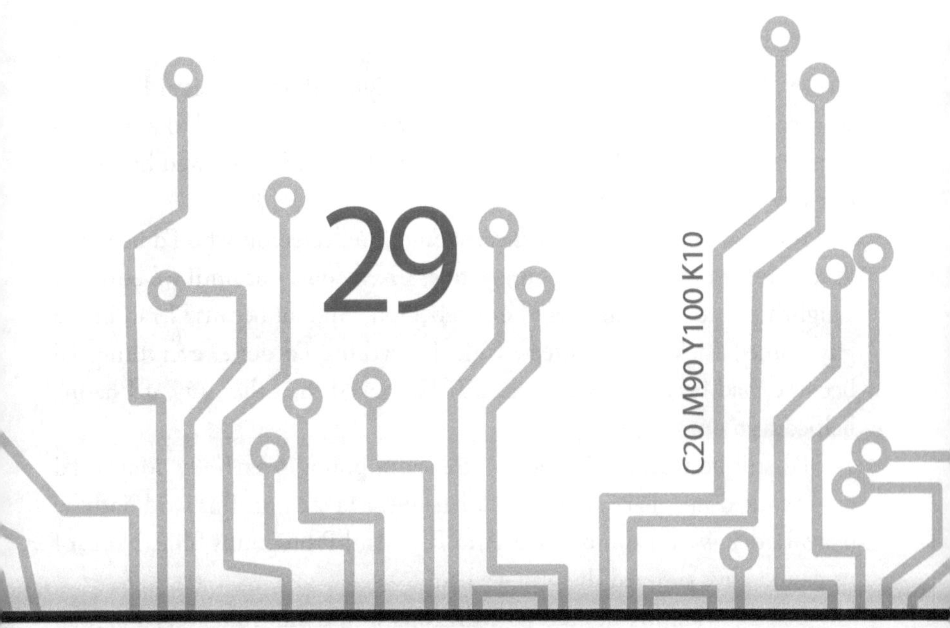

The following morning, I took another shower, since we had the access, and dressed in clean clothes again. I briefly considered taking my sword, but I suppose it would be awkward in the carriage.

"Be careful," Lainey said as she straightened my collar. "If there is a traitor, and they know about your appointment, there might be another trap waiting for you."

She stepped back to look at me. "Are you sure you don't want me to go along? Or maybe you should take Caedan? Show this woman that we have people from multiple cities?"

I shook my head. "She had her reasons, and I don't want to mess it up." Even saying it, I felt a little guilty for not clarifying the reasons.

"You could take the cat," Caedan said from the couch. "She didn't say not to bring a pet."

"I don't think Glacier would obey me." I looked to where the big cat lay snoozing in the sunlight.

Lainey laughed. "I could try to tell her, but I don't know if she'd listen."

"Yeah. I'll go it alone."

I gave Lainey a kiss, then slipped out into the street. Marcus not only gave me directions to the theater the Lady had designated, he gave me the best gift yet: an actual map of the city. Why didn't we have these in Viridia? We probably did; I had just never thought to ask anyone. Before becoming a rebel, I'd never traveled far beyond the neighborhoods where I lived and worked. I knew the location of almost anything else I needed to know. Except where Kelly lived. I was so pathetic back then, I'd followed her home one day to learn her address.

As I walked the streets of Incarnadine, I reflected on who I'd been last year. I didn't even have the courage to ask Kelly out, not until we both got caught up into the madness of our rebellion. And all because I ran into a guy named Rick on the street. Ugh. Everything I'd done, everything I'd become, had been spurred by him. If I'd looked the other way, if I hadn't helped him out…

I'd still be working in the bicycle shop, pining over Kelly. Maybe I'd have worked up the courage to ask her out. Maybe not. But we'd both be okay. Loden would still be alive. And Peri. And Protogonus Blue. None of us would have suffered the way we had.

But we wouldn't be free. The dragons would still rule everything, all of them. Hunter and so many others would still be dying in the Pit. And I would never have met Lainey.

That one thing, in and of itself, made it all worthwhile. No, I didn't mean that. I wouldn't want to trade lives for the chance to meet a girl. Of course not. But even if our mission eventually failed, at least I would have this time with her. That much, at least, was a very good thing.

So here I was, heading off to meet another beautiful young woman. Idiot. I almost turned around and went back. But the mission… We needed Lady Rust. I argued it back and forth in my head until I found myself standing in front of the Mahogany Birch Theater. And what kind of weird name for a theater was that, anyway? Weren't they both some kind of tree or something?

I didn't have much time to think about it before I saw the carriage approaching. On the cobblestone street in Amaranth, it had almost looked like it belonged. Here, on the concrete of Incarnadine, it looked completely out of place. It pulled to a stop at the curb. The driver nodded at me without saying a word. I glanced around, then reached up and opened the door.

The carriage was empty.

Alarm bells went off in my head. Was this another trap? But that made no sense. If the Lady wanted me somewhere, she could have taken me there herself. And Sangria couldn't be behind this. He didn't have that kind of power.

"Where is the Lady Rust?" I asked the driver.

"Waiting. Get in."

I hesitated long enough to make the driver turn and look at me. Then I climbed into the carriage and shut the door. It began moving at once. I sat back and waited, wondering again what I'd gotten myself into.

The carriage drove for twenty or thirty minutes, taking numerous turns. For all I knew, the driver was going in a circle. Or he could be taking the most direct route to our destination, whatever that might be. The ride seemed a bit more smooth this time. Perhaps we only drove on solid roads. I wondered why Amaranth wanted to keep such archaic means of transportation in place… and then I remembered her odd speech patterns. The female dragon seemed to want to live in the past. Was that why she went along with Onyx? Some romanticized version of their past relationship?

The carriage came to a stop. I waited a moment, but no one opened the door. I considered it for a moment, then threw caution to the wind, opened the door, and stepped right out. I stopped at the sight before me.

I'd seen fancy houses before, but nothing quite like this. Words like "mansion" and "estate" came to mind. The central house sported three stories, though the wings only had two. The walls were tan, highlighted in white trim and a reddish-brown roof. Two columns supported an arch over the front door, surrounded by tall windows. I'd never seen an outdoor chandelier until that moment. The door opened as I approached.

An elderly man in a black suit nodded to me, then pointed. "The Lady awaits you in the gardens, sir."

"Thank you." I walked under an even more unbelievable chandelier and past a white stairway curling up to the next floor. More columns flanked a short hall with black marble floors. I passed through an enormous living space decorated with furniture I would be afraid to even touch. Double glass doors stood partially open, so I stepped out onto a stone pathway that led through another arch, for which I could see no reason, and into the gardens.

White pillars lined a long stretch of the greenest grass I'd ever seen. On either side of the grass grew three rows of bushes of successive heights. Beyond them lay larger trees with branches drooping over past the columns and bushes.

The Lady Amara Rust stood near the end of this grass pathway, reaching for one of the overhanging branches. She wore a lighter red dress than before, though still showing as much bare skin as ever. Something like a cross between a sweater and a scarf lay over her shoulders. She turned as I approached.

"Ah, there you are, Beryl. Tell me: do you know much of gardening?"

"I know almost nothing whatsoever about gardening."

"Oh, good." She laughed. "A man who studies gardening likely has little else to excite him in life, wouldn't you say?"

"I'd say my life is plenty exciting right now."

She stepped forward and smoothly took my arm in hers, turning me back toward the house. "I'll take that as a compliment then."

I'd meant it in general, about my life as a whole, but… all right. Sure.

"Come. Let me show you some of what my old money has provided." We walked back into the living area, where she took a turn to the left. As we did, she described a few of the furniture pieces, telling their history. I pretended to listen, but found myself growing very warm. Was it the house or her presence? It seemed that every move she made—leaning over to point at something, gesturing past me, pulling me closer to walk around something—was designed to draw my attention to the curves and nearness of her body.

Lainey. Think about Lainey.

"Do you swim?"

I almost jumped. "I, uh, had a very bad experience with swimming just yesterday."

She led me through another set of double doors into an enormous atrium, enclosed with glass panels. A crystal-clear swimming pool filled most of the space, with a few flowering trees scattered throughout. A fountain bubbled into a separate round pool that overflowed into the main one.

"Yesterday? After our meeting?"

"Yes. We were chased by the Scarlet Brigade only moments after we left you. We had to escape through an underground tunnel into the canal."

Her mouth fell open. "How did they find you so fast?"

"That's what we were wondering. Do you think Sangria tipped them off?"

She wrinkled her brow. "I don't think he would. While he has his faults, he seems quite dedicated."

"Then I don't know. Maybe someone else saw us."
"Or maybe I told them, to test your capabilities."

"Then I don't know. Maybe someone else saw us."
"Or maybe I told them, to test your capabilities."

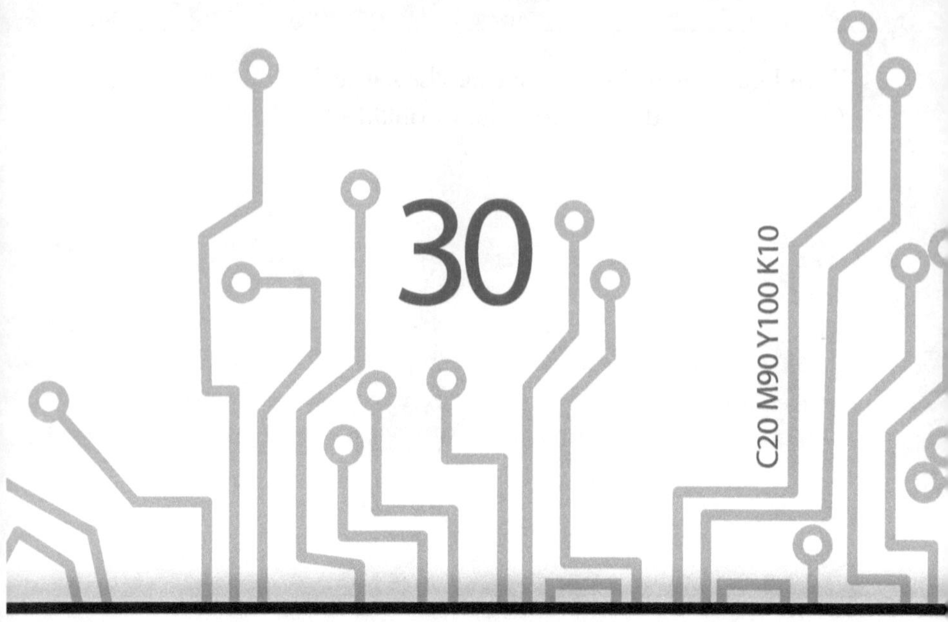

I stopped, and Lady Rust released my arm. She walked on to the round pool and bent down beside it.

"Did you?" I asked, wondering how fast I could run out of this house.

"No, but the thought did cross my mind." She dipped her hand in the water. "This water is kept very hot, for a different experience. There are water jets around the edges that can be activated for massage."

"Why would you want to turn us in?"

She turned her head to look at me. "I don't want to turn you in. But I will admit: I wondered if I might find some way for you to prove you are truly capable of all the stories about you."

"Are you asking me to perform for you?" I glanced around the atrium. I suppose I could demonstrate some jumps or something.

"Perhaps later." She got to her feet again and joined me. "Let's continue our tour." Again, her arm slid into mine, and we turned back to the doors.

"I, uh, didn't you want to hear about the Books of Lore?"

"Of course. Tell me all about that adventure."

While I told her about our heist and the subsequent chase with Incarnadine, the Lady guided me back inside and up the curved staircase I'd noticed earlier. She led me into what appeared to be a kind of study room. The walls and ceiling consisted of a polished red wood, while the floor had more of a tan look to its wooden tiles. Shelves lined the walls, divided by black pillars with gold capitals. A desk and chair sat near the full-length window, but Lady Rust led me to a long, curved couch near the opposite wall.

"And then I kind of crashed the Sky Claimer," I finished, "but I had help, so I survived."

She shook her head. "Such extraordinary events. Nothing like this has ever happened in The Circle's history. At least, not that I'm aware of."

"Well, we are trying to change everything, you know." I ran my hand on the back of the couch, amazed at the softness and smooth texture. If Marcus and Cerise had a couch like this, I'd never leave it. Wealth had its privileges.

"Indeed you are." She leaned back on a couch pillow and crossed her legs. "And now you want to move against both Onyx and Incarnadine."

"We're discussing plans."

"I have informed my agents to be on the lookout for Onyx in his human form, as you described him. It's only been one day, obviously, but no one has reported anything yet."

"I appreciate it. If we can locate him without him knowing, maybe we can catch him unawares. The dragons are vulnerable in human form."

"Are they? Then they don't possess all their, ah, dragon power in that form?"

I looked across the room from us and pointed at a display between some of the shelves. A set of decorative maces hung in a pattern. "If I were to take one of those weapons and strike Onyx in his human form, it would hurt him as much as any other human. I could kill him that way. But if I were to strike him in his dragon form, he might not even notice it." The disk from Auric bumped against my leg as I shifted. I almost mentioned it, but Lady Rust reached her hand out toward the side of my head, then pulled it back.

"Didn't you say Onyx spit acid in your face?"

"Yes. So they do possess those abilities in human form."

"Somewhat vulnerable, and somewhat not, then." She sat up abruptly. "But how rude of me. I have yet to offer you anything to drink."

"Oh, that's okay, I—"

She jumped to her feet and pulled a silk rope hanging near one of the shelves. A moment later, the door opened, and the older man I'd seen earlier stepped inside with a short bow.

"Drinks, please," the Lady instructed. He nodded and stepped back out. Lady Rust turned back to me. "Are you comfortable? Can I get you anything else?"

"No, no. I'm really quite comfortable, thank you."

"Excellent." She sat back on the couch beside me, a little closer, I noticed. "It may come as quite a surprise to you, but more often than not, I'm very alone in this huge house. Aside from the servants, of course."

"That is surprising. I'd think you would be very popular."

"Because of my money?"

"Sure, and, uh, because you're an attractive young woman." I didn't see any reason not to say it.

She smiled. "Are you trying to flatter me now?"

"Just stating the facts."

The servant returned with two flute glasses. Lady Rust took them and thanked him. As he left again, she offered one to me. I took it and looked at the almost clear liquid bubbling within. Seeing her drink, I also took a sip. I wasn't sure what it was, but the flavor was strong and sweet. I took a larger swallow.

"Now, tell me about your plans for Incarnadine," she suggested.

"We don't really have much of a plan yet." I took another sip. "We've been inside the Flame before, like I told you, so we think we can do it again. Maybe we can find a weakness there, something to exploit." I'm not sure why I didn't tell her about Onyx's blackmailing.

Lady Rust rose and placed her own glass on the desk. She walked toward me, and my vision shifted a little. I blinked. What was that?

"Is there a problem?"

"No, I—" Sleepiness suddenly pulled at me. "I'm feeling… tired."

"Let me take that." She took the glass from my hand. Good thing. I think I might have dropped it. I don't know why I felt so tired all of a sudden.

"Go ahead and sleep," she told me. "We can talk more later…" If she said anything else, I didn't hear it.

When I woke, I found myself lying in the largest and softest bed I'd ever felt. I sat up, fighting another blur of vision, and looked around. The bedroom, larger than the Vermeils' entire apartment, continued the red and tan decor I'd seen in the study. But here, a red carpet contrasted with tan walls. Directly across from me, Lady Rust stood beside an enormous fireplace, looking up at a photorealistic painting of Amaranth that hung above it. She wore a deep purple robe—not the same shade as those I'd come to worry about—setting off her red hair and pale skin in dramatic fashion.

"What happened?" I asked. "How long did I sleep?"

She turned, smiling. "Ah, there you are. Your escapades from yesterday must have tired you more than you thought. You've been out for over an hour."

"Yeah, I guess so." I blinked again and rubbed my temples. I didn't remember being very tired until that moment in the study. The drink?

I started to get up, but she hurried to the side of the bed. "No, no. Rest as long as you need," she insisted. I struggled to control the direction of my eyes as she leaned across the bed. "My house is your house. In fact, if you want to bring your entire team here, I see no reason you could not operate from this place."

My eyes widened. "That's… very generous of you. But didn't you say it would be harder to explain multiple guests?"

"Yes, but we can work something out, I'm sure. Maybe find a way for you all to come and go without using the main gate."

"That's, that's great. I, um, I'm surprised. You've kept these local rebels separate from you. What's changed?"

She sat on the bed and put her hand on my chest. "You, Beryl. You're different than they are. I want you here. On a regular basis."

I swallowed. "To, uh, make plans together?"

"Why are you so dense?" she asked in a harder voice all of a sudden. "I'm propositioning you, idiot. You said you found me attractive, didn't you?"

"I did. Yes. But—"

She leaned toward my face. "Then what's the problem?"

"I, uh, I have a girlfriend."

"She doesn't need to know what you do here."

I took her hand. I couldn't deny how unbelievably attractive I found her in that moment. The pull I felt toward her was stronger than anything I'd ever experienced.

"You want me, don't you?"

"I, I do, but… I can't. Lainey is—" I pushed her hand away.

"Oh, this is pointless." She threw her head back. "Lie down!" she ordered in a commanding new tone. To my shock, I obeyed.

"How did you—?"

"You will obey my words, Beryl. Do you understand me?"

"I—yes."

"I had hoped to be further along before the big revelation, but we're wasting time." She regarded me with a fiery gaze. "I am Amaranth, fool. And you will do everything I ask."

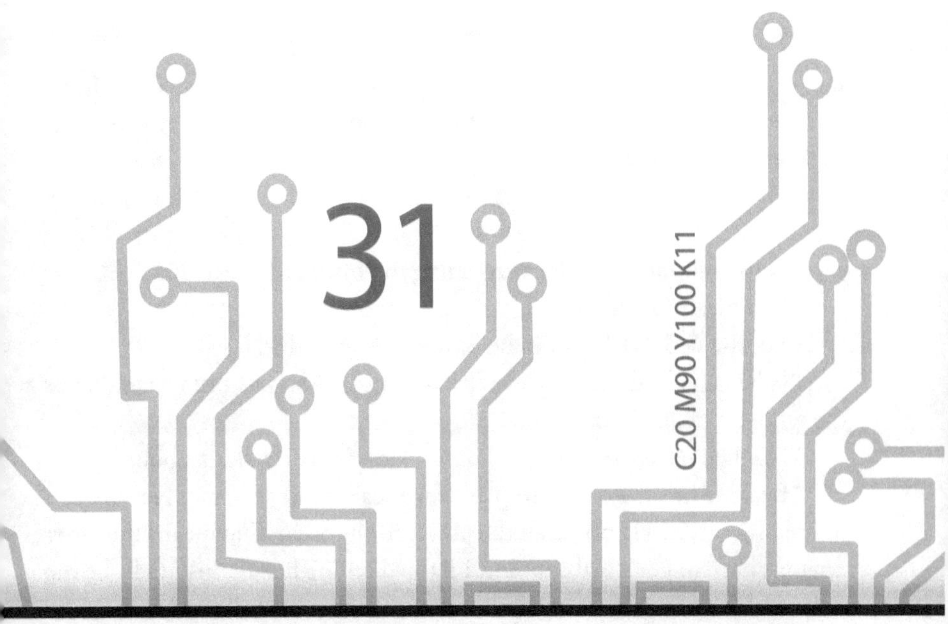

She couldn't be serious. Could she? Lady Rust leveled her gaze at me.

"Trouble believing?" She rotated her head and blew toward the ceiling. A tongue of flame burst from her mouth, then vanished as quickly as it came. She looked back at me. "Or should I do the full transformation right here?"

"Uh… you probably don't want to destroy your nice house."

"No, I don't. It really has been 'in my family' for over a century." She chuckled and touched my scar. "Fascinating the cybernetic work taking place below here… though it doesn't seem to have made you any smarter."

I tried to get up, but my limbs wouldn't obey me. "I don't get it. You're funding the rebellion against yourself?"

Lady Rust—Amaranth—traced the scar, touching the edge of my cybernetic eye. I flinched and blinked. I did possess some muscle control, then.

"Humans are rebellious by nature," she explained, "especially the male of the species. Knowing this, I sought out those who might be inclined to lead such a rebellion and took control over them. As their 'patron,' I guide their movements, letting them think they've won occasional victories, none of which really harm me. And if any of them do show even the hint of being a truly charismatic leader…" She snapped her fingers. "I remove them. Thus, I give them an outlet for their rebellion and make sure it never causes me any real difficulty." She smiled. "And it's fun. Can you believe, in all these years, no one ever thought to even connect Lady Amara Rust with Amaranth the dragon?"

I didn't know what to say. It all made sense, in a twisted, evil sort of way.

"Now. Tell me your plans regrading my brother Incarnadine."

"You mean Onyx's plans?"

She frowned. "What does he have to do with this?"

"Is he here?" I darted my eyes left and right. "Has he been watching us the whole time, laughing at me?"

"No, he's never been to this house. Why are you talking about him?"

"Because he's the one with plans for Incarnadine, not me. Haven't you figured it out yet? He wants all the power for himself. That means the other dragons have to go." At this point, I figured telling her all this might be the only way I could get out of the situation. Plus, sowing discord among the dragons was always a good thing.

"I know Onyx's ambitions, but he is under my care and control for now. He would not do anything without my approval."

"Wow, has he got you fooled. I guess I don't feel so bad about him fooling me now." Throughout the conversation, I kept trying to break her hold over my body. To my surprise, the first body part to respond to my thoughts was the cyb hand. I managed to twitch three fingers.

She studied me for a few moments. "Your tone of voice and method of speaking has changed. I cannot believe anything you say in this manner."

"Of course it's changed! You've got me magically restrained or something!"

"Then speak the truth!" she said in that commanding tone again. "Does Onyx seek to move against Incarnadine?"

"Yes."

"And you. Do you wish to kill Incarnadine?"

"Of course I do."

"Then what is your plan?"

"I told you." The compulsion to tell her everything almost overwhelmed me, but I held back. "I don't have a complete plan. Just ideas."

"I have ideas as well." She ran her fingers down to my chin and turned my face toward hers. Then she bent down and kissed me. I didn't kiss her back, but it wasn't easy to resist. Fewmets. She was beautiful.

Amaranth pulled away a few inches, and her red hair cascaded around both our faces. "Is that so unpleasant? You could still enjoy the rest of this evening with me."

"I have a girlfriend," I repeated.

"Who you'll never see again. You may as well enjoy pleasure when it is offered to you."

"Why would you do that?"

Her smile this time almost terrified me. Something dark lurked behind that smile. And then she spoke: "You mentioned not knowing how Amaranth's draconics came into being."

If I hadn't already been effectively frozen, I would have felt chilled.

"I give birth to them myself, of course. But first, I need a human male to start the process." She shifted on the bed, letting her robe gap further. "As it happens, one of my draconics was killed in a tower north of here. It seems only just that you would be the one to… sire his replacement."

Revulsion rose up inside me. For a brief moment, whether in my imagination or not, I saw her smooth pale skin flicker into red scales. She ran a finger along my chin. The horror of the moment forced me to think of something else to say. Anything.

"Why do you sound so different in your dragon form?" I burst out.

She kissed my cheek. "What do you mean?"

"Your language. You speak completely different."

"Thee would prefer I spoke thus?" She pulled back and laughed. "Dost thou find that more attractive?"

"No. I was just wondering."

"It's all part of the act, dear. I live two lives, as Amaranth the dragon and Lady Amara Rust the wealthy patron. It wouldn't do for both of them to sound the same, now would it?"

She started to roll herself on top of me. I had to stop this, somehow. What was she using against me? Was it like the magic Bice and Troilus Green used? If so…

I triggered a boost to my heart. Once again, something exploded through my entire body and outward, like a rush of electricity. Amaranth cried out and fell back off the bed. Free, I scrambled off the other side myself. I stumbled back several steps, a little surprised to notice my socks and shoes were gone.

"What was that?" Amaranth leaped to her feet and faced me. "How did you do that?"

"Secrets. We all have them." Even as I said it, I winced. Did I really need to quote Rick?

"Lie back down on the bed!" she commanded. But this time, I felt no compulsion to obey.

"No."

Her mouth opened a little in shock. "I… see. Your implant allows you to defy me somehow. Impressive. But there are many other ways to get what I want."

I slipped my cyb hand into my pocket and palmed the disk from Auric. No, I needed to save that for Onyx. Still, I held on to it. At least I had something as a last resort.

Amaranth took a step to the side. "In a few moments, I will walk through those doors over there into the garden." She pointed, but I didn't look. "I will transform into my full dragon form. Then I will seek out each of the rebel cells within this city. I told them all to hold meetings this evening. I know each of their locations. In the space of a few minutes, I will burn them all down. No one will survive… except Sangria. I will keep him alive for a few minutes, just long enough to tell me how he contacted you. Then, while he burns, I will follow that information to your safehouse in Incarnadine. My brother will not mind when I burn it to the ground as well."

She took another step to the end of the bed. "While I am doing that, you will fight your way through the Scarlet Brigade who await you outside this house. You will no doubt succeed, but it will take time. And then, using your cybernetic implants and whatever ingenuity you may have, you will rush across the two cities." Her smile grew. "And you will be too late."

"All of that because I don't want to sleep with you?" I tried to joke, but her description frightened me. She could easily follow up on her threats, and it would happen exactly as she said. In dragon form, she could be at all of those locations in seconds. I didn't even know how to get home from this place.

"No. Because you defy me. Submit to me now, give yourself up, and your friends may yet live." She took another step around the side of the bed. "Including your… girlfriend.

"Now." She clapped her hands. "You have thirty seconds to submit to me. This is your last chance. Submit, or everyone dies."

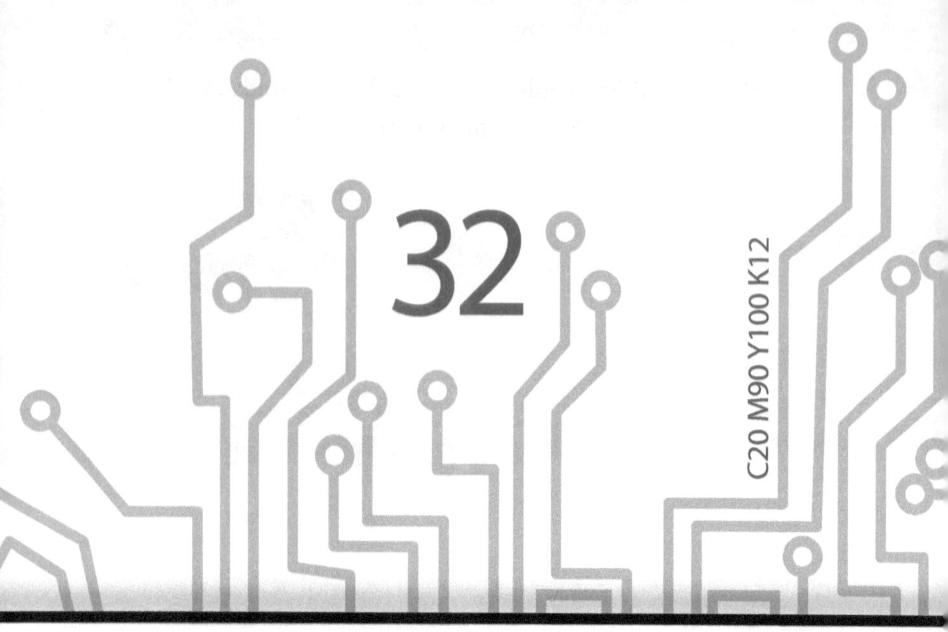

I could see only one way out of this, and I didn't like it. I took a step toward Amaranth. "If you would just—" I began.

"Ten seconds."

"I submit!"

She narrowed her eyes. "Do you indeed?"

"You're going to kill everyone I care about! I can't let that happen."

"Prove it." She beckoned me to come to her. "Kneel."

I obeyed. I stopped in front of her and dropped to one knee. As I did, I slipped Auric's disk from my cyb hand to the other hand. It felt cool as the bare skin on my palm activated it.

I stared up at Amaranth, who cocked her head to look down at me. She lowered her face near mine. "And now, you will do everything I want."

"Whatever you say." I bowed my head.

She reached under my chin and lifted my face. Her lips touched my forehead. In that instant, I gave my right arm a boost to speed it up. I pushed myself upright, kissing her on the lips. Her eyes widened. My hand slipped through her hair and to the back of her neck. She reached for mine as well. And then I slapped the disk onto her skin.

Amaranth shrieked and stumbled back. I pulled free and watched. She put both hands to the back of her neck. "What is this? What have you done?"

I didn't answer at first. Let her find out herself. She snarled at me and a puff of smoke escaped her lips. For a brief instant, her skin seemed to flicker into scales again, then it snapped back. She staggered as if struck.

"You're trapped in human form now," I said. "You can never become a dragon again, unless I remove that disk."

"You lie! Nothing can stop me!" She bent over and hugged herself, trembling. Her skin turned red. Two appendages ripped through the back of her robe, the beginning of her wings. But in an instant, she snapped back fully human again, and fell to the floor.

She tore at the disk with her fingernails. "Get this off me! How? How is this possible?"

"Not bad, huh?"

Amaranth rose up on her knees and glared at me with utter fury. Her eyes turned red and smoke poured from the edges of her lips again.

I held up my hand. "That disk is locked into you, but also locked to me. I'm the only one who can remove it."

She got to her feet. "Then I'll make sure to leave one of your hands intact while I incinerate the rest of your body! My scientists can take it from there."

"Pretty sure it doesn't work that way." I backed up toward the outer doors. I wondered if that were true. Auric said I was the only one who could remove it, but what if all she needed was my skin?

"Where did you get this? You do not possess the knowledge to create such a thing!"

I spread my arms. "You've seen the tech used to enhance me. Do you think anything is beyond the mind that did that?" I suppose I could have told her I got it from Auric, but he'd wanted me to use it on Onyx. He might not be too thrilled if she showed up at his city demanding he fix this.

Amaranth straightened and folded her arms across her chest, composing herself. "We seem to be at an impasse then. You have gained an advantage, but I still possess the ability to destroy all that you hold dear."

"And if you make one move toward doing that, then you guarantee I will never help you remove that disk."

"Very well. What will it take for you to remove it?"

If I removed it at any time, I removed the only thing keeping me safe from her wrath. "Yeah, I think we'll wait on that." I looked around and found a chair. I sat down and relaxed. "I like you this way better. No flying over the city burning buildings down."

"Name your terms," she growled through gritted teeth.

"Let me think… obviously, no reprisals against the rebels or anyone associated with me. Oh." I realized the best outcome to the situation. "And I want Onyx."

"What?"

"Give me Onyx. After I cut off his head, I'll remove the disk."

"That is never going to happen. I will never surrender one of our number to humans."

"Huh." I scratched at the back of my head. "And what will happen if I were to send a message to Auric or Atramentous about Onyx being here, and you trapped like this?"

"Do you wish to create a new Blasted Lands?" She took a step toward me. "Because that is what will happen."

"Maybe. Or maybe I'll just tell Troilus Green in Viridia. He doesn't have dragon powers now, but he'll send assassins or something."

"I do not fear him. Your threats are impotent."

"If you say so." I got to my feet. "Well, I'll be off then. Have fun being a human full-time."

"You're not leaving this house."

"Then bring me Onyx," I countered.

"Why should I? All I have to do is keep you here. I have experts in torture at my disposal. After a few hours in their company, you'll be begging to remove this device." She laughed and uncrossed her arms. "You have me in your power, but you're completely under my power as well."

I cocked my head. "I wouldn't say that." I triggered boosts to my legs and ran. In seconds, I was out of the bedroom and down the curved stairway. I shoved the front doors open and raced down the driveway to a closed iron gate. Beyond it, I could see several of the Scarlet Brigade waiting.

She did expect me to fight my way through them. Or so she'd said. So they couldn't be that bad. As if in response to my thoughts, a crossbow bolt shot past my head. I added more boosts to pick up speed, keeping ready to dodge any more I saw coming. And then I was approaching the gate. I leaped in mid-stride, kicked off the top rail of the gate, and plummeted to the other side. I was moving so fast, I almost forgot to throw new boosts into my legs to cushion the impact.

At least a dozen of the red-clad soldiers surrounded me. Their uniforms differed from the Crimson Elite in multiple ways. Most noticeably, the Brigade did not wear helmets, but some kind of hood and facemask combo instead. The reds were also darker, leaning more toward rust. Of course. Not sure why I hadn't noticed that before. Several of them carried crossbows, but most held some kind of baton with a metal tip glowing red. It didn't take much thought to figure out what those could do.

"Gentlemen. I believe your lady requires your assistance inside." None of them moved. Oh well. It was worth a try.

I channeled more boosts and ran toward the nearest soldiers. I dodged two more bolts. Then I was too close for them to risk shooting at me. Their lack of helmets left them vulnerable to my fists, a good thing, since there weren't any walls nearby to throw them against. I hadn't really used this new cyb hand in close quarters fighting like this yet. I punched the nearest soldier in the chin, and he went down. Another advantage: I didn't feel a thing.

I elbowed a second one in the stomach. But as he doubled over, something struck my left shoulder from behind. I let out a scream when my skin burned. I dodged away, and spun around.

"Now you've been marked," the soldier growled, "branded for her Ladyship, as surely as any chromark."

I believed it. I would certainly keep a scar on my shoulder from that. The pain was almost as bad as the time a draconic breathed fire on my hand.

"Your lady is a dragon who keeps people enslaved!" I snapped. "She's pure evil!"

"She is a goddess. And you are a heretic and a fool. Now!"

Another half dozen of the Scarlet Brigade ran around a corner. I had been about to run that direction, but they kept cutting me off. There were too many of them. They moved in, surrounding me in two half-circles. The inner circle of six soldiers held their branding irons aimed toward me as they advanced. Half of the outer circle readied crossbows.

I glanced behind me. Another mansion stood some distance from the road, behind another iron fence backed up by a line of trees. Maybe I could leap for the branches.

Two of the soldiers in the second half-circle raced up behind the first and threw something. I moved to dodge it, but it exploded in mid-air a few feet away. A net of some kind shot out of the device and tumbled on top of me. I fell with it tangled around all of my limbs as the branding irons moved in.

33

With no time to spare, I boosted all of my limbs and flailed outward. The net tore easily, but pieces still clung to me. Only inches from getting branded again, I leaped up as high as I could and twisted backward. A tree rushed to meet me. Twisting in mid-air wasn't easy, even with my implant. I slammed into a horizontal branch, knocking the wind out of me. Two crossbow bolts slammed into the branch next to me. I flipped over it and tumbled down into the brush.

Bushes and undergrowth obscured me from the soldiers for a brief moment. Another bolt narrowly missed my leg. I rolled away from the direction of the fence, gasping for air. Shouts and threats pursued me, but it would take them a minute or two to get over that fence or find the gate.

As soon as I could breathe again, I scrambled to my feet and ran. I bypassed this particular mansion and aimed for the opposite fence. I leaped it with ease and raced down the road. I didn't pay any attention to my directions at first, concentrating on putting distance between myself and the enemy. I took turns at random, but still making sure I didn't head back toward Amaranth's place. After about fifteen minutes, I slowed to a stop and caught my breath.

I needed to get back to my team. After that, we could send word to warn Sangria and the rebel cells, if they would even believe my story. Amaranth might strike out against them or us, or she might not. I didn't know how to judge her state of mind. What I'd done to her had to be the worst thing she'd ever experienced in a thousand years. She would want revenge. But I'd warned her against it. She was smart. Maybe she'd wait.

What would she tell Onyx, though? Would she even tell him what I'd done? If she admitted that kind of weakness in front of him, he might take advantage of it. I couldn't decide if that were good or bad.

Which way to home now? It was getting dark already, but I could see for some distance through the various buildings. However, I couldn't see the Flame, my sole landmark. Without it, I didn't know which way to go.

If I remembered the maps right, the city of Amaranth lay on the north side of Incarnadine, and, maybe, a little to the east. So if I headed south, bearing a little to the west, I could find the canal and cross over. The sun sets in the west, right? I turned toward the sunset. Facing west, that meant south would be… to my left.

I set out, jogging down the city streets. I'm not sure why, but there seemed to be far fewer people out on the streets in Amaranth than in any of the other cities I'd visited. I didn't take time to think about it. I needed to get home before Amaranth, just in case. I picked up my pace.

It took me an hour to find the canal. Crossing it proved to be easier than anticipated. Only an inch or two of water stagnated at the bottom, and the sun had long since set completely.

Once inside the city of Incarnadine, I soon spotted the Flame and worked my way across town. To my dismay, it took at least another hour to get to the apartment building, even boosting my legs on a regular basis. I stumbled through the Vermeils' door almost exhausted.

"Beryl!" Lainey grabbed my shoulders, and I screamed.

"Sorry, sorry." I pointed to the left shoulder. "Burned. Hurts." I staggered across the room and fell on the couch.

The others gathered around me. Bice, with my permission, peeled my shirt off. He examined my shoulder while I tried to listen to all of the questions.

"Wait, wait," I pleaded. "Marcus. I need you to get a message to Sangria as fast as you can. Do you have a system for that?"

"Um, yeah. I can get something to them pretty quick. What is it?"

"Tell them—" I winced as Bice probed the burn wound. "Tell them not to trust Lady Rust, and change everything so she can't find them."

"Lady Rust has turned against us?"

I closed my eyes. "Lady Rust is Amaranth the dragon in human form."

Everyone reacted to that. I waited for a moment, then interrupted again. "Don't tell Sangria that part. Just tell him she's turned against us, and the dragon knows about them. That's enough."

"You've got to tell us more than that," Cerise insisted.

"I will, I will. Just… get that message out, Marcus. Their lives may depend on it."

He nodded and ran out of the apartment.

Cerise settled in on the chair across from me. "Now tell us everything," she insisted.

Lainey brought me a glass of water, which I downed in a hurry. I don't think I'd had anything to drink since Amaranth gave me that drugged stuff. Bice worked on taking care of the wound while I talked. I told them almost everything, leaving out the part where Amaranth, uh, propositioned me.

"Why did she even reveal herself to you?" Lainey wondered. "That doesn't seem very smart. She could have gone on deceiving all of us."

"Yeah, I don't… I don't quite understand that myself."

Bice pulled away. "That should do it. Nasty burn there. It's going to leave a scar for sure."

"At least it wasn't my face this time."

"So you had to use the disk on her instead of Onyx," Caedan summed up. "All right. How do we use this to our advantage? Should we try to sneak back in and kill her, now that you know where she lives?"

"I'm sure she'll take precautions against that. I'll be surprised if she stays there."

"Should we take precautions?" Bice asked. "Does she know this location?"

"Only if Onyx tells her. She mentioned trying to get our location from Sangria, so he hasn't told her yet."

"But will he?" Cerise pressed.

"I don't know. With the doubts about Onyx I fed her, I'm hoping she's leery about trusting him. I'm almost completely certain she won't tell him what I did to her."

"A dragon would not confess to a weakness unless she has to," Bice said. "She'll keep that a secret as long as she can."

"So what do we do then? Does this alter our plans at all?" Caedan asked.

My shoulders slumped. "I don't think it does. I think I wasted Auric's gift."

"Don't say that," Lainey protested. "You've trapped a dragon in human form! That's a big deal in the long run, no matter what happens right now."

"She's right about that," Bice said. "But you're also right about it not altering our plans. Amaranth was never a big part of them, one way or another. We're still blackmailed by Onyx."

"But he can't depend on Amaranth to help him as much as she might have," Caedan said. "She's trapped as a human, and he can't become a dragon without attracting the others. That's a good thing."

"Which leaves only Incarnadine for now. I guess we should continue with Onyx's plan, or at least start working on it." I pulled my shirt back on.

"We can take our time with that, though," Bice said. "We don't have to get on it right away. You need rest again, for one thing."

"I'll rest when the dragons are all dead."

Bice shook his head. "Don't start down the angry, bitter road again. I thought you'd gotten past that."

"I have. I was just… never mind." I thought I was being funny, but my sense of humor didn't always seem funny to everyone else.

"Good thing," Cerise said. "I still have no idea how we're going to get anyone inside the Flame to plant the stuff, let alone how we'll evacuate everyone when the time comes."

"One step at a time," Bice replied. "We'll figure it out."

"Let's talk more in the morning," I suggested. My eyes were growing heavy. The others agreed, and we began preparing for bed.

Marcus returned a few minutes later, breathing hard. "I sent the message," he announced. "They should have it very soon." He held up a piece of paper. "But I found a message waiting for me. It's from Onyx."

If Onyx knew about Marcus's method of sending and receiving messages from Sangria, that could not be a good thing at all. "What does it say?" I asked.

He handed it to me. "See for yourself."

"Hello Marcus," I read aloud. "Please inform Beryl that circumstances have been altered. I need the job done sooner than I anticipated. You have three days."

34

"Three days?" Cerise exclaimed. "We can't possibly figure it out in three days!"

"That doesn't even give us time to get anyone else to help." I let my head fall back against the couch cushion.

Bice held up his hands. "All right, all right. Look at it this way. Day one, tomorrow: we spend all day making plans and double-checking everything. Day two, Thursday, we plant the explosives. Day three, Friday, it all comes together."

"Day four, we all die," Caedan added.

"If something goes wrong, we die a lot sooner than that," I said.

"Pessimists. You're all pessimists." Bice shook his head. "Go get some sleep."

Lainey sat on the floor and leaned against the couch where I lay. "Nice trick, getting a small injury so you get the couch."

"You can have it if you want." I started to move, but she stopped me.

"I'm teasing." She put her hand on my arm. "Are you all right, otherwise? I mean, after Rick's betrayal…"

"I'm okay. I'd known her for a single day. It wasn't like we had any kind of friendship already for her to betray."

Lainey rested her head against the couch cushion and my arm. "That's good."

I wanted to say more, but I fell asleep before I realized it. My life seemed to zig-zag between high-energy, insane moments and absolute exhaustion and sleep following them. I was either in life-threatening danger or passed out.

This time wasn't anywhere near as bad as some others. A solid night's sleep got me rejuvenated, especially once I took a shower the next morning. Bice changed my bandage while we ate breakfast. Cerise left for work, and the rest of us gathered in the living room to brainstorm.

"All right," I said. "Step one: we have to get inside the Flame with the explosives. Thoughts?"

"We could pretend to be making some kind of delivery and walk in through the front door," Caedan suggested.

"You wouldn't get any further than the front desk," Marcus said. "You'd have to check in with Cerise or whoever's working the desk. They'd take custody of the delivery and get someone who works there to take it where it belongs."

"We could still use that," I said. "If we have it sent somewhere we could find it later, and then we slip in separately from the packages."

"Is that the only way in?" Lainey asked.

"No." Marcus spread the first floor plans of the Flame onto the carpet. "There is a back entrance for large deliveries."

"There you go!" Caedan exclaimed.

"There are guards on duty at all times." Marcus pointed to the entrance on the plan. "Here and here. Then the delivery driver has to check in with the administrator on duty. The deliveries are then taken through this door, which slopes down into"—He pulled the page away to show the next one—"the basement level."

I leaned forward. "I remember seeing a basement level in the elevator but never thought about checking it out."

"There's not much to see there. It's mostly storage."

"I like that idea," Bice put in. "According to Onyx, some of the charges have to be planted in the basement, anyway. It makes sense to start there."

"We can make the delivery with my theater's truck," Marcus added. "I should be able to find costumes for at least two of us to be the, uh, deliverymen."

"Okay, but how do we get past the administrator to make the delivery? We won't be on the list," I pointed out.

"Cerise can help us there. We just have to come up with a name and details for the delivery. I'll stop by to visit her for lunch today, give her the information, and she'll add it to the list."

"That simple?"

Marcus shrugged. "Even after our adventure last year, they still have trouble believing someone would want to break into the Flame. With the war officially over, they've relaxed their security again."

"Good for us," Caedan said.

"Right. So we have a way to get the explosives into the building. Next step: planting them where they're supposed to be."

Bice leaned forward. "Onyx gave us a pretty detailed plan here. There are sixteen separate explosive devices to plant. Six of them go in the basement. Five go on the first floor, and the remaining five on level… fourteen."

"Why fourteen?" Caedan wondered.

"It's almost like cutting the building in half," Marcus said. "It's twenty-three or twenty-four levels, I think."

Bice shuffled through the papers and found the right one. "There's another reason." He spread out the plan for level twelve. "Look what they keep on this level."

Lainey looked over his shoulder and read, "Weapons Research."

"Ha!" Caedan laughed. "So he's expecting a really big explosion there."

"A lot of Incarnadine's weapons involve fire," I said. "Makes sense."

"So we wait until tomorrow night," Caedan said. "Beryl breaks the lock. We sneak inside, plant all the explosives, and sneak out."

"It won't be that easy," Marcus cautioned. "There is security at night. And sometimes, you'll find scientists working late."

"Not to mention the draconics." I looked over the plans. "We'll be careful. I'll take the fourteenth floor devices. I've been upstairs before, and I'm the one most able to escape." I didn't mention that I'd noticed Cybernetics Research was on level fifteen. I might check it out and find Loden's research on my own.

"You had Rick's help last time," Bice said.

"The last two times," I admitted. "But this will be simpler. I'm not trying to find stuff and wandering all over the place."

"Okay, then Lainey and I will handle the lower floors," Caedan said. "If we run into trouble, Glacier will protect us."

The big cat, curled up by the wall, lifted her head at the mention of her name.

I almost argued the point. I didn't like putting both of them in danger. But it made sense to have two people. The job would be too big for one, and if one got caught, the other could help out.

"All right… let's say, by some miracle, this all works the way we want it to," I said. "That leads us to the biggest question of all: how do we get everyone—the humans, that is—out of the Flame on Friday?"

We looked at each other in silence.

"Start a riot?" Caedan offered.

"I don't think that would work a second time. And it didn't get people out of the Flame either."

"The problem is that most types of threats or impending problems would cause them to keep people inside, not send them out," Bice said.

"The only way they'd leave is if they thought they were in some kind of danger," Marcus added.

"So we tell them the building's about to blow up!" Caedan mimicked an explosion with his hands.

"That makes kind of a twisted sense, telling them the truth." I smiled, thinking about it. "But would that work? Would they believe it? And would they really send people out?"

"It would have to be absolutely convincing." Marcus tapped the plans with his finger. "They would have to be certain they were truly about to die. But then they would bring in people to search for the explosives. We'd still end up killing some humans."

"What if you cut the electricity?" Lainey said. "If the power went out, would they all just stay there in the dark?"

"No." Marcus looked at her and rubbed the scruff on his chin. "When it didn't come back on right away, they'd want to get out."

Bice pulled the basement plans to the front again. "The building has its own massive generators down here," he pointed out. "We would need to sabotage them, maybe at the same time we place the explosives."

"Wait, wait, wait," Caedan interrupted. "We're doing this wrong. We're assuming we blow it up on Friday just because Bice mapped it out that way last night." He paused and grinned. "Why don't we just blow it up in the middle of the night? Fewer people to get out!"

"You're right," Marcus said. "The only people there will be security and the late-working scientists."

"So we plant all the explosives, and then cut the power." Bice pointed to the generators again. "The scientists, left in the dark, will evacuate."

"They'll have to take the stairs. That'll take some time." I remembered what that was like.

"Once they're out, we bring it down." Caedan whooped.

"When the first devices explode, any security guards left should run for the doors," Bice said, tracing paths on the plans.

"It all comes down." Marcus shook his head. "I think this could actually work. Amazing."

"And then I walk into the debris with my sword," I said. "All alone."

"You will not be alone!" Lainey exclaimed. "I'll be right behind you with my rifle!"

"We're doing this in the dark now," I pointed out. "Will you be able to see in the dark?"

"There should be some fires burning," Caedan said.

"I don't care." Lainey folded her arms. "You're not doing it alone."

I nodded. "Okay. I don't want to argue with you." I didn't want her to come, but if I died there, what would happen to her anyway? I would need to talk to Caedan and Bice about that. We needed to plan for the worst.

"All right," Marcus said. "So what's our delivery company? The biggest one around is Carmine."

I didn't see any reason to use anything else. The most common name would arouse the least suspicion.

The rest of the day was spent in preparations. Marcus visited Cerise at lunch and gave her the information to put on the next day's schedule. He also provided some red make-up, with which everyone practiced giving each other fake chromarks. We couldn't make a delivery to the Flame without looking like we belonged. Bice hand-lettered a pair of signs for the delivery truck's doors. Marcus and Caedan headed to the theater in the afternoon to attach the signs and load up the truck.

While Bice napped, Lainey and I took Glacier outside to let her run around a bit. I'd spotted a park nearby that did the trick, at least for now. The park appeared to be rarely used or tended. The grass hadn't been mowed in quite a while. We found a bench to sit on while the cat ran about.

Lainey snuggled up next to me, and I put my arm around her. For a brief moment, we were just two young people enjoying each other's presence. No schemes, no dragons, no danger. I wondered if there were people in the world who enjoyed times like this every day. What would it be like to be free? And normal?

"The plan seems to have really come together," Lainey said.

"Hm? Yeah, I guess so. When Caedan brings back one of the explosive devices, and we learn how to use it, that will about do it."

"I feel like we're leaving something out." She played with a lock of my hair.

"We probably are. Plans never go entirely the way you want them to."

"Onyx wants us to do this. Incarnadine doesn't know about it. And then there's Amaranth."

"Amaranth has her own problems now." I really didn't want to talk about her. I was still annoyed that I'd been force to use the disk on her instead of Onyx.

"But could she cause problems for us tomorrow?"

"She doesn't know where we are, and we're not even in her city."

"And now she can't fly to the Asylum to go after Chance."

I brightened. "Hey, you're right. That's a big positive. If Onyx wants Chance, he'll have to go himself. And he'd have to risk getting seen by the other dragons again."

"Then Kelly and Chance are safe."

"Most likely." I relaxed. That was good news. It took one of my biggest fears away. I turned and gave Lainey a quick kiss on her cheek. "Thanks for pointing that out."

"Oh, you can do better than that."

"Think so?" I leaned in and gave her a much longer kiss.

When we finally broke apart, she gasped. "Glacier!" She pushed free and ran off. She ran behind a decrepit pavilion, and I lost sight of her. I wondered what the cat had done now.

"Beryl Dragonslayer."

The voice, along with a sudden wind, made me jump from the bench and whirl around. A figure in dark purple robes stood beneath a nearby tree, facing me. I stepped around the bench and peered closer. I still couldn't see anything under the hood. Did these guys have faces?

"What do you want now?" I demanded.

"What did you do to Amaranth?" As before, the voice almost didn't seem to come from the figure, but from the air around me. It wavered in broken, inhuman tones.

"You seem to always be watching. Don't you know?" I took a step closer.

"You used something against her. What was it?"

They didn't know everything. And they didn't see everything. They didn't know about the disk, which means they hadn't watched my visit with Auric. Interesting.

"Why do you care?"

"You upset the balance of power here. It interests us."

"Why? What is your purpose in The Circle, anyway? You're not from here, so what are you doing?"

"Monitoring. What have you done to Amaranth?"

"I trapped her in human form." I didn't see a problem with telling them that; they'd discover it easily enough. But that also meant they weren't watching when I visited Amaranth. Or at least weren't listening. Could they maybe see and not hear?

The figure did not answer. Frayed lengths of its robe waved in the air, and the wind grew stronger.

"Listen," I began. "You—"

"Where is my father?" Lainey rushed up beside me and shouted at the figure. Glacier bounded onto the bench and growled, watching the intruder.

"Lainey Roberts…"

"Answer her question," I demanded.

"Your father is… occupied. He failed in his duties and pays the consequences."

"I want him back." Lainey folded her arms over her chest.

The figure didn't answer.

"If you use your boosts, you might get to him before he vanishes," Lainey whispered to me.

"Maybe." The last time, she'd tried her best to keep me from going after the purple robes. "What would I—"

I didn't finish the question, as Glacier decided to act instead. She leaped from the bench, rushed across the ground, and pounced at the purple robe.

The mysterious figure side-stepped. Folds of the robe—I couldn't tell if it had actual arms inside them—brushed against Glacier, redirecting the cat's momentum away. Glacier landed several feet past the purple robe.

But during that exchange, I acted. I boosted my legs and shot forward.

I am not clear on what happened next. I found myself entangled by lengths of purple cloth. Cold air, like ice, struck every inch of my exposed skin. Not even my cybernetic eyes could track what was happening as the purple robe shifted around me. I tried to grab it. My right hand caught nothing. The purple cloth seemed to glide over my skin and try as I might, I couldn't grasp anything.

But my cyb hand caught hold of a length of frayed cloth and held it.

In an instant, the rest of the robe moved, as if its owner spun away from me. The wind blew harder. The air itself moved, warping my vision around the figure.

"He's trying to get away!" Lainey cried, running toward me.

My cyb hand still held a length of the robe. I pulled on it and met resistance. Despite appearances, something was real and solid in there.

Lainey tried to grab at it as well, but her hands passed through without catching anything.

The purple robe seemed to fold in on itself, losing its human shape. The warping effect grew stronger. And then it vanished, leaving one torn, frayed length of purple cloth still in my hand. At the same instant, Glacier leaped through where the purple robe had been. She landed between Lainey and I and shook her head in confusion.

Lainey and I both turned our attention to the cloth I held. It looked completely normal now. I reached out with my right hand to feel it. It wasn't that I couldn't touch it at all: my fingers brushed against a silk-like surface. But I couldn't take hold of it, as if it flowed away like water. Lainey tried to touch it too, with no better results.

She touched my cyb hand instead. "You actually got a piece of it. That's amazing."

"Is it?" I let it dangle toward the ground. Glacier pawed at it, but her claws didn't catch either. "Only my cyb hand seems able to hold it. Why would that be?"

Lainey tried grasping it again. "I don't know." She looked up at me, and a couple of tears slipped from the corners of her eyes. "But it shows us something very important, something we didn't know."

"What's that?"

"They have a weakness." She put both hands on my cyb hand and smiled through the tears.

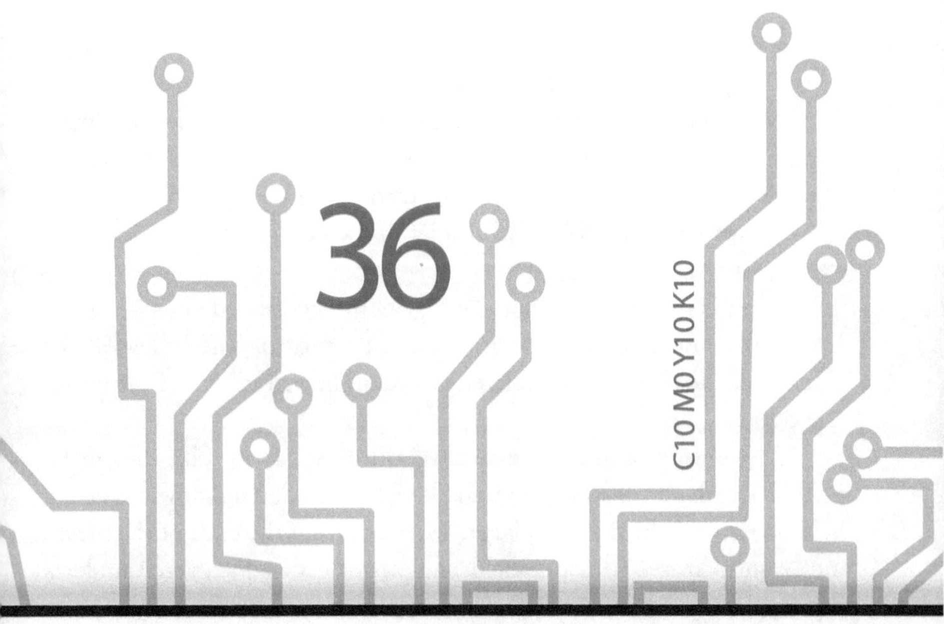

It would help if Lainey would tell me more about these creatures, but she refused again. "Not yet. I'm… not ready to go against my father's wishes."

"Even though they're the ones who took him away? You seemed awfully ready to take that one on for him."

"I shouldn't have. It was foolish. But you…" She patted my chest. "You get my emotions going."

"Is that a good thing?"

She leaned in and gave me another kiss. "Sometimes." She pulled away. "I think we should get Glacier back inside now."

"Okay." I held on to the purple cloth all the way back to the apartment. Once there, I dropped it on the table for Bice to examine, while we told him the story.

He tried to pick up the cloth without success as well. I picked it back up with my cyb hand again. It seemed to be the only thing that worked.

"Let's try a few things," Bice suggested. He found a wooden spoon from the kitchen and tried to lift a corner of the cloth. No luck. Then he tried a pair of metal tongs. This time, he managed to lift it into the air a bit before it slid off.

"It's metal," I said. "Only metal can actually touch it somehow."

"That may be the most bizarre thing I have ever seen in my life." And considering all Bice had seen, that was saying something.

"Next time, I'll go straight for the neck with this hand," I proclaimed, holding my cyb hand up. "We'll see how the purple robe handles that."

"Maybe we won't see them again," Lainey said.

"We attacked one. Will they just let that slide?"

"I don't know."

I guess her emotions weren't "going" now. She seemed nervous again.

At that moment, Marcus and Caedan returned. They'd loaded the truck, ready for tomorrow's delivery. Caedan showed us one of the explosive devices.

"They're very simple," he explained as I picked it up. Like the one I'd used in Viridia, it consisted of several long blocks of an unknown material, held together with wire. Two larger wires ran from the ends of the blocks into a small panel. This one held only a single switch, covered under a flip-top.

"Look on the back," Caedan said. I flipped it over and saw a long strip of some kind of paper. "It's glue. You pull off the outer covering, and you can stick this to anything."

"That'll be handy for hiding them."

In the background, I noticed Marcus discover the purple cloth on his kitchen table. He tried to pick it up, and stared in confusion when his hand went through it.

"What happens when you throw the switch?" Lainey asked.

"That makes them active. They don't explode right away, obviously, or we'd never get them all planted."

"Not to mention blow ourselves up," I observed.

Marcus tried again, with both hands, to grab the cloth. It slid through his fingers again, leaving him baffled.

"So how do we set them off?" Lainey took it from me gently and looked it over.

Caedan produced another small device. This one looked like a set of controls. "This will apparently set off all of them at once, assuming they're active. The instructions say it has a limited range, though. We'll have to use it within around a hundred yards of the building."

"And then run."

Marcus tried three more times, growing more frustrated and confused with each failure. I got up and walked to the kitchen.

"Let's study the maps," Lainey suggested. "We should memorize where to place them, so we're not wasting time looking it up while we're there."

"Good idea."

I casually picked up the cloth with my cyb hand, just to see the look on Marcus's face. I balled it up and tossed it toward Caedan. "Hey, what do you make of this?"

Caedan reached up to catch it, then fumbled three or four times, trying to snatch it out of the air. It eluded his grasp, of course, and fluttered to the ground.

"Purple! Is this from one of those robed guys? I never get to see them!"

"Be glad that you don't," Lainey said.

Caedan tried to pick it up. "What is with this thing? I can touch it, but I can't… hold it!"

"I know!" Marcus exclaimed.

I picked it up off the floor. "What do you mean? It works for me."

Bice and Lainey laughed, but Bice couldn't let it go any further. "He's playing with you two. We already figured out that only metal will hold it. We have no idea why."

"Let me see it again," Marcus said. I deposited it on his table, and he bent over to study it. "We use all kinds of cloth in the theater. Some forms of silk will slip right through your hands if you're not careful, but nothing like this."

"Can you cut it?" Caedan asked.

Marcus found a pair of scissors and tried to cut off a piece while I held it. The scissors could grip the cloth, but try as he might, Marcus couldn't cut through it. "How'd you get a piece off?" he demanded.

"I just held on to it." I lifted the cloth to see the edges myself. Now that he mentioned it, I couldn't tell where it had torn. The one end was frayed, but it had been like that when I grabbed it. The other end… "It looks straight, like it was cut, not torn."

"It vanished away," Lainey said. "But for some reason, it couldn't take that part you were holding."

"Beryl, can I take this to the theater tomorrow morning?" Marcus asked. "I want to show it to our costumes manager and see what she thinks of it."

"Sure. Just don't tell her where you got it."

"You might want to bring along some tongs to pick it up," Bice suggested.

I placed the cloth into a small plastic storage container for Marcus, which he sealed shut along with the tongs. He promised to let us know if he found out anything.

"The maps," Lainey reminded us. She and Caedan studied the layouts of the basement and first floor while I memorized the fourteenth floor. Even with this, I resolved to stuff the map into my pocket. I didn't trust myself that much.

When Cerise returned that evening, we compared notes over dinner and related the day's events. "I feel like the mom who comes home and finds out what crazy things her kids have all been up to!" she complained. "One of these days, I'll get to have the fun."

"This isn't fun," Marcus protested. "We're talking about incredible danger!"

She leaned over and kissed his forehead. "I love you, honey, but I do hope you're leaving that attitude at home tomorrow when you make the delivery."

"That I can do," he promised. "It's just another acting job."

"I'm not an actor," Caedan said. "I guess I'll just have to stumble through it."

"Who is going in the truck?" Cerise asked. "The two of you?"

"Marcus has to drive," I said. "The second worker will be either Caedan or Bice. I guess it should be Caedan, since he has more of the look of someone who moves heavy boxes around."

Caedan flexed.

"And I'm too identifiable with my scarred face, fake chromark or not," I finished.

"I'm ruled out again," Bice said.

"You've been an essential part of this whole trip," I exclaimed. "We couldn't do any of this without you!"

"Plus, you got to go swimming," Caedan said. "I missed that part."

Bice shuddered. "I would have happily traded places with you."

"Have we covered everything?" Cerise asked. "Are we confident in the plan? Anything we might have missed?"

We looked around at each other. I couldn't think of anything else.

"The one unknown factor is Amaranth," Bice said. "If she shows up anywhere along the way, it could throw everything off."

"If she shows up in the Flame, we just let it fall on top of her too," Caedan said.

"Anywhere else, I'll deal with her," I said. "If I'd had my sword yesterday, she'd already be dead."

Bice gave me a skeptical look. "Do you think you can run your sword through a human woman?"

"She's a dragon!" I protested. "But… I see what you mean. No, I won't hesitate. If I get the chance, I'll kill her. Onyx too."

"And tomorrow night, we kill Incarnadine." Caedan shook his head. "Who'd have thought we'd be discussing killing so many dragons."

I picked up the sword. "The purple robes call me Beryl Dragonslayer. I aim to earn that title."

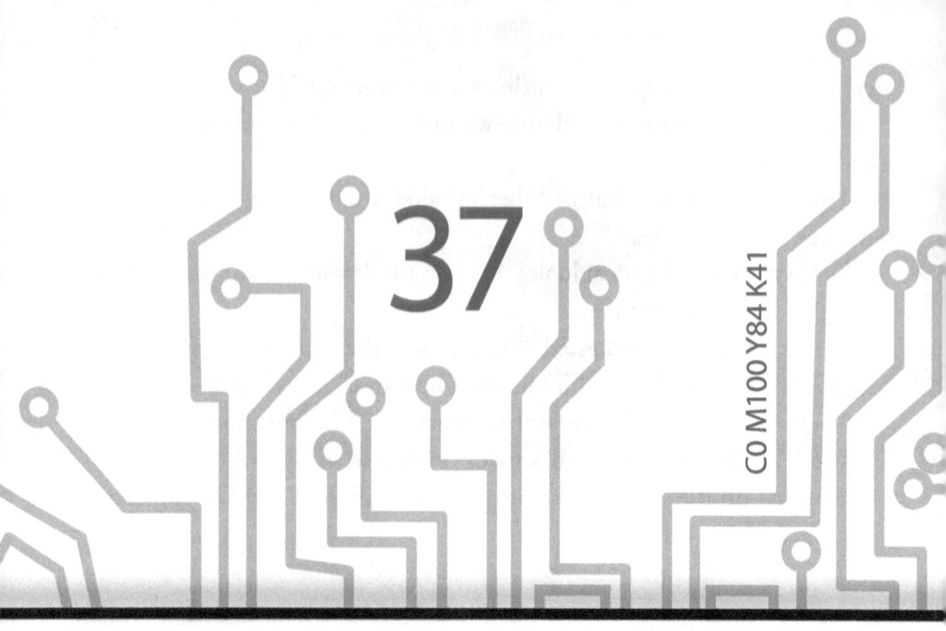

I tossed and turned on the floor that night. Cerise's words about what we might have missed kept me awake. What had we missed? What could go wrong?

Me. I could go wrong. I had other agendas I couldn't help thinking about.

Two things tempted me: the missing Book of Lore, and Loden's notes. For the Book, I knew where it might be kept, but getting there could be as nasty as the last time. It might not be worth it… except it reportedly covered the beginning of The Circle, when the dragons first came here. We could learn a lot from that.

As for Loden's notes, Onyx had promised to give them to me, that he'd gotten them back from the Incarnadine scientists. But of course, I couldn't trust him. The scientists would have made copies. All I had to do was find them. And cybernetics research was only one floor higher than where I'd be planting explosives. Everything depended on timing, and with my boosts, I could move faster than anyone. I could plant all the devices, and run up the stairs while Lainey and Caedan were still working.

Maybe it wasn't the wisest course of action, but it had a reasonable chance of success. Didn't it? Then why wasn't I talking to Bice about it? I stared at the ceiling in the dark. Because I knew he'd tell me not to risk it. We had a plan. Stick to it. Impulsive actions always tended to get me in trouble.

If this worked, what would happen next? Onyx would show up, I suppose. And what would stop him from forcing us to do something else on his behalf? Fewmets. We should have a plan in place to abandon the apartment. If Don and Lovat found a new place for us to live, we should gather up everyone and head there. Marcus and Cerise wouldn't be happy, but we needed to get out from under Onyx.

Unless we could kill him. And I'd already used the one potential advantage I'd probably ever get. I should have found a way to kill Amaranth instead of use the disk on her. Ugh. I felt trapped. Trapped with no way out.

We'd been trapped in the tower too. And in Viridia. We'd escaped then; we could escape now. Somehow.

My brain considered and rejected a dozen or so ideas until I finally fell asleep.

In the morning, Caedan and Marcus donned their Carmine Delivery uniforms. Caedan thought it hilarious that we'd decided to identify the crates of explosives as elevator repair parts. I didn't care, as long as it worked.

Marcus took the container with the purple cloth and they headed out to the theater. The rest of us had little to do until the evening. I brought up the topic of escape to Bice and Lainey.

"I've been so focused on getting past the dragon, I hadn't thought about afterwards," Lainey said.

"I've considered it," Bice admitted, "but unless we can persuade Cerise and Marcus to leave, I think we're trapped here."

"Cerise won't have a job after we destroy the Flame," Lainey pointed out.

"True. But she's pregnant. And Marcus has a job. And friends and family."

"They don't really have to leave the city," Bice mused. "Only Onyx knows their names, and he only knows this apartment. All they really need to do is move across town."

"He's watching this place, though," I said. "How can they move without him seeing it?"

"Maybe we can deal with the watchers?"

I got up and walked around the room. "Maybe. But he'd just send new ones. He seems to have plenty of followers for some reason."

"So we get rid of the watchers and move them, all in one day. It's not impossible."

"No, it's not." I nearly tripped over Glacier, who occupied more space than I thought she should. She just kept growing. "But I wish we'd talked more about this earlier. It's too late to make those plans now. We'll have to wait until after we take down the Flame."

"And you're worried it'll be too late." Bice poured himself a glass of water. "I don't see that we have much choice right now, Beryl. These are things that we have to discuss with the people who live here."

"I know, I know." I continued to pace.

Lainey stretched out on the couch and read the script for a play Marcus had left sitting out. After a few minutes, she lowered it and frowned at me. "You need to relax, Beryl. You're not going to do anyone any good walking circles around the apartment."

"I can't help it. I'm not good at waiting. When are they making the delivery again?"

"Not until noon," Bice reminded me. "They're less likely to have people pay much attention to them at lunchtime."

"I hope so." I stopped and looked through the kitchen window. "What if I went back to Auric and told him what happened with Amaranth? Do you think he'd give me another one of those disks?"

"He might be outraged," Bice said. "He wanted you to act against Onyx. I don't think he means ill to the other dragons."

"He threatened all of them."

"To stop them from fighting amongst themselves." Bice shook his head. "No. While Auric's always been a strange one, he's still committed to the status quo. He wouldn't be happy to hear about Amaranth. Not to mention Incarnadine, if that works."

"We could tell him Onyx did that."

"I don't see us going back to Auric any time soon. Why even speculate about it?"

I spread my arms. "Because there's so much, Bice! I'm trying to find a way through it all, to protect all of us and still accomplish our goals. But we have so much going on and so many enemies to deal with. I mean, I still don't understand what's going on with Troilus Green!"

Bice got up and joined me. Without another word, he reached out and drew me into an embrace. "Let it go, Beryl. You can't solve everything. You just do the best you can, let others do their best, and trust the rest to work out somehow."

"I wish I could," I whispered into his shoulder. "I wish I could trust." At times like this, I did wish Bice was right: that there was a god or gods above it all, and nothing like the dragons.

Lainey got up. "Come on. We're taking Glacier to the park again. You need some air."

We spent a couple of hours at the park this time. Lainey refused to let me talk about mission stuff and only focused on ourselves and our relationship. It might have been the nicest morning I'd had in months. When we returned to the apartment, I felt much better about everything.

Until noon came and went, that is. The stress amped back up while we waited to hear about the delivery. Finally, at almost two o'clock, Marcus and Caedan returned. I demanded to know how it had gone before they could even shut the door behind them.

"It's all good," Caedan assured me. "We made the delivery. It's all waiting in the basement for us."

Marcus went into further details, describing his interaction with the administrator who double-checked his list more than once. Guards watched them carefully as they unloaded the crates. Afterwards, Marcus had to sign a receipt.

"So I wrote 'Richard Onyx,'" he finished. "Hope he doesn't mind."

I laughed. "Perfect."

"I did scribble the last name a bit, so they may have trouble reading it. I mean, 'Onyx' isn't exactly a name you'd run into around here. But I couldn't resist."

Caedan tossed his delivery company hat onto the table. "So now what? Nothing to do until it gets dark?"

"You should all probably get some rest," Bice suggested.

"Just a minute," Marcus said. "I showed that cloth to the costumes manager. She flipped out, wanting to know where I got it and whether I could get any more."

"I'm not surprised." I took back the container he offered with the purple cloth inside.

"That's not all. She put it under these big magnifiers she uses for close stitching. You'll never believe what we saw in the actual weave."

I waited. Marcus let the dramatic silence go a bit too long.

"It's cyb, Beryl. There are tiny cybernetics woven into the cloth itself."

Cybernetic cloth?

"Is that even possible?" Caedan asked.

"Beryl has cybernetics running under his skin," Lainey said. "So why not?"

I opened the container and looked at the cloth again. If the purple robes used cybernetics, it took away some of the weirdness of their actions. It meant at least part of what they could do happened because of technology, not some new type of magic. And if they used technology, then there could be ways of countering it.

"It's crazy," Marcus said. "If you ever get hold of more of that stuff, I'd love to examine it more closely."

I promised he could, if it ever happened.

We now had at least five more hours of waiting again. I hated it. Bice again recommended we try to rest, so to humor him, I stretched out on my sleeping bag. And promptly fell asleep. Guess not sleeping the night before might have made me a little tired.

As the sun went down, we prepared for our infiltration. We dressed in dark colors. Caedan brought his former Cerulean Corps weapons: the baton and shock projectile, or whatever he called it. He'd apparently picked up a newer model during his last trip home. Lainey slung her rifle over her shoulder. I brought my sword. I left one of the talkers with Bice, in case of emergencies, and had Lainey carry the other.

"Our thoughts go with you," Bice said. "We'll be waiting here anxiously for you."

"You might want to be waiting ready to run," I said, "in case anything goes wrong."

"I have every confidence in you."

I didn't know how to respond to that. We slipped out of the apartment and down to the street.

"What good does it do us to wear black if we're being followed by a giant white cat?" Caedan wondered.

"Because that's all people will see," Lainey said, "and it'll freak them out."

She had a point.

I don't think I'd ever seen the Flame at night. Four massive spotlights, tinted red and positioned on top of other buildings, illuminated it on each side. Smaller lights on the building itself lit up each of the fire-shaped balconies I knew so well.

We made our way around to the back of the building, where Caedan pointed out the single guard on duty. Cerise gave us the schedule; he shouldn't be relieved of this position until midnight. We got as close as we could without being seen, then Lainey walked out in the open.

"Hi!" she called. "I think I'm lost. Can you give me directions?"

The guard pointed his hand crossbow at her, then raised it when he saw a girl. "You're in a weird place to be lost," he said. "You should—"

Caedan fired his projectile weapon. Wires shot out and struck the guard, followed by a burst of electricity. His muscles locked up, and he fell to the ground, shaking.

"Bring him," I ordered, running to the door. A quick boost to my cyb hand let me break the lock and swing it open. Inside, we bound and gagged the guard. Lainey insisted we let him go when we were done, so he could escape in time.

"We've got about four hours until his replacement shows up," Caedan observed, checking the time. "Let's get busy."

We descended a stairway to the basement where we found the crates of explosives exactly where Caedan and Marcus had unloaded them. No one had bothered with them, much to my relief. I gathered the five devices I would need and put them in my pack.

"Okay, I'm heading upstairs," I told the other two in a low voice. "I don't know how long it'll take to get there without running into trouble and then plant the explosives. If I'm not back by eleven-thirty, then get out of here."

"We'll come find you," Caedan said.

"No. If I'm not back, it means something has gone horribly wrong. Get out and blow this place."

"We won't blow it with you inside!" Lainey protested.

"If I'm caught, it won't do any of us any good for you to get caught too."

"Then don't get caught," Caedan said.

I started to say something else, then changed my mind. "We're wasting time. Let's do the job and get out." I turned and almost fell over Glacier, who chose that moment to walk behind me. I shoved her out of the way and hurried to the elevator.

With Caedan's help, I repeated the method Rick used the last time to open the doors. I jammed my cyb fingers into the gap until I could get enough leverage, and then we pulled them apart. We both looked up the elevator shaft.

"Sure you don't want to just ride it?" he asked.

"It might attract attention. Besides, I've done it before, so I know what I'm doing now."

I ignored the massive cables in the center of the shaft and focused on the frame surrounding the doors. I took a breath, triggered a boost, and made my first jump. I caught hold of the next floor's tiny platform, boosted my arms, and vaulted up onto it, catching the frame for stability.

Every three floors, a pair of emergency lights gave just enough illumination to get by, but too much to activate my new night vision. As before, the shaft was even colder than outside. Good thing I wore warmer clothes this time.

In fact, everything was easier this time. I jumped, grabbed, pulled, and balanced myself to the next floor. The cyb hand made the grabbing much simpler. And I could hold on without strain. On the other hand, I hadn't been carrying a pack full of explosives and a sword on my back, last time.

The hardest part was keeping track of the floors. I knew which floor I needed to reach, but counting them while climbing wasn't easy. Jump. Grab. Pull. Balance. Three. No, wait. Two. The basement didn't count as a floor. Did it? No, it didn't. I remembered the inside of the elevator from the last time. The first floor was the lobby. That meant I had to climb fourteen levels to get to the fourteenth floor. Right?

After a lot of effort, I reached the level I thought was the fourteenth. I fumbled around until I found the roller and pushed it. A lock pulled out from the doors. Balancing on the rim, I caught the inner door and pulled it open a few inches. Seeing nothing except a hallway, I pulled the doors the rest of the way open and stepped through. My legs relaxed from being on solid ground again.

I checked the directory next to the elevator and confirmed: fourteenth floor. At least I got that right. Directly across the hall, I faced a set of double doors leading into the weapons research lab. A dim light shone from under the doors, not enough to indicate late workers. I checked the handle. The lock broke with ease, and I slipped inside.

I don't know what I expected to see. Racks and racks of strange and exotic weapons, maybe? Instead, I saw mostly desks and workbenches. Some of them held a lot of scattered parts, some held devices that looked almost like weapons, and many were just empty. A few lights provided the dim glow I'd seen from outside. I assumed some of them remained on at all times as some kind of safety measure.

Remembering the diagram, I set down my pack and took out the first explosives device. I mounted it under the first workbench nearest the door and flipped the switch to activate it. I'll admit: I half expected it to blow up in my face as soon as I flipped the switch. It would be just like Onyx to sabotage me that way. But I suppose it wouldn't work with his stated goal. Even so, the longer we stayed in the building with active devices, the greater the chance they might all go off. I fully expected Onyx to be somewhere nearby. He might have known the exact moment we entered the building.

I hurried through my assigned task, finding the locations for the five devices. This one laboratory covered almost this entire floor. The fifth device brought me to an area I hadn't noticed earlier.

It appeared to be a kind of testing room. I opened an extremely thick door and stepped into a long, mostly empty chamber. Scorch marks covered the walls, floor, and ceiling. Some of them looked as if something had exploded, rather than fired a controlled burst. I wondered if those were intentional detonations or accidents.

On a table near the door, I found three odd weapons, apparently left behind for future testing. I picked one up and held it by its handle, amazed at its compact design. It couldn't be more than eighteen inches long, and not very bulky. A nozzle at the front was followed by a long canister attached to the primary weapon's length. A type of shield folded out in two pieces near the end, presumably to protect the operator from the heat.

Impulsively, I aimed it toward the other end of the room and pulled the trigger. A narrow burst of flame erupted from the nozzle and struck the opposite wall. Intense heat flooded back at me. A few seconds later, the flame died off. The small weapon couldn't hold much in the way of fuel, I suppose, but it was certainly effective.

I planted the last device, hesitated, and then stuffed one of the remaining weapons into my pack. It might come in handy.

I checked the time. I'd gotten the devices planted in under ten minutes, even with my distraction. Surely that left enough time to check out the cybernetics lab. I slipped out into the hall, found the stairs, and ascended to the next floor.

While the hallway looked much the same, the layout for this floor was different. A number of doors led to multiple labs smaller than those on the weapons research floor. A brighter light shone from one of them. Someone was working late.

I avoided that door and checked out the next one. Another broken lock later, I wandered through a room vaguely similar to the lab we'd investigated in the Emerald Ascendancy a few months ago. Using my flashlight, I sorted through a pile of papers. Nothing caught my eye, at least nothing I could understand.

Loden's notes wouldn't be just lying around. I looked around the rest of the room. Where would they keep something that valuable?

The door opened and bright light filled my eyes. I blinked and tried to see straight against the sudden illumination. I drew my sword, and saw… red.

"I wondered who would be wandering in here in the dead of night," the towering draconic said. "I never expected to see you here again."

Zidanta Red. I'd encountered this one multiple times last year. It ripped my eye out, revealing it was cybernetic.

"And I thought you were dead," I answered. I'd put a sword through its neck, and then Incarnadine flooded the hall with flames. But I guess it made sense that the red draconics would be immune to fire.

The draconic tapped a metal band around its neck. "You tried your best. I see you've replaced the eye as well… though I can't say much for your new facial marking. The rumors say you're dead. That you fled Viridia months ago and were never seen again."

"I've been busy." I shifted around a table and bumped against a coil of some kind of cable. I didn't have much room to maneuver here. That worked in the draconic's advantage.

"Yes, I imagine so… Why, in the name of holy Incarnadine, would you dare return?" It flexed its claws and stepped fully into the lab. "Why risk the wrath of my dread lord again? You barely escaped last time."

"You kept one of the books. I wanted the complete set."

"You won't find it in a cybernetics lab." Zidanta Red pointed at me. "But it is the perfect place to explore your own enhancements. My scientists would love another look at your eyes. The one you left behind was… damaged."

"Not my fault. Your holy dread lord shouldn't spout fire all over the place." And it was only in that moment that I realized: the missing book had been on the floor in the hallway when Incarnadine breathed fire. It couldn't possibly have survived intact. Fewmets.

Coming here was stupid. The book was ashes. I wouldn't find Loden's notes without help, if they were even here. And now I had to deal with this beast. Why did I make such enormous mistakes all the time?

I didn't have time to debate. I boosted everything and charged, leaping across the table. Zidanta Red dodged the first swing of my sword and countered with a backhanded slap. It would have snapped bones if it had connected directly. As it is, my own speedy dodging didn't protect me entirely. The impact against my side threw me across the room onto another table. I slid across, knocking random mechanical parts to the floor.

"Your friend won't be coming to rescue you this time." The draconic moved toward me, but its footsteps appeared sluggish to my racing mind.

"I won't need him to deal with you," I shot back.

The beast grabbed the table and flipped it. I leaped clear just in time and charged again. Removing the table gave me more room to maneuver.

As the draconic reached forward to grab me, I dropped to the floor and slid between its legs. My sword sliced open its thigh as I passed.

I scrambled back to my feet as it spun around with a bellow. I only hoped no one else could hear us. If I hurried, I could still take him down and get out of here. Lainey and Caedan should be done by now, but they would be waiting for me. There was still plenty of time left before the deadline I'd given them.

Zidanta Red threw up its left palm and screamed something. I knew what he was doing before it happened. Resomancy. The weird power. But now I knew what to do: I triggered a boost to my heart again.

The wave of power swept over me—I could tell only by its effect on the debris around me. I felt nothing myself. I grinned. As long as I had enough of a warning, I could counter the power.

"How is this possible?" The draconic stared at me. "No one can resist resomancy!"

"No one but Beryl Dragonslayer!" I cried, lunging forward. Actually, I think all I said was, "Uh, surprise?" Then I did lunge forward. I stabbed my sword straight through the monster's palm, then landed with both feet on its chest. With its injured leg unable to balance, it fell back from the impact.

I landed on top of it, and somehow kept my balance. I yanked the sword free, intending to bring it back down through the draconic's face. But it grabbed me with its right hand and threw me off. I smacked into the fallen table and rolled back to my feet.

"This is ridiculous," Zidanta Red growled as it pulled itself up on one knee. "What do you hope to accomplish here?"

"Well, since you ask…" I maneuvered to my right, catching my breath and trying to think of my next move. The door was to my back now. With the draconic's injured leg, I could run, and it wouldn't be able to catch me. But then it might raise an alarm, summoning more guards. They might even find the explosives. At the very least, more of them would be in the building when it came down. "I'm here to kill your boss."

The draconic regarded me with its usual indifferent expression. "Incarnadine cannot die. He is a god."

"You mean like Caesious? Or Viridia? Dragons can die. They're just harder to kill than most."

"And you think that you"—it gestured at me with a bleeding hand—"can do this? You?"

"Yeah. Me." I shifted back to the left. I knew what I wanted to try, but I would have to time it right. "I'm going to take all the dragons down, one at a time."

"Your enhancements have clearly driven you insane. I will have to mention this to our scientists."

I stared at the draconic. It still thought it was going to win this. It couldn't stand, and one of its hands had a hole in it, but it still thought it would win. Amazing. Was I missing something?

I got my answer a second later. Zidanta Red leaped to its feet and charged me. The leg injury apparently wasn't as severe as it had seemed. Even with my boosts, I barely managed to duck under the swinging claws, but I collided face-first with the monster's chest. This time, I hit the ground. I swung wildly to keep it from clawing me. I grabbed an ankle with my cyb hand and yanked, not to pull it down, but to slide myself out of the way.

I kicked the back of the draconic's knees with both feet and used the momentum to flip myself backward. I planted the sword in the floor and came to a stop. That may well be the coolest move I've ever made, and absolutely no one saw it.

Zidanta Red spun around. "Your enhancements make you fast, but it can't last forever. Sooner or later, I will catch you." A tongue of fire puffed from his mouth after his words.

"Not if I catch you first."

I lunged forward, pulling myself with the sword at first, then yanking it out of the floor. With all the boosts to my speed I could manage, I reached out, dodging between the draconic's claws. Flames erupted from its mouth, right above me. My cyb hand caught hold of its lower jaw. I boosted both arms. I jerked the jaw down, and brought my sword in from the side. The point of the blade stabbed through one side of the reptilian head and out through the other.

Okay, maybe that was the coolest move I've ever made.

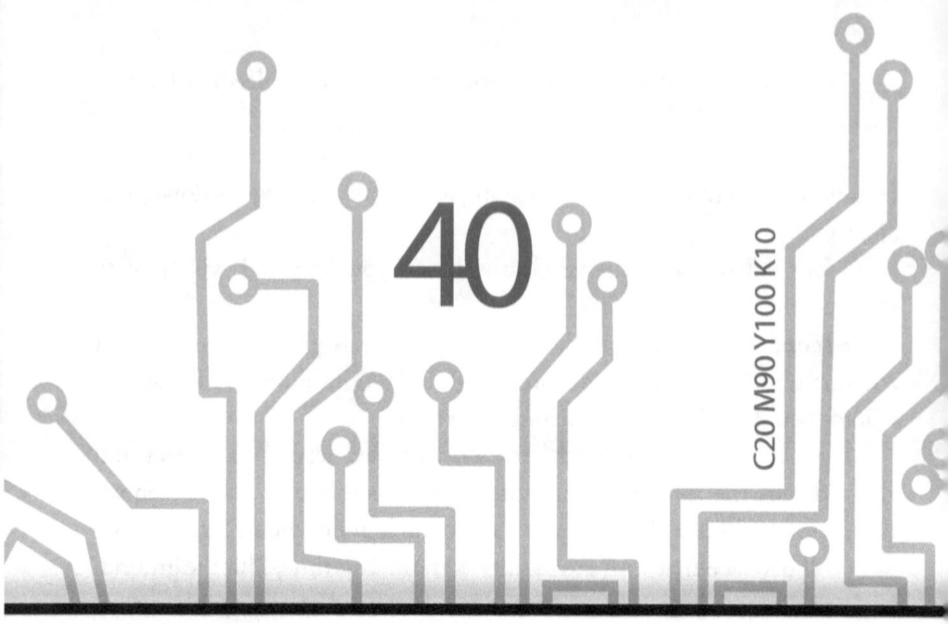

40

The draconic fell, dragging me down with it. The last bit of fire caught my sleeve. I disentangled myself and beat on my arm, putting the fire out. My arm was hot, but didn't seem to have been seriously burned in the brief moments of ignition. My cyb hand was fine, of course, except for being covered in blood and draconic spit. Gross.

I found someone's abandoned jacket and used it to wipe my hand and sword off. Nice jacket. Or it was, anyway.

I'd wasted enough time in a fruitless search. I jogged down the hall to the elevator. At this point, climbing would be another waste of time. I decided to risk it. I pushed the elevator button and waited. When it arrived, I pushed the button for the basement.

The ride down took longer than I'd like. I kept my sword in hand and bounced around inside the elevator, unable to stand still. Too much nervous energy after the fight, I guess.

When the doors opened, I walked out and looked around. Glacier sat on top of some crates, watching me with a lazy look in her eyes. Caedan and Lainey emerged from hiding when they saw me. They hurried close, then stopped.

"Whose blood is that?" Lainey asked.

I looked at myself. Yeah, trying to wipe it off hadn't worked very well. And I was missing a sleeve. And smelled like smoke.

"Um, it was a draconic. It won't be bothering us any more."

"You keep running into those things." Caedan shook his head and laughed. "It's like you're cursed or something."

"They keep running into me!" I finally sheathed my sword. "Is everything ready?"

"Yeah. We just need to sabotage the generators and get out of here."

"What time is it?"

"Almost eleven."

Really? It didn't seem like anywhere near that much time had gone by.

"Let's do it."

Caedan led the way from his memory. When we reached the generators, I had no idea what we were looking at. I didn't even want to try to understand.

"If I flip this one big switch, all the power will go out," Caedan explained, pointing. "But we don't want them to just flip it back on, so we need to do as much damage as possible."

I flexed my cyb hand. "Point me in the right direction."

Lainey took out a flashlight and waited. Caedan pulled the switch and everything went dark. With Lainey's light, I ripped apart everything I could get hold of. It wasn't a huge amount of damage, but we only needed enough to last for an hour at the most.

"Let's get out of here."

We dragged out the bound guard and took him with us. I untied his legs and kept him moving by threatening him with the sword. Outside, we crossed the street, hurried down to the nearest intersection, and turned right. An empty four-story office building lay just ahead where we'd watch the destruction.

"We'll let you go in a few minutes," I told the guard. "Right now, we're saving your life."

He glared at me over his gag.

I glanced back at the Flame. The spotlights from the other buildings still lit up its exterior, but no lights came from the structure itself. I heard some voices griping from near the exit. Good. People were leaving.

Inside the office building, Caedan tied the guard's legs again. We left him on the first floor and climbed the stairs to the third. We made our way to a window and looked out over the streets. A handful of people were leaving the area of the Flame, walking down the street and talking with each other.

Caedan set his bag down and took out the device to set off the explosives. He looked at me.

"Not yet. Give them a little more time." I watched the people move on. Those must have been working near the bottom floors. Anyone near the top would take longer to get down the stairs. Sure enough, about five minutes later, another group exited and passed off in the opposite direction. That might be it.

"Someone's going toward the building," Lainey said suddenly.

"What? Where?"

She pointed and stepped to the side so I could see. A woman, all alone and wrapped in a thin jacket, walked directly toward the Flame.

"Fewmets!" I watched her get closer. "Maybe she's just out for a walk, curious about the darkness. Maybe she'll keep going…"

She stopped on the sidewalk right outside the Flame and stood still, staring up at it.

I made an angry growling sound. Glacier responded in kind. I started toward the stairs. "I'll get rid of her. Caedan, hold off until we're out of the range. But if I'm not back in ten minutes, set it off."

"I told you: I'm not going to blow you up."

"I don't mean that, idiot. I mean, I may have to force her far enough away without bringing her back here. But you've got to blow it soon, before they get a repair crew over to fix the generators!"

"Oh, right."

I stampeded down the stairs, past the bound guard, and out into the street again. The cold night air struck my face with more force this time, shocking me. I gasped and ran toward the woman and the Flame. I slowed as I drew near.

"Excuse me!" I called. "Miss? Excuse me! I need you to—" A street light reflected from her red hair.

She turned around and smiled at me. "There you are. I knew you had to be around here somewhere."

Amaranth.

A thousand questions ran through my head. Did she know about our mission? Had Onyx told her? Did she do something to Onyx? Why was she here all alone? What should I do about it? Should I leave her to be buried when the building came down?

"You need to leave," I burst out.

"This is my brother's home. I'm perfectly comfortable here." She walked to meet me. "But you, on the other hand, do not belong." She waved a hand in the air.

Four of her Scarlet Brigade converged on our location from the shadows. Each held a crossbow aimed at me.

I glanced up at the darkened Flame. Caedan would have to set off the explosives soon. He'd have no choice.

Amaranth followed my glance. "I'm assuming you're the reason the Flame is dark. Did you steal something again?"

"I'll tell you whatever you want to know, if"—I pointed down the street—"we go that way a couple of blocks."

"Where you have friends waiting in an ambush, no doubt. Just how stupid do you think I am now?"

What could I do? The soldiers were already closer than they had been outside her mansion. I couldn't think of any trick that would break free of the situation without getting shot at least once. Even that might be worth it, to get away from the exploding building.

"I've had time to reconsider your demands," Amaranth announced.

"Great. Where's Onyx?"

"I won't give him up to you. But allow me to make another counter-offer," she said in a rush.

My eyes kept flicking to the building. "Go ahead."

"I can offer you all the knowledge of a thousand years. Every secret of the dragons." She took one step toward me, and now had my full attention. "Where we came from. What's outside The Circle. How we formed the cities. How our magic works. How the draconic magic works. I'll tell you all of it."

Wow. "Um, that sounds like a pretty good deal. I'm assuming you tell me all this before I remove the disk."

"Unfortunately, yes," she growled.

"And how do I know you won't just kill me the second I remove it?"

"I give you my word. No harm shall come to you—"

"Or my friends."

"No harm shall come to you or your friends from me, or those who serve me."

My eyebrows were all the way up. "Wow, you're desperate. Let me think here…"

"I encourage you to think quickly."

The sound of Lainey's rifle split the air. One of the Scarlet Brigade screamed, dropped his crossbow and fell, clutching his leg.

"There's my ambush," I told Amaranth. "Send your soldiers away, or they'll all fall one by one."

"What was that?" one of them demanded, looking around in every direction.

I hoped Lainey was well hidden. She would have to be close to make that shot in the dark.

At that moment, lights erupted as the Flame came to life again.

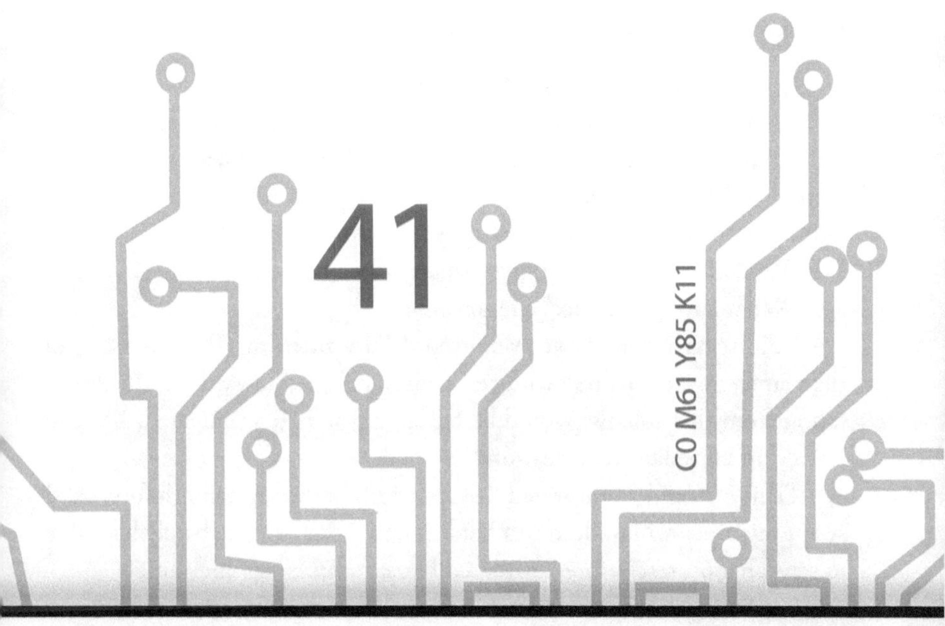

Lights shone out from the lowest level of the Flame. The small spot-lights illuminated its fire-like balconies. A red glow shone out from the top. "Now, Caedan," I whispered. He couldn't wait any more.

Another shot rang out. The soldiers had enough and ran. I grabbed Amaranth by the arm and dragged her with me.

"Let go of me! What are you doing?"

"I'm saving your life! Run!"

"I should immolate you this instant!"

I didn't know what that meant, but it didn't matter. The first explosion erupted from behind us. I risked a glance back and saw the lights go out just as quickly as they'd come on.

"What was that?" Amaranth demanded. She pulled hard against me and spun to look herself.

Fire and light and devastating sound erupted out from the first floor. All of the windows in the front half of the building shattered, followed by similar explosions through the other walls.

Amaranth and I, only two blocks away now, stared up at the massive structure as it began to shift. "Come on," I whispered to myself. Where were the rest of them?

In answer to my question, a ring of fire exploded out from mid-way up the building along with an even louder roar. The explosives I'd planted on the fourteen floor ripped the entire structure in half. The lower floors collapsed down into the devastation caused by the first explosions, tilting only a little as they crumbled, smashing together like pancakes. The upper section did the same, falling down into what was left of the fourteenth floor, then tilting in the opposite direction. Toward us.

"Run!" I shouted, yanking at Amaranth's arm.

"What have you done?" she screamed.

I didn't have time to answer, even if I'd wanted to. The top floors of the Flame, now consumed with real flames, plunged toward us. The devastation from this collapse would be far larger than I'd anticipated. I hoped Lainey and Caedan were clear on their end.

"This is stupid," I muttered. I stopped and jerked Amaranth forward. I swept my other arm underneath her legs and lifted her. She barely had time to screech a protest before I triggered boost to both legs and ran.

I sprinted down the street as fast as I could. Amaranth looked over my shoulder and gasped. "Faster!" Funny how her tone changed when she realized our genuine peril.

The sound behind us was unbelievable. The impact as the first parts of the building—floor fifteen, I assume—struck the ground shook every-thing. Then the rest of it came crashing down, smashing apart, ripping the fronts off other buildings, raining debris and fire in every direction.

Something heavy struck the back of my leg. It buckled and we went down. Even then, I rolled to try to protect Amaranth. I'd told Bice I wouldn't hesitate to kill her, but in that moment, she was a woman in my arms, needing protection. I couldn't help myself. We rolled across the con-crete, tearing clothes, scraping knees and elbows and anything else that hit the ground. My head bounced off the surface, filling my vision with stars. I lost my hold on Amaranth. More debris, some of it heavy, struck me as we came to a halt.

I tried to cover my head with my arms. Then I heard Amaranth scream-ing something above the cacophony around us. In an instant, the debris stopped hitting us. I lifted my head and looked up.

Amaranth knelt beside me, clothes torn, skin bleeding, hair disheveled, with her arms held high. All around us, concrete and steel and bricks and flaming debris cascaded down through the night. But a canopy of hardened air protected the two of us. We were completely shielded. The whole process only lasted a few seconds, but my boosts were still channeling, making it seem like everything happened in slow motion.

The debris stopped falling and an enormous dust cloud rose around us. Amaranth muttered something else and her power pushed out, keeping the dust away from us. Only then did it occur to me to wonder about the magic or resomancy or whatever it was. I distinctly remember someone telling me the dragons couldn't use it themselves. Yet here Amaranth knelt, throwing it out like she was used to it.

She turned her face down toward me, and I could see the strain it had taken on her. "You absolute fool," she growled in clipped tones. "What have you done?" Her eyes rolled back in her head, and she fell forward.

I caught her before she hit the ground. Her magic collapsed with her, and the dust blew around us, filling the void it left behind. I needed to get moving, to head toward the center of the disaster and wait for Incarnadine. But what to do with her? Amaranth had saved my life. She'd also made an offer I couldn't just ignore. I needed to find her if I made it through this.

But I couldn't just stash her in a doorway or something. Already, I could hear sirens approaching and voices yelling in the distance. If Caedan were here, I could leave her with him. But he was blocks away. I sighed, already tired from the exertion of the night. Then I bent down and picked up the dragon queen.

Step by step, carrying her in my arms, I maneuvered my way back through the debris, toward the base of the Flame. Another dragon would be coming soon, if Onyx had been right. I needed to be there, ready and waiting. I hoped Lainey was all right and able to watch me with her rifle. I would probably need her if I were going to get out of this alive.

"Onyx," Amaranth murmured without opening her eyes.

"Nope. His worst enemy," I answered. Where would Onyx be, anyway? He couldn't be far. If only we'd been able to figure that out.

I coughed. Dust hung in the air. I squinted, trying to keep it out of my eyes. I couldn't see more than a couple of yards ahead. But if I kept following the debris, I should reach the spot I needed. I suppose if the Flame had been a more traditional building, it would have fallen almost straight down when the support pillars were destroyed. But since it had such an odd shape, it had partially collapsed straight down, and partially to the sides. As I walked, I caught glimpses of serious damage to all of the other buildings along the street. The entire front had been torn off some of them.

A breeze picked up, blowing the dust along. At the same time, everything grew brighter, though I couldn't tell why at first. A moment later, I figured it out. Someone had turned the giant spotlights down toward the destruction instead of into the sky where the Flame had been. The more dust that cleared, the more I could see. Only three of the spotlights remained.

I reached the front steps leading to the lobby of the Flame. Ahead lay the largest pile of debris, though it seemed much shorter than I'd expected. How much of it had been flattened or forced down the tunnel into Incarnadine's lair?

I laid Amaranth down on a flat chunk of concrete and drew my sword. She looked so vulnerable in that moment. So human and frail. And very, very female. One quick stab with my sword and another dragon would be dead. But I couldn't do it. I couldn't bring myself to kill a woman, regardless of whether I believed her earlier offer or not.

I sighed and turned back to the debris pile. I switched my sword to my cyb hand. I would need all the reach I could get. Rick's cyb hand helped him kill Caesious. On impulse, I took one of the fire launchers from my pack and held it in my right hand. I didn't know what use it might be against a red dragon, but I'd take any help I could get.

The dust still floated in the air, though not as thick as before. If Lainey were in range, I couldn't see her anywhere. At least the spotlights would help her see into this mess. Some of the broken pieces of the building created bizarre shapes in the shadows and dust. In the distance, I heard voices yelling at each other. The sirens grew closer.

I climbed on to a higher pile, took a stand, and looked around.

Directly in front of me, the debris shifted. Something enormous moved beneath it.

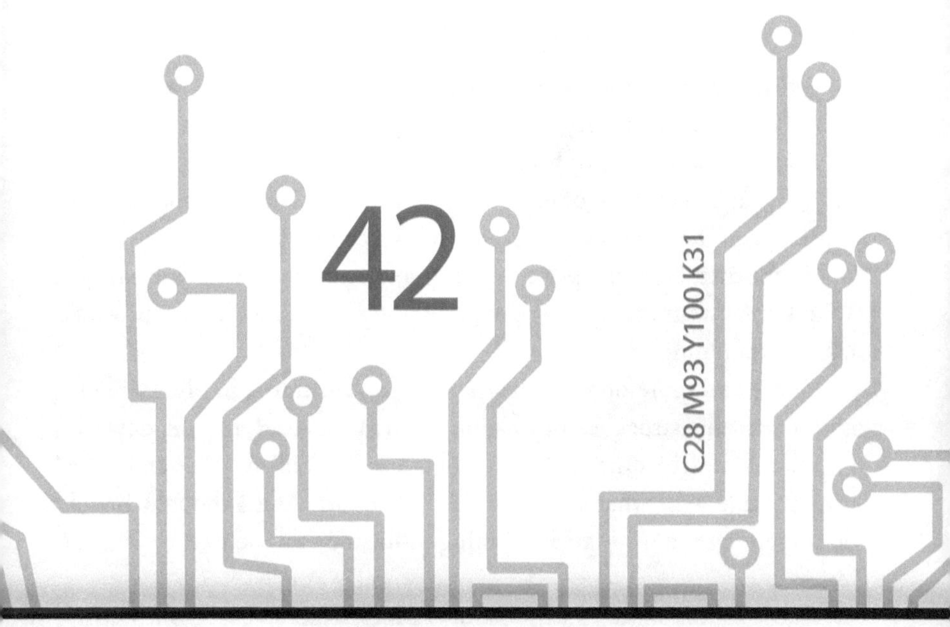

"My great-grandfather told me of a story that was ancient when he was young," Loden told me once. "In the story, a dragon was killed… by a single man with a sword."

At the time, we all agreed the story was ludicrous. Even if someone could get close to a dragon with a sword, he'd never be able to cut through its armor. And even then, the dragon's heart was so deep inside its body, a single man had little chance of reaching it.

Yet that was precisely what I was hoping against hope to do here.

The debris field shifted again. I sidestepped to avoid a large chunk of concrete as it slid past me. I glanced back at Amaranth to make sure her position was still safe.

Rubble rose up, sending more chunks of wreckage sliding away in all directions, then it receded. I knew exactly why it was happening. It rose again, and I could almost sense the strain coming from beneath. It was a lot of weight, even for a dragon.

Fire erupted up through the debris, melting everything that could be melted. I staggered back several steps as a wall of heat struck me.

The wreckage bulged, sank, then exploded upward, sending more debris—some of it on fire—in every direction. The gigantic head of Incarnadine the dragon appeared, shoving more rubble out of the way. It swiveled back and forth, pushing concrete and steel with its nose and chin. The red dragon looked much worse than the last time I'd seen him chasing after me. Massive gashes, some of them scarring, some of them new, decorated his head and neck. One of his horns was missing the tip. As he turned his head, I caught a glimpse of his cybernetic eye—or rather, the socket where it belonged. The eye itself hung loose from a batch of cables.

I crouched behind a piece of wall. No reason to show myself just yet. Who knows what the sight of a man standing around with a sword would inspire from him?

More and more of the dragon's neck pushed through. The spotlights illuminated his struggle. Incarnadine twisted his head and bit down on one chunk of debris the size of a small house. He pulled it free and tossed it to the side with what seemed to be little effort. And I thought I could do something against that? Everything inside me told me to run. This was insanity.

More rubble shifted and slid away as Incarnadine pushed one massive clawed left hand through it. Except one finger hung limp. Blood poured from another broken claw. The dragon lifted the injured hand high, pulling through a tattered wing. It looked like one of the purple robes: frayed and shredded at the ends. He would never be able to fly with that wing again. If he survived this, his people would have to replace so much with cybernetics.

Every movement stirred up more dust. Even with the spotlights, I had difficulty seeing everything. Incarnadine leaned hard to the left and pulled out his right hand. I couldn't see what was wrong with it, but he wasn't using it as aggressively as his left. Was it injured even worse?

In some ways, the spectacle awakened a deep feeling of sadness in me. There was something so… pathetic about it. Not in an insulting use of the word, but in the sense of inspiring pity. I watched a horribly-wounded animal struggling to survive. If I didn't know who it was—and it wasn't so gargantuan—I would be genuinely sorry for it.

Incarnadine braced his left hand and right elbow against the ground and pushed, trying to pull more of himself out. With every effort, he shifted the rubble and stirred up more dust. Debris skidded. Walls collapsed. Small fires erupted. Just getting to the dragon across this dangerous pile of wreckage would be a deadly challenge.

With another immense effort, the dragon pulled the top half of his chest through the debris. He collapsed on top of it, rolling to his right and exposing his chest in my direction.

Onyx was right. Huge sections of the dragon's torso lacked his protective scales, including the left breast, where I assumed I'd find his heart. Enormous gashes criss-crossed his entire chest, evidence of the fight with Atramentous. In a few places, I could make out scales beginning to grow back, but not many.

He was vulnerable. He was weak. He lay on his side there before me, struggling to regain his breath and energy. This was the moment.

I let loose with the implant, sending boosts in every direction throughout my body. I vaulted up and raced toward the dragon. Even as I ran, more rubble shifted from his earlier movements, cascading toward me. But in my heightened state and speed, it all appeared to move like thick syrup. Each footstep struck a solid spot and lifted up again before that spot could move. I planted one foot down at an angle and launched myself in the other direction to dodge protruding chunks of steel. But I kept moving toward the dragon, always toward Incarnadine.

Was anyone watching me? I had to believe Lainey was. I hoped Caedan could see as well. Amaranth might have regained consciousness by now. Aside from the three of them, I doubted anyone else could see through the dust clouds, even with the spotlights. Whether I lived or died—and whether Incarnadine lived or died—would have few witnesses.

Incarnadine's massive head began to lift. He turned his good eye in my direction. What did he see? A human being moving faster than any human could? Did he recognize me? Did he understand what I intended?

It didn't matter. It was time. I was destiny incarnated against Incarnadine. He died now. At my hands.

My sword plunged deep, followed by my cyb hand.

Incarnadine shifted, and let his head fall back down, not even looking in my direction. I dodged as his massive left hand pawed the area, pushing some of the rubble away. My sword thrust was nothing to him; he assumed I was a piece of the wreckage pricking at him. I pulled the sword free. Blood spurted out. To me, it was a torrent. To him, it was a trickle.

What had I been thinking? What had Onyx been thinking? The red dragon's size made it impossible for me to kill him. Maybe if I had an extremely long spear, I could get through to the heart. But even then, would a poke in the heart be enough to kill him?

I took a few steps back and looked up at the dragon. Up close, I saw many more scars and missing scales, but none of them would help me. My eyes followed his neck up to the massive head. Then I spotted the dangling cybernetic eye. An insane idea popped into my head. I sheathed my sword, but held on to the fire launcher.

I glanced around. Despite the breeze, the dust clouds persisted. I could see Amaranth still lying where I left her, but no signs of anyone else. The sirens continued, somewhere nearby, along with the occasional yell.

Watching my steps, I backed up a little more. With more boost energy coursing through my limbs, I ran forward and leaped. I caught hold of a scale with my cyb hand, and used it to hurl myself higher. I landed on the side of the dragon's neck and kept moving.

Incarnadine didn't even move in reaction at first. My feet running along his scales was even less noticeable. Like a bug crawling across my clothes. But one foot landed on a scale-less spot more sensitive, I guess, because the dragon moved, twisting his neck. I leaped into the air to avoid the movement. When I landed, I caught hold of another scale, waiting for him to stop. I moved with the rotation of the neck, barely breathing for fear of being noticed. At last, he came to a stop, letting his head settle on the rubble again.

Now I moved again, as fast as I could, racing up the last bit of the neck, dodging past spikes and finally his giant horns. The metal plate around his cybernetic eye lay before me. I took one last leap, landed on the metal, and slid. I caught hold of the rim and flipped down… into the empty cybernetic eye socket.

That got a reaction. Incarnadine reared his head up, as I struggled to maintain my grip inside. The socket was smaller than I'd anticipated. I barely had room to maneuver, and a slick goo covered everything. My cyb hand caught hold of an enormous metal bar and I held tight.

Incarnadine roared. I wanted to slap my hands over my ears. My proximity to the sound deafened me. If he roared again, I didn't hear it. Both ears filled up with pain instead.

The dragon's massive hand slapped against the outside of the eye socket. I lost my grip from the impact, fell out, kicked off the palm with a quick boost, and seized hold inside again. In another instant, the dragon might figure out that he could stick a claw into the socket. I didn't know what I could do against that. I had to move fast.

I yanked myself to the very back of the eye socket and aimed the flame projector. For a second, I hesitated, trying to determine the nearest spot to the dragon's brain. Not directly back, but at an angle from the socket. I couldn't let go of my grip to fold out the heat shield, so I narrowed my eyes and pulled the trigger. The flow of fire shot out, burning its way through the dragon's inside toward its brain. The heat almost overwhelmed me.

Incarnadine shook his head violently. I knew he screamed, because I could feel the vibrations, but I couldn't hear a thing. I slammed back and forth against the inside of the socket, but since I didn't have far to move, it didn't hurt too much. The flames ran out, and I dropped the empty weapon.

I'd burned a hole up to the dragon's brain, but I couldn't tell how much damage I'd done to the brain itself. He continued to shake his head back and forth, even smashing it against the ground in an effort to jar me loose. If I wanted this to work, I had to time it exactly right.

I twisted around, facing the newly burned hole with my head, while my legs bent, bracing against the opposite side of the socket. I drew my sword with my right hand and discovered how much it hurt from the burning. I gave it another boost to keep my grip through the pain, but I would have to switch hands to make this work.

I waited, holding on for my life as Incarnadine continued to thrash about. At last came a moment where he paused, perhaps trying to evaluate whether the cause of his torment remained.

In that moment, I released my hold, switched the sword to my right hand, sucked in a deep breath, boosted my legs, and lunged upward. I leaped into the newly burned hole, jamming my body up into its narrow space, sword extended. This time, I knew. My sword and cyb hand both penetrated deep into soft tissue that had to be the brain. My entire body stretched through the dragon's head, encased in burned brain tissue or whatever it was. I had nothing to hold on to any more.

Incarnadine's head warped back and forth in violent spasms. I slid back out into the cyb eye socket. I tried to catch hold of something solid, but I was covered in foul-smelling gunk and blood. With the next movement of the head, I plunged out of the socket and fell.

The wreckage of the Flame rushed up to meet me. Unable to twist around, no boosts would help me out of this. I slammed into the debris and rolled. Something, a piece of steel most likely, punctured my side, but I kept going. I finally came to a halt, still clutching my sword in my cyb hand. Ignoring my injuries, I looked up.

The red dragon, his lower body still trapped beneath the rubble, thrashed about in his death throes. I mean, it had to be that, didn't it? I'd burned a hole and stabbed into his brain! That had to be enough to kill him!

His head whipped back and forth. His arms and tattered wings tore through the rubble, tossing steel and concrete into the air and whipping up even more dust clouds. I could barely make out what was happening.

His mouth stays open in a perpetual scream, some of which I could almost hear, I think.

Then his head and neck curved all the way back, impossibly back. Surely the neck was breaking with that bizarre movement. Its entire body stiffened and shook all over. And then it collapsed with a massive impact. My perch of concrete flipped into the air, taking me with it. I twisted hard to avoid it coming down on top of me. Even so, as I hit, I rolled again. The chunk landed right where my legs had been.

I gasped for breath, the pain in my side making it difficult. I used the sword to pull myself up on to my knee. Taking short, fast breaths, I at last looked back up.

Amidst the dust clouds and the bright lights, I could make out the form of Incarnadine, the great red dragon. He lay completely still in the ruins of the Flame. I couldn't believe it. I staggered to my feet and almost fell immediately. The rubble was still unstable. Fewmets, I was unstable. I took a step and then another step. I tried to boost my legs for stability but failed. I must have overloaded my system yet again. But maybe it was worth it. Maybe…

I drew closer to the dragon's body and stared. He truly didn't move. His chest didn't rise from breathing. No steam or smoke flowed from his mouth or nostrils. A nasty-looking goo oozed from the empty eye socket. The same horrible-smelling substance, mixed with blood, covered me and the sword.

He was dead. Truly. Incarnadine was dead. Despite everything else, no matter what else happened, I, Beryl, had killed a dragon. I let the realization, the awe, the glory of the moment flow over me.

And then I collapsed in pain and nausea. I vomited two or three times. My head spun. I almost lost consciousness. My whole body ached from being pummeled inside the dragon's eye socket. My muscles ached from the strain put on them by the prolonged boosting. My ears hurt. My right hand throbbed with pain from burns, and I had a stab wound in my side. Plus some other damage I probably hadn't realized yet.

I don't know how long I stayed in that spot, mostly on my hands and knees. At some point, I finally sheathed my sword, though it would require a lot more cleaning later. I threw up a few more times. I may have even blacked out for brief moments at a time. I don't know. I wanted to celebrate, to cheer the downfall of a dragon. But I felt sick, in more ways than one. The brief battle had taken a lot out of me.

Lainey and Caedan found me there. They were both covered in dust head-to-foot. Glacier came too and sniffed at the dragon. Lainey crouched down to look in my face. Her mouth moved, but I couldn't hear her. I pointed to my ears and shook my head. "I can't hear anything," I tried to say, but I couldn't tell if the words actually left my mouth. Caedan said something, and she nodded her head. She pointed at me and made a gesture I didn't quite get, but I think she was asking if I was okay. I shrugged.

Lainey pointed at me and then held her nose. I knew what that meant and rolled my eyes.

Caedan offered his hand. I took it and let him pull me to my feet. I staggered and almost fell at once. Lainey caught my other side. All together, we slowly descended from the pile of wreckage.

Glacier bounded past us, stirring up her own small clouds of dust. She stopped beside Amaranth, who still lay where I'd left her but covered in so much dust as to be unrecognizable. The cat nudged her with her nose, but the dragon queen didn't wake up.

I let go of Caedan and pointed at Amaranth, then mimed carrying someone. "Bring her." He raised his eyebrows at me, but picked her up.

One dragon dead and another in our custody. I'd say this was a good night's work.

44

Much slower than I'd have liked, we made our way out of the debris field. When we finally broke free of the main dust clouds, we met a cacophony of activity. Crimson Elite, firefighters, and medical personnel ran this way and that. No one tried to check our chromarks—none of them were visible, anyway—and no one demanded any answers from us. They pointed us to a triage tent if we needed medical attention. I considered heading that way to let them look at my stab wound, but I was covered in something more than dust, and that would raise questions.

Instead, we turned a corner and ducked down an alley, like we always did. Since I first met Rick, I think I'd spent far more of my life in alleys than actual roads.

Caedan, carrying Amaranth, led the way. But I couldn't keep up. The pain in my side grew steadily. Darkness appeared around the edges of my vision. At last, I started to fall. Lainey caught me and helped me sit on the ground. My vision blurred again. When Lainey and Caedan looked at me, mouthing words I couldn't hear, I pointed to my side and twisted so they could see.

Immediately, they engaged in a spirited conversation. I think I heard a few sounds come through from it, but it might have been my imagination. After a few moments in which they pointed back and forth while debating something, Caedan picked Amaranth back up and hurried away. Lainey knelt beside me and took a closer look at my side.

She said something else, shaking her head. I think her lips formed the word "blood." That made sense. I'd probably lost too much blood. And then I lost consciousness too.

I woke up to find Glacier licking dragon gunk off my arm. Lainey shooed her back. I took a deep breath and felt something tight against my side. I looked down to see a makeshift bandage wrapped around my lower torso. I wondered where Lainey had found a clean towel or whatever it was. Even here, blocks from the Flame, dust covered everything. And then I realized the sun had arrived. Morning.

I didn't hear their footsteps, but Bice and Caedan suddenly appeared in my vision. Bice talked with Lainey as he knelt beside me. This time, I know I heard some muffled sounds from their voices, but nowhere near loud enough to recognize words.

Bice examined my side, then checked over the rest of my body, ignoring the dirt, blood, and grime that covered every inch of me. He discovered my burnt hand and also figured out something about my ears, pointing to them while he talked with the others. Finally, he put his hands on either side of my face and looked me in the eyes. He spoke slowly, mouthing each words with exaggeration to help me get it.

"We've got to get you back to the apartment."

I nodded, understanding that much, at least.

Bice put his arm around me, again not caring about the mess, and helped me get back to my feet. With careful steps, we resumed the walk. It took us another hour, stopping frequently so I could rest, to make it all the way back to the apartment building.

Inside, I noticed Amaranth, cleaned up somewhat, asleep on the couch. More conversations took place, now including Marcus and Cerise. I hoped Bice apologized to them for the mess I was making of their apartment. I tried to say it myself, but I don't know how it came out.

Bice and Caedan took me to the Vermeils' tiny bathroom. They stripped off my filthy and ruined clothes. Caedan took them away. Bice helped me into the shower and turned on the water. I screamed when it hit my side. I could even hear myself a little. Bice did his best to at least rinse me off, and scrubbed away some of the worst spots. When I got out, wrapped in a towel and barely conscious, he cleaned my face. If I'd been more aware of everything, I'd probably have been massively embarrassed at all this. But as it was, I felt on the edge of darkness the entire time.

Lainey came in, looking a little cleaner herself, and helped Bice put fresh bandages on my side and hand. They discussed my ears, I think, judging from the pointing, but didn't do anything about them. Then they made me swallow a few pills. With help, I exited a filthy bathroom and managed to get to my sleeping bag on the floor.

Caedan pointed at the woman on the couch, clearly annoyed, and said something. He probably wanted me on the couch. I didn't care. I was out two seconds later.

I woke up from the piercing pain in my side and cried out without thinking. Lainey appeared in my vision and said something. This time, I know I heard my name in there somewhere. "Side hurts," I said, the words sounding almost coherent.

"Bice!" Lainey called. I got that much. Then she said something else, but the only word I caught was "pain."

Bice appeared a moment later and offered me more pills. I dutifully swallowed them with some water and went back to sleep.

I didn't know what was going on around me, but I learned later that I slept all that day and through the next night. Surprisingly, so did Amaranth, except she never woke up like I did. The others debated what to do with us. Bice was very worried about the side injury. If they couldn't get me out of the city and back to Hunter, he was almost ready to take me to a hospital. Apparently, getting stabbed in your side is a pretty serious thing.

Cerise figured out what to do. She contacted a medical friend and persuaded her to come to the apartment. While everyone else hid in the bedroom, Cerise explained to the doctor that I was a friend from Viridia who'd been caught in the destruction. She'd added bandages over my burned face, and suggested they'd been afraid to take me in since my chromark had been burned off. I don't know how she explained away my cyb hand.

The doc examined the side injury and told Cerise what to do to help me avoid infection. Beyond that, she wanted to take me in for x-rays and deeper examination, but Cerise expressed fear at the prospect. Reluctantly, the doctor gave her a bunch of drugs to help me out and left.

Hunger and thirst finally woke me up the next morning. Before I could even sit up, Lainey brought me some hot tea. I took a sip and sighed as the liquid warmth spread through me. A few minutes later, I managed to sit up against the wall and eat a little. My hand still hurt, but the true agony came from my side. Every movement seemed to aggravate it, sometimes bringing tears to my eyes. I swallowed more pills, which helped a little once they kicked in.

My hearing had improved, but only on my right side. While Lainey talked in a louder-than-normal voice, I turned my head back and forth.

"I can't hear a thing from the left ear," I said. I'm pretty sure I was speaking louder than usual too, but my voice sounded odd in my head, unbalanced.

Lainey frowned. She leaned in beside my left ear, then pulled back. "You couldn't hear that?"

"Not a thing."

Bice settled in to a chair next to me. "Beryl, in order for me to understand your injuries, I have to know what you did. Right now, I have no clue what could have happened to your ears."

In order to understand him, I had to keep my right ear turned partially in his direction while watching his lips intently. It was annoying but better than the total silence I'd endured earlier. Maybe my left ear would come back over time.

I was about to tell Bice the whole story when Cerise joined us. She knelt down by my side and insisted on checking my temperature and the condition of my bandages. Once that was done, she looked me in the eye, leaned in close, and said:

"Beryl, I don't know if I want to hear the answer to these questions, but... Who is this woman on my couch, and why hasn't she woken up yet?"

45

"Oh, that's Amaranth," I said, looking over at her. "I don't know why she hasn't woken up."

"That's Amaranth?" Caedan exclaimed from across the room. "You mean I was lu—admiring a dragon?"

I laughed a little, which hurt a lot.

"You brought a dragon into my apartment?" Cerise demanded.

"No," I said, closing my eyes and leaning back against the wall. "Caedan did."

"What? You told me to!"

I turned my left ear toward the wall so I could hear them better. "I don't remember telling you anything."

Caedan muttered something I couldn't hear at all.

"So why bring her here?" Marcus asked.

"She made me an offer." I covered my right ear while speaking to see if it changed the way my voice sounded in my own head. It still sounded weird.

"I'll bet she did," Caedan said.

"She offered to tell us everything about the dragons and their history," I went on. "Where they came from and why. In return, I take the disk off."

"Do you believe her?" Bice asked.

"I don't know. But you were right: I couldn't kill her."

Caedan stepped up beside the couch and looked down at the sleeping dragon. "I get it," he said. "I do. But if she's a dragon… I mean, isn't that our whole purpose?"

"You killed Incarnadine!" Lainey burst out. "Another dragon is dead! Do we need to kill this one too?"

"All right, all right," Bice said, raising his hands. "Everyone wait a minute. Before we debate any more, let's get the whole story."

"We've told them up to the point where Caedan flipped the switch and brought down the Flame," Lainey explained. "But none of us know what happened to you next."

I took a deep breath and then told the story. Right away, Bice was shocked to hear about Amaranth's use of the resomancy power. "That doesn't make sense," he repeated multiple times.

When I got to the eye socket, Caedan lost it. "You did what?"

"I climbed in the eye socket where his cyb eye fell out."

"You…" Marcus shook his head, open-mouthed. "I thought you were crazy with the flying thing last time."

"But that's totally insane!" Caedan threw his hands in the air, narrowly missing a light fixture. "Why would—Why would you even think of doing something like that?"

"The brain," Bice said. "He was going for the brain."

I nodded and went on, explaining what I had to do and what happened next. "And I guess it worked," I finished.

"Incarnadine is dead," Marcus confirmed. "They haven't wanted to say anything, but…"

"Once the sun came up and the dust cleared, everyone could see him lying there," Cerise said. "He's dead." She sat down on one of the dining chairs. "I just can't believe it. The dragon is dead."

"Three dragons are dead," Caedan added. "Three dragons. Unbelievable."

Bice looked down over the couch's occupant. I could see what he was thinking. I was thinking it too. One quick stab or slice or even something simpler… and it would be four dead dragons. He blinked and shook his head, turning back to me.

"Now at least I understand your ears," he said. "You probably ruptured your ear drum, at the very least."

"Will my hearing come back?"

"Once it heals… maybe. We'll just have to wait and see. Hunter will know more."

"Are we leaving then?" Caedan asked.

"I don't know." I looked around the room. "I'm assuming you haven't heard from Onyx?"

"Not a word," Marcus said.

"Should we wait for him?" Caedan asked. "Why not just clear out while we can?"

"He knows where we live," Lainey said. "And we can't leave Cerise and Marcus."

"We did what he asked," I said.

"And do you seriously think he'll keep his word?" Caedan demanded.

"Now that he's used us, he's likely to want to use us again," Bice agreed. "He has no reason to let us go."

"Yes, he does." I pointed to the couch. "We have her."

Everyone else looked at Amaranth. For a moment, no one spoke.

"You think that'll matter to him?" Caedan asked at last.

"She's been sheltering him. She's his only ally. Without her, he doesn't stand a chance against the other dragons."

"We were his allies too," Caedan pointed out.

I couldn't argue with that. Would Onyx betray Amaranth as easily as he'd betrayed me? He had kept his plans for Incarnadine a secret from her. Come to think of it, he'd kind of implied that he'd betray her eventually. But not just yet.

"What are you suggesting, exactly, Beryl?" Bice asked. "That we force Onyx to do what we want, or else we kill Amaranth? How long will that work?"

"It only has to work long enough to get us out of here," I argued. "And protect all of us. By now, the others may have found a new place for us to hide. Once there—"

"And are we taking her with us?" Bice interrupted. "Do you want to keep a dragon in our very midst?"

"It's temporary!" I insisted. "We'll work out a deal for our protection. Onyx leaves us alone, Amaranth tells us the secrets we want to know, and then we're gone."

"It seems… dangerous," Cerise said.

I started to spread my arms out but winced from a burst of pain in my side. "Does anyone have any better ideas?"

"I don't," Bice said. "But that doesn't mean it's a good idea."

"Beryl can't travel just yet, anyway," Lainey pointed out. "He needs time to heal."

"That shouldn't be a factor," I protested.

"Really?" She narrowed her gaze at me. "You think you can walk across The Circle in your present condition?"

She might have a point.

"Marcus. Cerise." Bice looked to our hosts. "What are you two thinking?"

"Well, I'm out of a job," Cerise said.

"But we don't want to leave the city!" Marcus added in a hurry.

"The only problem is Onyx," Cerise went on. "He knows us and knows where we live. As long as that's true, I don't see how we can ever be safe."

"You're welcome to come with us," Bice said. I struggled to hear him since he wasn't facing me. "I know it sounds hard, and I know you're worried about the baby." He smiled. "But we do have a good doctor with us now, and we've had one birth already."

"I don't know if that one counts," Caedan said, eyes wide.

Cerise and Marcus exchanged looks. "I just don't know," Cerise said.

"Well, we probably have a couple of days, at least, to make that decision," Bice said. "Now what about—"

"Where am I?" Amaranth rose up on her elbow. "Who are you people?"

I boosted my legs enough to stand, ignoring the burst of pain. "You're here with my friends," I told her. "That's all you need to know."

Her eyes locked on me before roaming around the room again. She paused on Bice, recognizing him from our earlier time with her, then locked in on Lainey. "No mark," she murmured.

"Before you say anything else, you need to understand something," I said. "You are only alive because I kept you that way and brought you here."

"Who did?" Caedan muttered.

"If you want to keep living, you'll do as I say."

Amaranth gave a little snort. "I remember saving your life," she countered. "Sacrificed a lot of my energy to do that too." She sat up, letting the blanket fall away. Her torn clothes showed more skin than I was comfortable seeing. I reminded myself repeatedly that she was a dragon.

"You're right," I said. "And I appreciate that."

She folded her arms, then looked toward the others standing in the kitchen area. "Wine!" she snapped.

"We don't have any wine," Marcus said. "Cerise can't drink it right now, and—"

"Whatever." Amaranth rolled her eyes. "Bring me something to drink. I don't care what."

Marcus poured water from the tap into a glass and brought it. Amaranth gulped down a swallow, glared at him, then drank most of the rest.

"You destroyed the Flame," she declared. "How has Incarnadine responded?"

I met her eyes. "Incarnadine is dead. I killed him."

"You lie."

Caedan held out my sword, and I pointed to it. "I drove that blade into his brain. His body lies in the ruins of the Flame."

"It's true," Cerise broke in. "People are mourning in the streets." She pointed at the window. Something outside caught her attention and she stared.

"We need to talk about—" I began.

"The Crimson Elite are moving in," Cerise interrupted.

The sound of a cybernetic hand knocking on the front door followed her words.

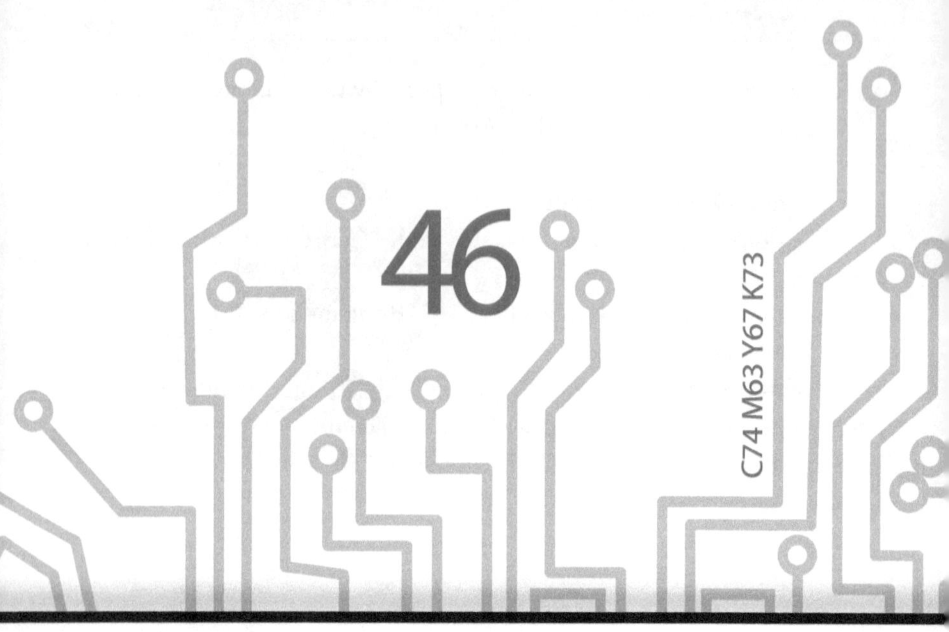

"It's Onyx," Marcus said.

"What?" Amaranth stood up.

"Listen to me quick," I said. "If you want the truth about all of this, head into the back room and listen. Don't let him see you here. I'll get him to talk."

"Why should I? He'll get me out of this."

"He forced me to kill Incarnadine. He provided the tools to destroy the Flame. Hide back there and listen. If he doesn't admit it, you can come out and do whatever you want."

Amaranth studied me. Onyx knocked on the door again. Finally, she gave a short nod and moved toward the bedroom. Cerise went with her.

I gestured to the door, and Caedan went to get it, still holding my sword. I took a few steps, then sank down on the couch, gasping from the pain. Lainey moved around behind me and put her hand on my shoulder.

Caedan backed from the door, holding the sword aimed at Richard Onyx, who entered with a grin. Upon seeing me, he applauded. "I knew you could do it! You are amazing, Beryl!"

"It wouldn't have worked without the explosives you provided," Caedan said, a little too loud. I almost rolled my eyes.

"Yes, of course. But Beryl... Beryl truly is a dragon slayer now. How does it feel, Beryl? To fulfill such a lifelong dream?"

"You tell me. Seems you're the one getting dreams fulfilled," I growled. I wanted to wipe that grin off his face so bad.

"It's true. I am. But!" He reached into his pocket and produced some folded up papers. "You did what I asked, and here is what I promised in return." He dropped the papers on to the easy chair. "The other half of Loden's notes. I'll be very interested in your reaction." He looked at Caedan. "Pay attention when he discovers what it means. I want to know what his face looks like."

"And now you leave us alone," I said. "All of us."

"That was never part of the deal."

"Not true," Bice countered. "You said if we didn't do the job for you, then we would all die, and then you would go after Kelly and the child. But you said if we did do it, none of that would happen."

"Ah, Bice. You have the memory of a dragon. Very good." He held up a finger. "But you'll notice I never said I wouldn't ask you to do something else."

"We don't work for you, Onyx!" Caedan snapped, still holding the sword aimed at him.

"Of course you do. I know where you are. I have complete power over you. When next I need your particular skills, I'll let you know."

"What then? You'll ask us to kill Amaranth?" I asked.

"Maybe." He cocked his head. "Although now that you mention her, she's been missing for a couple of days. I can't help but wonder if she had a very poorly-timed visit to dear old Incarnadine. Wouldn't that be something? Two dragons dead at once!"

"If she finds out, or if the other two dragons find out what you did, you won't stand a chance." I had to admit: at this point, I was impressed with Amaranth's self-control. I'd fully expected her to charge into the room and possibly attack Onyx herself.

"I have more resources than you know." He reached out and tapped the extended sword with a cybernetic finger. "Speaking of which, tomorrow at noon, there's going to be a gathering at the ruins of the Flame. I've specifically invited all of the red draconics from both cities. You'll want to be there to see what happens."

"Why?"

"Secrets." He chuckled. "You know the rest."

"What is your endgame, Onyx?" Bice asked. "You want to rule all of The Circle? Get revenge on the other dragons?"

"We've been over that, Bice. I take back what I said earlier. Maybe your memory is getting worse, after all."

"That can't be all of it," I said. "What about the purple robes?"

He lost his grin. "What are you talking about?"

I started to lean forward, but the pain stopped me. "You know exactly what I'm talking about. The purple robes, the sorcerers or whatever they are, from outside The Circle. I know you've had dealings with them."

Rick didn't say anything for a moment. "You know, Beryl," he said at last. "There are old tales that speak about the dangers of seeking too much knowledge. Sometimes, it's far better to live in ignorance." He looked pointedly at Loden's notes on the chair. "Case in point."

He hadn't denied it. He was working with them, somehow. But for what purpose? Why is it every time I learned something new, it led to another mystery?

Rick turned to go. "I'll show myself out. Don't forget: tomorrow at noon. You don't want to miss it."

Caedan lunged forward, jabbing the sword in front of Rick, who stopped. "Why shouldn't I take your head off now?"

"Same reason as last time I was here." He gestured to the window. "Soldiers. Fire. Apartment building. Innocent people die. Blah blah blah. You know the drill."

"Let him go, Caedan," I said with a sigh. "It's not worth it."

"Yes, Caedan. Keep being the dumb muscle. Obey those with brains."

Caedan glared at Rick and didn't move the sword.

"Caedan…" Bice called.

Finally, Caedan moved the sword. Rick nodded at him and left the apartment. With the door shut, Cerise and Amaranth returned. The dragon wore one of Cerise's sweatshirts over her own torn blouse. Her eyes were narrowed. I could almost see fire pulsing from them.

"I see I owe you somewhat of an apology," Amaranth said. "It appears Onyx has never had my best interests at heart."

"That's an understatement," Bice observed.

"Why didn't you come out?" Lainey asked. "I kept expecting you to burst in and attack him." She came around the couch and sat beside me.

"No." She went to the kitchen window and looked out. "Like you, I am very curious about his schemes. What does he mean to do tomorrow with the draconics? I must be there to see it."

"We'll be there," I promised. "For now, whether we like it or not, we're on the same side, Amaranth. We can work together against him."

She turned back to me. "Then you should remove this thing from my neck. I can do far more against Onyx in my dragon form."

"He'll tear you apart with his new enhancements," I said. "He's got the physical advantage for now."

"Then we summon the others: Auric and Atramentous. Together, the three of us will take him down. You will be rewarded for your assistance in the matter."

I almost laughed, but I'm pretty sure it would hurt. "Rewarded? I think you're forgetting our ultimate goal."

"No. I am not." She put her hands on her hips. "In return for helping us defeat Onyx, you may have the three cities without a dragon to rule however you humans wish to rule them."

"What?"

"Half of The Circle will belong to you. The other half will be ours. As long as you recognize our existing trade arrangements, we can—"

"You can't be serious!" Bice exclaimed. "You would seriously trade away half of The Circle?"

"Why not?" Amaranth lifted her hands. "Their dragons are dead. It would be more work for us to govern two cities apiece, and I have no desire to do so."

"No, no, no, no," I said. "We want—I want—everyone free. Not just some."

"Half of The Circle," she repeated. "To do with as you like. You want them 'free'? Set them free. Or rule them all as a despot. I don't care. I want the betrayer."

For a brief moment, I considered it. Not as a despot or king or whatever. But to have three of the cities free. Just like that. Maybe we could live in peace with the dragon-ruled cities. Maybe they could be persuaded to change. Auric, for one, seemed more amenable than the others. Maybe…

"The purple robes would never allow it," Lainey said. Since she was on my left, I barely heard her, but I got the point of her statement.

Amaranth spun to look at her. "What do you know of the purple robes, girl?"

Lainey glared back at her. "I know enough. I grew up under them. They took my father."

"That explains the face, at least. Hmph."

"So you know about them, then?" I asked.

"Of course I know about them," Amaranth grumbled. "They work for my mother."

"What?" I must have heard her wrong. But the sudden explosion of similar questions from everyone else in the room implied that I hadn't. I looked at Lainey. She pulled her knees up to her chin and seemed to shrink back. She knew. She knew all along. For some reason, this was one of the things she and her father hadn't wanted to tell me.

Caedan pounded on the dining table. "Mother? As in: the mother of the dragons?"

Amaranth folded her arms and said nothing. Caedan, Marcus, and Cerise kept demanding answers.

Bice held up his hands until the others stopped. He stood facing Amaranth. "You can't just drop something like that on us and not expect a reaction," he said. "We know the purple robes come from outside The Circle. You're saying that your mother rules outside there, and these people are her agents of some kind?"

"Chroma!" I exclaimed. "Chroma! Auric called himself the first child of Chroma. But his draconic said it meant the place they came from or something. Is Chroma the actual name of your mother?"

Amaranth ignored Bice and looked at me. "I offered you an agreement," she said. "I will not tell you the history of the dragons unless you agree to remove this infernal device." She touched the disk on the back of her neck.

"Wait, wait, wait." Caedan put both hands in his hair. "What happened to setting half of The Circle free? Now we're back to just information?"

"I spoke hastily." Amaranth closed her eyes for a moment. "Yes. I apologize." She opened them again. "My original offer stands. I will give you all the secrets in exchange for removing the device."

"I, I haven't decided about that yet," I stammered.

"Very well." She turned and pushed past Marcus, heading toward the back. "I'll be in the bedroom when you make up your mind." She disappeared into the bedroom and slammed the door.

"If she thinks she can just take over my bedroom—" Cerise began, clenching her fist and taking a step.

"Cerise!" I called. "Let it go for a bit. She, um, she can breathe fire, you know."

Cerise stopped and looked at me with eyebrows up. "She can breathe fire as a human?"

I nodded and pointed at my face. "Onyx did this in human form, remember?"

She threw up her hands. "Fine. But only until we decide what to do next."

Bice bent over the easy chair and picked up the papers Onyx had dropped. "Maybe we should look at these," he observed, unfolding them.

"I don't know," Caedan said. "I mean, I want to understand Beryl's cyb stuff as much as anyone, but we've got a dragon in the bedroom to deal with. Not to mention"—his voice rose—"the bleaking revelation that there's a mother of all dragons waiting outside The Circle!"

I turned all the way around to Lainey, so I could be sure to hear her with my right ear. "Are you ready to talk about this?"

She shook her head and pulled her knees closer.

Fewmets. What could I do? I couldn't force her to tell me. But at the same time, it hurt that she wouldn't.

"Let's face it," Bice said. "We don't know what to do about Amaranth. Or Onyx. I propose we wait until this event tomorrow, see what Onyx is up to, and then proceed from there."

"I propose we get out of here," Caedan argued. "Let's make tracks for the Asylum."

I couldn't argue with him. I wanted to get back too. I wanted to make sure Kelly was all right. And Don and Lovat. We'd been gone for… a few days? A week? I'd lost track. It seemed like far too long. But at the same time, we couldn't just run.

"We can't run," I said aloud.

"I wouldn't say that," Caedan answered. "I'm pretty good at running. Pfft. You can run faster than anyone in the world!"

"You know what I mean. We can't leave Marcus and Cerise. We need to see what Onyx is going to do." I pointed back toward the bedroom. "And we have to decide what to do about her. Do we take her with us when we run?"

"I don't know!' Caedan waved his hands in frustration. "But we've got to do something! We can't just sit here!"

"We will! But Bice is right. Let's wait one day and see what Onyx does tomorrow. But!" I started to lift my right hand, remembered it was bandaged, and lifted my left forefinger instead. "We need to be prepared for whatever that is. That means being ready to run." I pointed to Marcus. "You too. If it's bad, we're out of here, and you're both coming with us. It's too dangerous for you here."

"But—" Marcus started.

"No! We have to be prepared. No arguments."

Cerise stepped to Marcus's side and took his hand. He bowed his head.

"Bice, can I see the notes?" I asked. "Let's think about something different, at least for a few minutes."

He came around behind the couch and leaned over to let me look over the papers with him. At first, I didn't understand a thing I saw.

"This… doesn't look like his other notes. Where are the wires and schematics and stuff?"

"This isn't cyber tech," Bice said.

"What is it?"

"It's genetics."

"What? Let me see!" Cerise broke free from Marcus and hurried over. "I did some studies in genetics some years ago, thinking I could get out of manning a desk."

"Why would Loden be writing about genetics?" Caedan asked. "How would that help with the cyb stuff?"

"The dragons wanted to understand genetics," I said. "Loden talked about that. And… I think I remember hearing the green dragon saying something about it."

"When you were in Viridia's lair?"

"Yeah. It's all a vague memory, but they said something."

Bice handed the pages to Cerise, who frowned as she studied them.

Lainey let go of her knees. "Do you remember the last part of the other notes?" she asked. "He was talking about your organs."

"I remember." But I didn't want to. "He talked about maybe using draconic organs, because human organs might not be able to handle the stress. But he couldn't have done that! Troilus Green was the injured draconic, and Bice didn't take any organs from it."

"No, no," Cerise said. "These first set of notes discuss that but reject it. I think… I think he was considering whether to combine or splice together human and draconic—"

"Splicing!" I exclaimed. "That's what they said. Something about splicing not working."

"What's splicing?" Marcus asked, looking over Cerise's shoulder.

"It's where you tamper with the genetic coding of something by combining it with parts of code from something else," Cerise said. "It's super advanced. I only heard about it as a theory. But this…" She tapped the notes. "This looks real. Like he genuinely was going to do it."

"Did he?" Bice asked.

"I don't know. I'm still trying to understand… Hang on. I'll skip on a bit." She flipped over the page and scanned over the notes on the back.

"That's what the purple robes do," Lainey said.

I turned to her again. "Gene splicing?"

"Genetics," she said. "I really don't know any more about that. Honest."

"I still don't get it," Caedan said. "Your implant is about your brain and your muscles, right? You boost them. So why was Bice worried about your organs? You don't boost those."

"Except one," I said, swallowing. "The strongest muscle in the body. The heart."

"You can boost your heart?"

"Sort of." I didn't want to go into it. I didn't like the direction this conversation was taking. "My heart is normal. Loden couldn't have given me a draconic heart. It would be too big!"

"Unless he took it from a young draconic," Marcus suggested.

I scowled at him.

Lainey wrapped her arm around mine and patted my chest with her other hand. "You have a good heart," she told me.

"No, no. I said he abandoned that idea," Cerise said, still perusing the notes. "He decided that—this can't be right—even a draconic heart wouldn't be strong enough."

"Considering what Beryl puts his body through, that makes sense to me," Bice said. "I don't know how he lives through what he's done."

"This is crazy," I said. "I don't have—"

"He made you a new heart!" Cerise interrupted.

"Beryl's heart is cyb?" Caedan asked.

"No, but parts of it might be." Cerise paced around the room as she read, much to Marcus's annoyance. "I think… I think he partially grew a new heart. With some help. He talks about someone named Hunter."

"We know him."

"Hunter thought your body would reject the heart, which is why…" She slapped the papers with the back of her hand. "Which is why he used cybernetic connections, so the heart itself is not organically attached. That's amazing!"

"Did he grow a draconic heart then?" Caedan asked.

"No." Cerise looked up at me. "It's a dragon heart."

"That's ridiculous. A dragon's heart would be immense." At first, my heart seemed to stop at Cerise's words, but logic prevailed. She couldn't be right.

Cerise rolled her eyes and slapped the papers against her thigh. "Come on, Beryl. I'm not saying he took a literal heart out of a literal dragon and put it inside you. Have you seen any dragons running around without a heart lately?"

"There's one in your bedroom," Caedan said.

"I just said that he 'grew' a new heart. This is where the genetics comes in." She waved the papers. "If he just gave you an artificial heart, or transplanted someone else's heart, then none of this genetic stuff would matter. It would be pointless scribbling. But it's not."

"How can you grow a heart?" Marcus asked for all of us.

"It's complicated," Cerise answered. "And theoretical, I thought. I don't know of anyone else who's done it. Theoretically, you could clone an existing heart with the modifications you want to make, but it would be very small. You would have to grow it in a donor, like an animal of some kind."

"So… you're saying Loden built a dragon heart, and then let it grow up inside a goat… before cutting it out and putting it in Beryl?" Caedan marked the different steps with a finger on the table.

"Essentially, yes. Something like that."

"My head hurts." Caedan went to look out the window.

"The scientists in the Emerald Ascendancy had access to pieces of the dragon," Bice said. "Old scales, and such. And the priests had access to his blood. It wouldn't have been hard to get the dragon's genetic... code, or whatever it's called."

"I don't understand," I said. "Why go to all this trouble? It sounds ridiculously complicated." Not to mention that I hated the very idea of having anything in common with a dragon, especially not the green dragon.

"It is," Cerise agreed. She sat down and flipped through the pages again. "But from what I can grasp here, he didn't think your regular heart could handle the constant strain your boosts would put on it."

"But I've only boosted the heart twice."

"Not like that." She sighed and put the pages down in her lap. "I mean, your heart has to keep pumping blood and keep your body going normally, right? When you do the crazy things you do, like running so fast, or jumping from high places, your body still has to deal with that. And your heart has to keep up with your body's movements, pumping more blood faster and faster. Even more so if you get injured, which you seem prone to do." She pointed at my side. "A regular heart just wouldn't be able to keep up. You'd die very young."

Lainey gave my arm a squeeze.

"So... Loden and Hunter rebuilt my entire body, patching it up, putting in this cyb system and the implant in my brain, and giving me a whole new heart to help run it." I looked up. "They basically built me into a weapon to use against the dragons. And then they left me in the hospital like they forgot all about me."

"Ouch," Caedan mumbled.

"No, they didn't." Bice put his hand on my shoulder from behind the couch. "They left you in my hands."

"What?" I turned to look at him. I knew Bice had been there when I woke up in the hospital. I even knew Loden had told him bout the implant.

"Loden asked me to help you during your recovery," Bice explained. "Yes, he told me about the implant, but no more than you originally thought: that it was there to help you walk. He told me about the accident and your parents' death. And he emphasized how much you meant to him."

My heart ached, and not because we'd been talking about it. "Then why didn't he spend more time with me?" The question had been eating away at me, unasked, for years.

"I can't say for sure, but I think I can guess now." Bice shook his head. "You're right. He made you into a weapon. But you were still young. Too young. You needed time to grow into a man, to live some more of your life, before he came back and pointed you at the dragons." Bice squeezed my shoulder. "I think he was afraid that if he spent time with you, he wouldn't be able to help himself. He'd force you into being that weapon before you were ready.

"Don't get me wrong!" Bice hastened to add. "I'm not saying he thought of you only as a weapon. He cared about you greatly. And that, I think, is part of why he stayed away. He was torn between wanting you to grow up and have as normal a life as possible and the desire to see his work come to fruition."

I lowered my head. I guess it made sense. Still hurt, though. "I have fake eyes. A fake hand. Cyb tech running throughout my body. And a heart that's made from a dragon. Loden wanted me to become a man? I don't even know if I'm human!"

"We've had this conversation. Of course you're human."

"How can you say that? What about me is human any more?" I realized I probably sounded deranged, but I didn't care. "You can't say my heart any more, because clearly, that's not even remotely human. My brain? It's plugged into cybernetics! So who am I? What am I?"

Bice walked around the couch and knelt in front of me. "You are a human being, Beryl. Your body parts are not what define you. I've known many people who have lost arms or legs and they're still human. Even those who've had their brains damaged. The dragons and their minions think those people are worthless. But they're not. They're human. They're alive. Just like you. No matter how much of you is repaired or replaced or augmented or whatever, you're still you." He pointed at my chest. "You have something that can never be replaced. A human soul."

"How do you know that?" I almost couldn't hear my own voice.

Bice's grin widened into a huge smile. "I have faith, Beryl. I've told you. The dragons are not gods. But that doesn't mean there isn't a power above them in this universe."

"…to me." Lainey said something, but she was next to my deaf ear. I turned toward her. "What was that?"

"You're human to me!" she said louder. "Do you trust me?"

"I—Yes, I trust you." I wrinkled my brow.

"Do you believe what I tell you?"

"Yes." Though I wished she would tell me more.

"Then I tell you you're human. Believe it."

"Lainey, it's—"

"Are you calling me a liar? You don't trust me?"

"That's not fair!"

"Why not? Who makes the rules here?" She pulled her knees up under her on the couch as she faced me. "Who decides who's human? Who decides who has a soul? Do you? Are you some kind of god?"

"No, of course not."

"Then you'll just have to take our word for it. So there."

I almost laughed. Between the two of them, Bice and Lainey knew how to show me their love, in different ways. I appreciated it more than I could say. I didn't feel human. But maybe, just maybe they were right. Maybe there was more to being human than a set of body parts.

"Great," Caedan said from the window. "Are we done with the emotional stuff now?"

"Yeah, I guess so," I answered with a bit of a chuckle.

He turned back around. "All right. It's all pointless, anyway. You look human to me. Why do we need to get all philosophical about it?"

"Everyone copes with stuff in their own way," Bice said.

"Right, right. Anyway. What are we going to do tomorrow, then? Can we get back to that? And the whole mother of dragons thing?"

"Caedan…" Bice warned.

"No, it's okay," I broke in. "We can talk some more now. I don't think we'll get anything else from the notes until we show them to Hunter." For one thing, we still didn't know where my boost energy came from. Genetics didn't explain that, did it?

"So… tomorrow?" Caedan asked.

"Tomorrow, we find out what Onyx is doing," I said. "And then we either find a way to stop him, or we run for our lives."

"Oh. All right. Well, as long as we've got a plan, then."

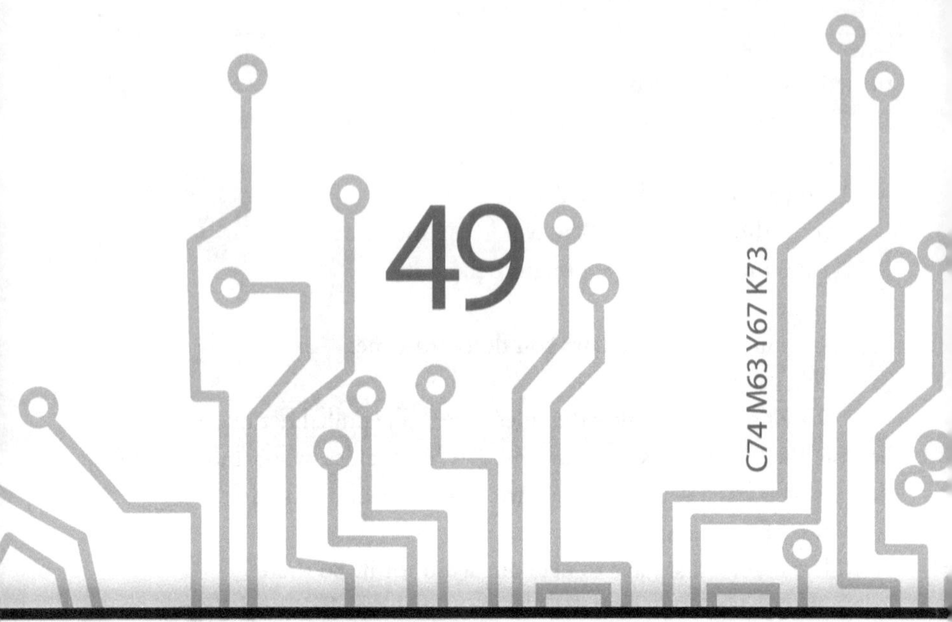

We talked a little more but didn't really make any more decisions. I needed time to rest and heal, and we needed to see what Onyx would do. No matter how anyone felt about any course of action, right now we had to wait.

I have news: waiting is hard. Lainey cuddled with me on the couch, as much as was practical with my injuries, and we talked for a while. That part was pleasant. But the rest of the day? Boring. Mind-numbing. Annoying. I hated it. I took a couple of naps, when my brain would let me. The rest of the time, I fretted over Onyx, worried about my other friends, and generally ruined my peace of mind.

Toward the evening, I got off the couch and tried to walk around the apartment. I didn't get very far. The pain, even with the doctor's pills, became unbearable after only a minute or so.

Amaranth emerged only when she grew too hungry to stay hidden. After eating something, she retreated to the bedroom again. Cerise wasn't happy about it, but I promised her it would only be for one night. Lainey sent Glacier to keep the dragon company.

Sleep did not come easy that night. My brain obsessed over all the new things we'd learned, from Amaranth's casual revelation about her "mother," to the bizarre statements about my heart. And Onyx hovered over it all. Every danger any of my friends faced, every compromised location, was all due to him. What could we do about it? I'd squandered Auric's disk, which raised even more questions about what to do with Amaranth. Over and over, my thoughts circled through all of these factors, never getting anywhere important.

Morning came. The other six took turns in the shower. I had too many bandages to try that again, but Lainey helped me wash my face and hair at least. Bice, Caedan, and Lainey had fake red chromarks applied. I would just have to keep my face hidden, as usual.

An hour before noon, we left the apartment. Marcus found a tall staff for me to lean on, probably a prop from one of his performances. Between the staff and help from Caedan, I managed to walk, albeit much slower than I'd like.

We mingled with the large crowd gathered at the ruins of the Flame. A huge portion of the population of Incarnadine had to be there. The body of the red dragon still lay where I'd left it. Some of the debris had been shifted about, but the devastation remained stark and unbelievable. In the light of day, we all stared at the ruins stretching out before us. Smoke still curled up from a handful of spots beneath the rubble.

But someone had erected a ramp on the opposite side of the Flame's remains, running out into the very middle. I suspected it would be used for a speech of some kind.

Over a dozen red draconics stood not far in front of the crowd, at the very edge of the debris. Now that I saw them together, I could tell the difference between Incarnadine and Amaranth's draconics. Incarnadine's looked more pure red, while Amaranth's had more of a… rust tone to them. Huh. You'd think I would have noticed that earlier.

"My children," Amaranth muttered. "Why did they answer his summons? What deception did he use this time?"

"Look!" someone exclaimed. I joined the rest of the crowd in turning my attention toward the ramp. A lone figure strode up toward its top.

Richard Onyx.

Murmurs ran through the crowd as people started to realize he bore a black chromark. Why would someone from Atramentous be addressing this assembly? Incarnadine's draconics reacted in a similar fashion, but Amaranth's, at least, knew Rick to be a guest of their queen.

He reached the peak of the ramp and stood with hands on hips, looking down at the crowd. A smile spread over his face. Once upon a time, I loved seeing that smile. It meant my friend Rick was about to reveal some crazy plan. He wore the same smile when we stood on a rooftop in Viridia and first thought of killing a dragon and blaming it on another one. But now… now I knew the truth about him. His chromark wasn't the only thing black about him.

"Behold Incarnadine!" Rick cried, pointing at the fallen dragon. In the silence and cool air, his voice carried well enough for even my hearing to understand him.

"In the past year, we have seen The Circle undone. Incarnadine is the third dragon to fall, after Caesious and Viridia. Nothing like this has ever happened before. What does it mean?"

The crowd murmured again. They didn't have a clue where this was going. I had a pretty good idea myself.

"It means these three were false gods!" Rick shouted. "If they could be slain like this, they were not worthy of our worship!"

"Nooo!" one of the draconics cried. "Our god will return to us!"

Rick looked down at the draconic, then made an exaggerated turn to look at Incarnadine's body. He turned back again. "I'm pretty sure that's not going to happen, my friend."

"Who are you?" a human shouted.

Rick pointed in the direction of the voice. "Now there's the right question to ask! Who am I? Why am I here? What right do I have to speak before such a gathering?"

"You don't!" a draconic responded. "Leave us, human! We come to honor Incarnadine!"

"And I come to tell you the truth!" Rick's voice rose. "Incarnadine is dead because he was not worthy of honor! Caesious and Viridia are dead for the same reason! And where is Amaranth now? She is not here because she sees what is happening. She knows! She has fled to preserve her own life from those who know that she also is one of the false gods!"

At this, a loud outcry arose from the draconics of both shades of red. They surged forward, starting to climb over the debris to get to this human who dared such blasphemy.

Black flames erupted around Rick, swirling around his perch on the ramp. The draconics halted. Many of them, like me, recognized the effect. Rick grew larger with each second. He fell to his hands and knees as those hands transformed into claws. The orb of black fire grew, expanding out larger and larger. Rick's face elongated, turning black as scales formed. Jaws lined with terrifying teeth appeared. Glowing liquid fell from his mouth into the ruins, sizzling and burning through the debris.

I noticed one important distinction from the last time I'd seen him in this form. Enormous scars ran the length of his front legs, the mark of the cybernetic implants that grew with him. A dragon with my abilities, exaggerated to that size. The concept terrified me.

In the midst of all of this, he turned his head. His eyes, those ancient eyes, seemed to find me in the crowd and bore into me, staring through the black flames. Whether he saw me or not, he knew I was there, witnessing his transformation for the second time. I clenched my fists.

The black dragon's claws sank into the debris as he continued to grow. A motion across his back preceded the eruption of his wings. They spread to an enormous span. He rose up on his hind legs and roared. The black flames rushed outwards, dissipating just before striking the crowd, though we all felt the heat. People screamed. Dozens fled.

Onyx, the lost black dragon, was announcing his presence before all, no longer in hiding, and no longer worried about the other dragons. But they still outnumbered him. Unless… a horrid thought entered my head. I looked to the sky.

And a second black dragon descended.

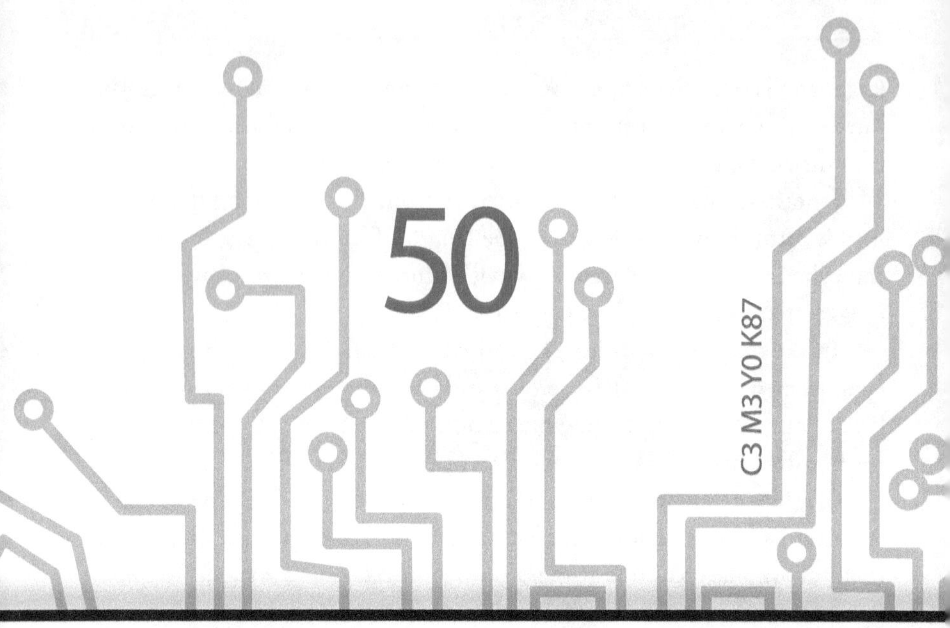

Atramentous, the other black dragon, came to a rest beside Onyx in the ruins. Some of his scales appeared to fade in and out as he landed. He rested one claw on top of Incarnadine's tail and laughed, an enormously deep sound that rattled some of the debris.

"Brother?" Amaranth whispered.

Silence descended over the crowd. For a very long time, no one said anything.

"What is this?" a voice said, just loud enough to be heard.

"I am Onyx, and I have returned. My brother and I are the true gods of this world," Onyx announced. "The other dragons have usurped our right long enough. Three have now been proven false, and the others will follow."

"Oh, will we?" Amaranth growled. She took a step forward.

Bice caught her arm. "You might not want to be seen just now," he cautioned. "Unless you think you can take on both of them in your current form."

She snarled at him but stepped back.

"Together," Atramentous announced, "we will rule the cities. No longer will one dragon rule over a single city. Onyx and I will share the responsibilities, and all of The Circle will worship its true gods!"

"Today, we enter a new age!" Onyx declared. "The priesthoods will be reformed. Travel between the cities will be opened up. Peace and prosperity will be extended to all who follow us! Very shortly, we will deal with the last remaining opposition to our rule. We will unseat that craven Auric and track down the coward Amaranth."

"Blasphemy!" a draconic screamed.

"Who said that?" Atramentous demanded.

One of the rust-colored draconics stepped away from its brothers. "Our mother and goddess Amaranth will return! You cannot take what is rightfully hers!"

"I would be careful of your words," Onyx said. "You draconics were summoned here for one reason only. This is your moment: the time where you swear your allegiance to your true gods."

"We will never follow you, usurper!" the draconic cried. "You are a blaspheming traitor! You—"

Onyx spit a flood of acidic flame. The protesting draconic was consumed in an instant. It didn't even have time to scream before its entire body burned away, leaving behind an acrid smell and a wisp of black smoke.

"My child!" Amaranth lunged forward this time, but Caedan and Bice caught her.

"He'll kill us all!" Bice hissed.

Fortunately, the remaining draconics were creating quite an uproar at the moment, or one of the black dragons might have heard Amaranth's cry. Many of them protested or shouted down the protestors. The human crowd didn't know what to say or do. Most only watched, wondering where this would all lead.

One of Incarnadine's draconics stepped out from the others. It stared up at the dragons, and then fell to one knee. "Power resides in the gods! And you have demonstrated true power. None can stand against the black dragons!" It lowered its head. "I swear to serve and obey."

One by one, the other draconics followed. They knew their resistance would be pointless now. *Better to serve the new power than die for the old one, I suppose.*

"Look." Lainey pulled on my arm and pointed. "Behind the dragons."

Just beyond the other side of the ruins of the Flame, a human figure stood. At first, I couldn't make out much because of a plume of smoke. And then another figure appeared beside it, and I could see. Purple. A third appeared and then another. In a few moments, over a dozen purple robes stood watching the proceedings.

Caedan turned to me. "I don't think we have a choice now."

I nodded. "You're right."

"We run?"

"We run."

With his help, I turned around. The seven of us slipped out of the crowd and hurried down the street.

Three dragons were dead, one was trapped in human form, and another had just been threatened with an attack of overwhelming force.

And yet… our freedom seemed further away than ever before.

Black dragons ruled all.

Darkness consumed The Circle.

Beryl's story continues in

Atramentous

For more information on the Dragontek Lore series,
and other upcoming books,
visit timfrankovich.com

Joining the mailing list is the best way to stay informed,
plus you get free stories!
(including Rick's story before he arrived in Viridia!)

If you enjoyed this book, please post a review
on Amazon, B&N, Goodreads, etc.
There's no better way to spread the word.

Author's Notes

Five books into the series. Wow. I didn't expect it to go this long, and I didn't expect people to still be reading. Yet here we are. And what more can I say now that I haven't already said in the previous four books?

I don't know of anything like these books on the market today… which makes it very hard to advertise. If you can help with that by telling your friends or leaving a review online (even just star ratings on Amazon), it would be greatly appreciated!

In the meantime, there's more to come. This adventure isn't over yet.

A special shout-out to the new fans from Comicpalooza! It was fantastic to meet all of you at our booth. I look forward to doing it again next year.

If you want to keep track of my progress on all my writing, you can connect on timfrankovich.com, my Facebook author page, Twitter, etc. But the best way, which keeps you informed and gives you exclusive previews, is to join the mailing list. Sign up on the website. (You'll get free stories too!)

Tim Frankovich has been exploring fantastic worlds since third grade, when he cut up a grocery sack and drew a Godzilla-meets-superheroes story. Since then, he's gotten a little bit better at the writing part (not so much with the drawing).

His goal as a writer is to transport readers to another world, make them care deeply about characters in dire situations, and guide them deeply into life itself.

At the moment, he is probably suitably conscious somewhere in Texas with his beloved wife, awesome four kids, and a fool of a pup named Pippin.